BEYOND JUAREZ

BEYOND JUAREZ

MARION SURLES

Love and Literacy

Published by Love and Literacy

ISBN 979-8-218-13998-8

Typesetting services by BOOKOW.COM

To my friends

who live with the constant pull of two cultures,

you are my heroes.

Foreword

The Families

Cristal's Family
Fina, younger sister

Iván, older brother, lives and works with a mechanic, Jairo

Pastor Miguel and Pastora Pati, foster parents to Cristal and Fina

Rubí, drug-addicted biological mother of Cristal, Fina, Iván

Yarely, Cristal's friend at UACJ

Itzel's Family
Carmen, mom, storekeeper

Humberto, dad, construction worker

Javi, Itzel's boyfriend and husband

Daniel's Family
Memo, younger brother

Araceli, mom, homemaker, bookkeeper for husband's business

Lucas, dad, construction worker

Adriana, Araceli's sister, Daniel's uncle

Burly, Daniel's friend at UTEP

Kevin, Daniel's roommate at UTEP

Acknowledgments

Writers at the Well, for your encouragement

My beta readers, helpers, and editors: Laquita Dettman, Margie Gonzalez, Helen Mabery, Jennifer Wagner, Kassidy Wagner, Cecelia Boswell, Vivian Menzel, Soraya Rdz Roman, Nancy Brown, Dottie Sharp, Linda Merkel, Lori Altebaumer, Carolyn Martin, Jennifer Muncey, Leslie Wilson, and so many encouragers

My husband who always supports me in all my crazy endeavors

Contents

Prologue

In 2019, two events in the United States rocked the world of the Hispanic immigrant population. Although unrelated, the events were a horrific reminder that this world is not our home. The characters in this book are fictional, but the massacre at a Walmart in El Paso, Texas, and the workplace round-up in north central Mississippi are true events which occurred only days apart. A political response is not a solution. Only by hearing individual stories do we begin to partially grasp the world of the immigrant. Lord, have mercy.

Let us have mercy.

Part I

2012–2015

Chapter 1

2012
Ciudad Juárez, México
Cristal

"CRISTAL, come out here," someone shouted from the street.

Cristal was pretty sure who was calling. She looked from her math homework to her foster mom Pastora Pati who gave her a sad smile.

"I'm here if you need me, baby. You can always use me as an excuse," Pati said.

Cristal stepped outside to see her mother, Rubí, leaning against the pallet fence that surrounded their tiny yard. The neighbor's pit bull, tied near their gate, was growling. The heat of the desert sun beat down on them all, showing no mercy.

"Cristal, I just need some money to make it 'til Monday. I'm starting a new job at a different maquila. I'll be assembling cellphones on day shift."

Cristal tried not to laugh or cry. How many times had she heard this same request? She watched her mom, jittery and unable to stand still.

"I'm sorry, Ma. I don't have any money. I just paid my entrance test fees for *prepa*. How did you buy your cigarettes anyway?" Cristal was a little bolder with her mom since she knew Pastora Pati had her back.

Rubí took a long drag and said, "I borrowed one from my neighbor. What business is that of yours?"

"You just asked me for money." Cristal shook her head, her pretty curls shiny in the sun.

"Go ask your preacher family. They're supposed to help the needy."

"No, Ma. They've helped you enough. I need to go study."

"Study! Look at you! You need to go fix your hair and make-up. How will you ever get a man when you look like that?"

Cristal tried to block out her last comment, running her fingers through her curls as she turned to go inside. "I'm going to study now, Ma." A tear ran down her cheek. She didn't want to be mean to her mother, but Pati always talked to her and her sister about boundaries. Pati was showing her a better love, a love in action that Cristal had never known. She trusted Pati who stepped up to be her mom since her own was unable or unwilling.

Her sister Fina was waiting inside the door. "What did she want?"

"The same as always."

"Come taste the flan I made this morning. It should be set by now."

Fina served a small plate of flan to Cristal and to Pati. They appropriately oohed and aahed.

"Fina, you are a great cook! You could sell this to a fancy restaurant in town," said Pati.

Fina was smiling. She loved to cook and often helped Pati in the kitchen with food to sell on the corner. Cristal was glad to leave cooking behind when they came to live with Pati after being taken by DIF, the child protective service. She always felt responsible for finding something for Fina and herself to eat when they roamed the streets as neglected kids.

"I want to study culinary arts when I move up to prepa. Is there a course?"

"We'll find one," said Pati. "You still have to get your math grades up. You use a lot of math when cooking."

Fina and Cristal smiled. They both struggled in school since they got such a late start. They were proud of how fast they were catching up to their peers. Thank goodness for Pastora Pati and her husband, Pastor Miguel. They were not legal foster parents, but the child services agency was glad to have the girls off the streets and in the care of loving, responsible adults. Their older brother, Ivan, lived in the next *colonia* with a mechanic who took him in. Ivan could easily open his own garage, but he was enjoying the feeling of a home there as well. God had watched over all three of them.

Chapter 2

2012
Ciudad Juárez, México
Itzel

RETURNING home to her *colonia* in Juarez, Mexico, on a public bus was normal for Itzel. She rode the bus to the next *colonia* the last four years to attend *prepa*, the best high school according to her papi. But now she was attending the University of Juarez. Riding a bus all the way to and from UACJ downtown where so much violence occurred was a big step. Itzel couldn't believe her mamá let her go. Of course, she had to return every night and not live in an apartment as some girls did. Too many girls disappeared in Juarez nowadays.

As the bus neared her neighborhood, more girls her age got on, but Itzel could tell they were not from the university. They came from working a shift at a *maquila,* one of the big international factories located along the border. Itzel recognized them by their ear protectors, a nametag, and steel-toed boots. She could easily be coming home from a maquila also, but her mamá pushed and punished her about her grades so she would not end up there. She knew she should be grateful, but she didn't want to admit it.

"Itzel, why're you so dressed up today?" her friend Adriana asked when she boarded the crowded bus. Adriana was her classmate since *primaria* who often stayed at her sister Araceli's house near Itzel.

"My first day of classes at UACJ started today."

"Wow, I can't believe you still wanted to study at uni after we dragged our feet at *prepa*."

"It's fun, so far. No homework yet. And lots of cute guys!"

"*Ay chihuahua,* Itzel, you always have an eye out for cute guys. What're you studying to be?" Adriana asked.

"I'm not sure. Maybe architecture or interior design."

"That sounds like a lot of work. Will it pay good?"

"They say it will. More rich people are building houses here since the violence calmed down."

"Yeah, but who knows if it will start up again?"

Juarez was considered the murder capital of the world, as competing drug cartels battled for control of the large city. About one and a half million people called it home, with new immigrants arriving daily from rural areas looking for work.

They got off together and walked the remaining blocks to their *colonia*. Adriana bought a bag of chips at Itzel's store and walked on to Araceli's house. Itzel sat down in the store to talk to her mamá, Carmen.

"I'm gonna need so much stuff for my classes," Itzel complained. "So many different notebooks and pens, special erasers, and specific drawing paper, plus books. They must think we are made of gold, or else they want to weed us out."

"Give me the list, and we can go this weekend," Carmen said.

"No, I need it all by tomorrow!" Itzel didn't mean to snap at her mamá. "It's so overwhelming. Sorry, Ma!"

"Okay, we can go tonight as soon as your papá gets home."

The young neighbor boy Daniel came in for tortillas. His mom, Araceli, often visited with Carmen.

"Hi, Daniel," said Carmen. "How's your mom?"

"She's fine. She's doing homework!"

"You must be so proud of her finally going back for her diploma," Carmen said.

Daniel shrugged, trying to conceal a smile of pride while complaining, "I'm having to do all the cooking."

"Aww, poor baby," Itzel said.

Daniel punched her arm on his way out.

"Go easy on him, Itzel. He's always carried a much bigger load than you."

"There you go again, Mami. Always comparing me to Daniel. I work hard."

"Yes, you do, but I don't think you are always as grateful for what you have as you should be."

Itzel rolled her eyes. Her mamá was always on her case. If she had siblings, she wouldn't always be in her line of focus. Then her whole demeanor changed when she heard her dad's truck pull up. Itzel ran to greet him just as when she was a little girl. She was definitely a daddy's girl. Now her mom rolled her eyes.

Chapter 3

2012

Ciudad Juárez, México
Daniel

"MEMO! Come move these greasy car parts off the table!" Daniel shouted at his brother as he finished attaching the propane tank to the stove. He chopped chiles, onion, and garlic while the meat browned in a skillet and the rice browned in another pot.

Memo moved the parts to the floor in the next room. "I'm almost finished. Then I can sell that car for almost double what I paid."

"Don't be tricking your customers with a glued together quick fix," Daniel said. "Remember all those cars we went through before Papá learned about cars. Don't be one of those guys."

"I'm not," Memo said, offended. "I wouldn't do that! My customers trust me."

"I'm just saying. It sucks to be taken advantage of."

"Jairo wouldn't stand for it either. He demands perfection before he agrees to put it on his lot. One day I'll have my own lot."

"And treat your customers the same way, I hope. Don't sell them something you know will break down tomorrow. You wouldn't be here if it weren't for a decent car to get you to the hospital every time you had an asthma attack."

"I know, I know. Why does everybody always have to remind me. I'm grateful, okay? What else can I do about it?"

"Pay it forward like Pastora Pati told us."

Memo rolled his eyes. He hated when his big brother tried to get all preachy with him. "Where's Mamá?"

"She's studying at the store for her Saturday class. Their Wi-Fi is cheaper than riding a bus to the school for free internet."

Daniel added water to the rice, turned down the burner, and picked up the book he was reading. Memo finished repairing and cleaning the parts, put them in a bag from S-Mart, and with great effort picked up a book to read. Memo was about to start his second year of *secundaria,* same as eighth grade on the other side. He didn't really like school, but he knew his parents' rules. He would finish school. Then he would open a big car dealership. He could sell to anybody. Being around all those strangers in hospitals so many times helped him become an extrovert.

Someone knocked and called from the fence. Daniel was surprised to see Pastor Miguel.

"Are your parents at home?"

"Papá is still at work, and Mamá is studying at the store using the Wi-Fi. They should be home soon. Is something wrong?"

"No, something is very good. It has to do with you."

"Me?"

"Let me talk to your parents first. I'll come back tonight."

Daniel was worried anyway. He liked Pastor Miguel. He coached his soccer team last year, and he always told a good joke. But still, why did Pastor Miguel want to talk to his parents about him?

Mamá came home soon after, and the three of them sat down to eat. Papá would be very late finishing a job.

"Pastor Miguel wants to talk to you and Papá," Daniel said. "He said it's about me, but not to worry."

Memo grinned. He knew he was the spoiled baby, and Daniel was the responsible one. Maybe Daniel tripped up this time.

When Lucas made it home and was finishing supper, Pastor Miguel knocked at the gate again. Araceli made him some coffee, and they all sat at the table.

"I've been getting information about a school in El Paso that is accepting good students from Juarez, and I thought of Daniel."

Araceli raised her eyebrows and looked at Lucas.

"The school has scholarships and some jobs at the school to help pay expenses. There would still be some other expenses not covered, but it would be a great opportunity."

"But would he stay there?" Araceli asked.

"No, he would cross the pedestrian bridge every day and walk about four or five blocks to the school. I think they have a van for the first few days, but the kids who cross together become friends and begin walking rather than riding the van. That's what I've been told."

"Will they teach him in Spanish?" Araceli asked.

"No, everything is in English, but there is a class for learning English too. The kids from the other side are mostly Spanish-speaking and are learning English at the same time. The school is sponsored by the Methodist church. It's called Lydia Patterson."

Lucas didn't say anything as the Pastor talked, but his mind was working. "How can he cross without papers?" he asked.

"He will need to get a passport, and the school will help him get the paperwork needed to cross on a student visa."

"It's a thirty-minute bus ride to the bridge, then time to pass through customs every day, walk another few blocks to the school, only to do it all again after school and a part-time job?" Lucas' tone sounded doubtful.

"I know it sounds exhausting, but some kids in the next colonia did it last year and really learned a lot. We could go talk to their parents about it if you are interested."

Araceli and Lucas did not respond. Daniel wanted to ask hundreds of questions, but he knew not to speak until spoken to. Finally, Araceli spoke. "It does sound like a great opportunity, but it seems so dangerous."

Before Lucas could speak, the Pastor said, "I understand. But before you make any decisions, think about it overnight and let me arrange a meeting with these two families who did it last year. They have more insight than I do. Daniel is such a good student and has matured into a responsible young man. I would love for him to have this opportunity."

They shook hands, and Pastor Miguel left. Only then did Daniel speak, "I want to find out more about it, but I really think I want to go." Araceli hugged him tight.

Lucas turned on a soccer match. He needed to let that idea simmer before saying anything.

Chapter 4

2012
UACJ
Itzel

UNIVERSITY was much harder than Itzel imagined. She felt like she studied all the time, but this time she enjoyed studying. She liked the independence and the demands. She also liked the many new young men on campus. They seemed different from the boys where she grew up, more confident and more courteous.

Itzel looked around the student center while she took a sip of her coffee. She watched as a professor in line paid for her tray, then turned as a student from the next aisle turned into her. The professor's tray spilled, and the student froze in embarrassment. The next student in line left his selections, grabbed napkins, and helped clean the mess before anyone else moved. The professor thanked him profusely and returned to refill her tray. The student paid for his food and sat at the table beside Itzel.

"That was really nice," she said. "I think boys from my neighborhood would have laughed and moved on."

"Well, I'm not a boy anymore," he said. "Boys from any neighborhood would probably do that too. It takes us a little longer than girls to grow up."

She smiled at him. "Where are you from?"

"Durango. You?"

"From here, Ciudad Juarez, but about thirty minutes from here by car, or an hour at least by city bus."

"Do you live on campus?"

"Noo! I ride the bus both ways every day. Do you?"

"I share an apartment with three guys from Durango also."

"Is this your first year?"

"Second. Last year was tough. I never felt like I got caught up. I can breathe easier this year with the scholarship."

"I hope to get one at Christmas. They promised me one if my grades are good. Do you work too?"

"Yes, I make the killer breakfast burritos at Crisostomo's. You been there?"

"No, I usually eat my mom's burritos on the bus and get a coffee or snack here in the afternoon. I get home in time for real food with my parents."

"Mama's girl. That sounds nice."

"I'm really more of a daddy's girl. He works construction and always took me with him to his work sites. I'd rather be there than in the kitchen," Itzel said as she picked up her tray.

"Where's your next class?"

"In the architecture building. I have a drafting class."

"I'll walk with you. I pass there to get to my motorcycle."

"Wow, a motorcycle? That's cool."

"It's cheap," he smiled. "Hey, what's your name?"

"Itzel. Yours?"

"Javier, Javi."

They shook hands, and Itzel felt a tiny spark run up her arm. She had to get to class and focus. She knew better than to pay attention to that spark. "I better run. See ya around." Itzel left Javi on the sidewalk as she hurried to class. She spread her papers out on the worktable and tried to block Javi's face from her brain and focus on her work.

Chapter 5

2012

Ciudad Juarez
Daniel

THE following Sunday afternoon, Lucas, Araceli, Daniel, and Memo rode with Pastor Miguel to the next colonia to visit the two families whose children were finishing their first year at Lydia Patterson. After introductions, Pastor Miguel spoke. "Would the boys like to go talk together, and the parents talk separately?"

The two boys got up and led Daniel and Memo outside. They kicked a soccer ball around while they talked.

"It's hard the first few weeks. I like it better now," said Samuel. "Getting up so early and getting home late is worse in the cold. Since we changed the clocks back, it's not so bad."

"How did you learn English?" Daniel asked.

"I'm still learning. I practiced a lot last summer on my phone, but that seemed to go out the window those first few days. I think I was in shock when everybody started talking to me in English only."

"Yeah, it's pretty intense at first," said Andrés. "I'm not gonna lie. I wanted to quit, but my mom kept telling me it would get better. It did. My grades still aren't as good as I had here, but I'm getting better."

"What about the other kids?" Daniel asked.

"Most of them are cool. They have a hard time with English too. They just don't have the extra hard part of having to cross the bridge every day," Samuel said.

"Are there any bullies?" Daniel asked.

"Well, I guess bullies are everywhere, but if we stick together, we won't have any problems," Andrés said.

"What about crossing the bridge or walking anywhere?"

"We all stick together. There are about 12 of us that get off at the same time from this side. We never have any problems," Samuel said.

Inside the parents got down to specifics. "The tuition is $500 a month. That's dollars! But don't let that scare you away. There are scholarships and part-time jobs for the students who need help. It's still a struggle, but we think it is worth it," said one of the dads.

"Yes, very worth it," his wife said. "You know how our schools are so lax about the teachers being absent from school and not really checking the kids' absences either."

Araceli and Lucas nodded, but they were still thinking about the $500.

"The teachers are rarely absent, and if they are, there is a substitute who keeps the kids working. It's not a free day. And not nearly as many holidays," the wife said. "Andrés complains about that, but he really likes it there. Plus, he has started learning to play the guitar and is on the junior varsity soccer team."

"It's not that it is a strict, serious place, but education is top priority. There are enough extra activities to keep the kids interested. Andrés is really coming along with his English too," his dad said with pride.

Samuel's dad spoke up next. "I know my wife worried a lot at first about the crossing and the unsupervised time getting to and from school. But I think Samuel has become more confident in himself in other areas because of handling the crossing. I'm very impressed with how much he has matured this year."

"He's still my baby, and I still worry, but I'm glad he has this opportunity," Samuel's mom said. "There are so many kids his age here dropping out and roaming the streets, too young to work and only getting into trouble."

Araceli knew all about those roaming kids. She remembered Toño bullying Daniel when he was younger. She also thought about her cousin who was killed when he got mixed up with the drug cartel.

The discussion continued with details about getting the passport, filling out forms, and getting uniforms. With their heads spinning from so much information, the little family climbed in Pastor Miguel's van to return home.

"Thank you, Pastor, for even considering Daniel for such a special opportunity. We will think it all through very carefully and give you an answer soon," Araceli said as they arrived home. "Buenas noches."

* * *

Daniel and Memo played soccer in the street until Mamá called them in. They washed up and ate supper in silence. Everyone seemed to be lost in thought. Suddenly Memo broke the silence, "Did somebody die?"

Even Lucas had to laugh at his youngest son. "No, Memo. You boys are just growing up."

* * *

Daniel was reading a book in bed when Mamá came to sit by him. "What do you really think about the change of school for next year?"

Daniel was quiet for a long moment. "Do you think I will get kidnapped walking to the bridge?"

Mamá hugged him tight. How could she tell him that would never happen?

"Daniel, I can only tell you that we will take care of everything we can control, and we will cover you in prayer for the things out of our control. I believe God may have a hand in this opportunity. I want to trust Him for your future, but I want to know that you trust Him too."

"I do, Mamá. I do."

* * *

Araceli wanted more advice. She knew Daniel was a good candidate for the school. He was so responsible about doing his homework without reminders. He was a natural teacher for Memo as he started school. Plus, he was so much help for her at home as she tried to finish her education. She wanted to talk to Abuelo. He always had good advice. Abuelo lived in Dallas, a time zone later. He often visited with mission teams, and he became an adoptive grandparent for her family.

That night Araceli made the call. Usually they texted at night, brief conversations about what she cooked, what the boys were doing, where Lucas found work that day. But this time she wanted to hear his voice.

"Bueno," said Abuelo, surprised at the call. "*¿Todo bien?* Everything okay?"

Araceli explained everything about the school, but Abuelo was having a hard time hearing her.

"I need new batteries for my hearing aids," he said. "I'm going to need surgery on my ear. I have a tumor."

"Oh, Abuelo, I hate to bother you with this now."

"No, I'm thrilled to hear your voice. Just wish I could hear you better. The tumor isn't cancer, so let me read about the school, and you text me some details. I'll let you know what I think in a few days."

Araceli hung up. After first meeting Abuelo when their house was being built by volunteers, Araceli welcomed him to their home at least twice a year. She worried about his health. She wasn't sure of his age, but she knew he didn't take care of his blood sugar and blood pressure like he should. *Why are men so hardheaded, always thinking they are invincible, forever young?*

Araceli texted him all the information they received about the school. The hardest part was telling him about the cost. How could they ever afford $500 a month? She would have to go to work. Maybe she could work during the week this time and not have to leave her weekend studies. She really wanted to receive her high school diploma this time.

After sending the text, Araceli began to think about another job for herself. She would have to be available to get Daniel off to school very early, and of course Memo a little later. Her younger sister was working at the *segundas*, a large flea market, on the weekends now and making good money. Araceli would like that, but it would interfere with her Saturday classes. Maybe she could cook and sell something during the week. Of course, everybody was always selling food, but were enough people buying?

She had a real job as she accompanied Lucas to meet new customers and help with the estimates and contracts. They were a team, but she felt she needed to do more. She heard her phone alert and was surprised by a text from Abuelo so quickly.

"Looks like a great opportunity for Daniel, and someone from our church is on the board of trustees for the school. Let me talk to him about scholarships. Tell Daniel to pack his backpack!"

Araceli's heart was pounding almost like the first time she met Lucas. She was so excited for Daniel, but she didn't want to get his hopes up until everything was in place. And, she knew she needed Lucas' blessing.

* * *

The next day, Araceli accompanied Lucas to do an estimate on a large home in downtown Juarez. Lucas couldn't read. Araceli tried to help him, but he couldn't grasp it. His math skills were amazing though, and his construction business was going well. They passed the bridge that Daniel would cross every day.

"That's a lot to put on a boy," Lucas said as he drove.

"I know. So early every morning and so late every night. He's only used to a half day of school."

"It's a big opportunity. He could learn English," Lucas said.

"It is. He could." Araceli didn't want to say too much. She knew her husband. He had to work it out in his mind first.

"I never got to finish sixth grade, much less high school in another country," Lucas said.

"Me either, but I would have liked to go further."

"It's a lot of money. We could use the money for lots of other things," Lucas said.

"Yes, but he's only gonna be this age once."

"He could always learn English at home. He could go to Prepa on our side. They teach English here too."

"They do and he could. He's been practicing some when the teams come through to build houses," Araceli said.

"But it's a great opportunity."

"It is."

"And you think he can handle it?" Lucas asked.

"I do, and the Pastor does."

"I guess he could try it. He doesn't have to commit to all three years, right?"

"Yes, that's right."

Silence filled the truck. Only the GPS voice broke the silence, "*en 500 kilometros su destino está a la derecha.*" Lucas parked in front of a gated house with a pink stucco wall surrounding it.

"Okay then."

"So, you agree to start the process? To sign for his passport?"

Lucas nodded. His mind was on the job ahead. Araceli wished she could compartmentalize like that sometimes. Her mind was racing ahead to the paperwork they would need to do and the trips to government offices that always took all day. But if God opened this door, He would make it happen.

Chapter 6

2012
Ciudad Juarez
Cristal

THE next afternoon, Cristal was breathless. She ran into the house shouting, "I passed! I passed!"

"*¡Felicidades!* I knew you would," Pastora Pati said, wrapping her into a big hug. The entrance test for *prepa* was not an easy given. Not everyone passed, and not everyone continued studying. Even though school was free, there were always extra fees, uniforms, and supplies. The team members who came from the other side of the border to build homes pitched in what they could. Every little bit helped.

"I'll try to get my schedule at S-Mart arranged for after school so I can help with all the extras," Cristal said as she saw the worry lines appear on Pati's face. One day, she hoped to be able to pay them back, maybe not in money, but at least by having a stable job, an independent life, and paying it all forward.

"Cristal, your job is to study and do your best in school. Don't worry about the expense. Right now, could you run to the store for me? I need some matches. This lighter gave out, and I can't light the stove."

"Sure, Ma," Cristal answered without realizing what she said. She reached for a few pesos and saw the look on Pati's face.

"Thank you, *mija*," Pati said. She hugged Cristal to her. "You are my beautiful girl."

Cristal skipped to the store, happy at the slip of calling Pati her mom. She stepped into Carmen's store as Daniel was coming out.

"Hey, Daniel."

"Hey," he said, but he kept moving, never up for a conversation.

"I got in to *prepa*. Will you tell your ma?"

"Yeah, I will."

"Your mom helped me a lot. You have a really nice family."

Daniel turned back. "Congratulations." He smiled at her. "I'll tell my mom."

"Thanks." Cristal couldn't stop smiling as she stepped to the counter.

"Hey, Carmen. I only need a small box of matches. Did you know I passed my test for prepa? I can't believe I passed the math part."

"That's great, Cristal. Will you take the bus to Zaragoza or walk to the one by the youth detention center?"

"I hope to Zaragoza, but I'll probably be walking. Where is Daniel going? I'm sure he passed his test as well. He's so smart."

"He was telling me he might be going to the other side to school."

"The other side of *the secundaria*?"

"No! He will be crossing into El Paso every day! I couldn't believe it. I mean, I know he reads all the time and will be a great student. I just can't believe Araceli is going to let her baby cross the bridge every day for school."

"That's so cool! His mom is so sweet. I remember her helping me learn to read before I finally got to go to school. She was so patient. She must be really proud of him."

"Yes, our little community is making progress. Here are your matches, no charge. Bring your first report card by for me to see. I bet you will do good too. Keep your eyes off the boys. That's what I have to remind my Itzel all the time."

Cristal walked home thinking about Daniel crossing the border. A group of girls from school passed her whispering. She greeted them but kept going. She always had a hard time making friends with girls. Maybe she didn't know enough about fixing herself up, make-up and hairdos. Maybe she needed a new look for *prepa*. Not for a boy, like Carmen warned, but to try to fit in better. Pati would know what to do. Or, maybe not, since she was a preacher's wife. A new hairdo was something her real mom would know about.

The week before school started, Cristal found her real mom selling watered down fruit drinks at the *segundas*. She was a pretty lady, Cristal thought. And to think that her mom already had two babies when she was her age now. How did she manage?

"Ma, I thought you were going to work in a maquila," Cristal said.

"It starts next week. I'm doing this until then."

"Ma, do you think you could do something with my hair before I start *prepa*? A new look?"

"Sure, *mija*. You got some money?"

Cristal didn't want to answer. "What time do you get off?"

"At nine. Leave me the money, and I'll pick up the chemicals when I get off."

"Ma, you know I can't do that. Tell me what to go buy."

"No, just meet me at the Guadalajara Pharmacy at ten tomorrow morning. We'll buy the stuff, and then we can go to my house to fix you up."

Cristal worried all night about this decision. She didn't tell Pati or even Fina. Did she want it to be a surprise, or did she know they would tell her not to do it?

The next morning, she met her mom as planned, but Rubí already held a bag of products.

"Are you sure this is the right stuff?" asked Cristal.

"I do this all the time. Besides, Lola owed me. You can pay me back and we'll be even."

Cristal didn't follow that exactly, but she resigned herself to her mother's plan. At her mom's house, Cristal grabbed a dirty towel and wrapped it around her shoulders. Rubí's housekeeping was the same as she always remembered. Rubí never washed clothes but waited for some group of volunteers to give her a new donation of new clothes. Rubí sectioned off Cristal's hair and began to paint each section with some very strong-smelling stuff.

"It kinda burns, Ma," Cristal said. "Are you sure about what she gave you?"

Rubí popped her across the neck. "Stop being a baby. It's time to grow up."

Cristal's eyes watered. She knew better than to come here. Why did she keep putting herself in these situations?

"How much longer?"

"Oh, all right. I'll finish it now, but it won't be as good as if you'd let me Keep the product on for the full time."

Rubí rinsed out the product and rubbed in a conditioner that also smelled funny but at least didn't burn. After ten more minutes, Rubí rinsed the conditioner and reached for the scissors.

"I don't know Ma. I think I want to leave it long. Let me get used to the color change first."

"Okay, you owe me 500 pesos for the products."

"Ma, that's all I have. I didn't think it would cost that much!"

"Beauty is expensive." She held out her hand. "Pay me."

Cristal handed her mom her hard-earned money. She walked home slowly. *Rubí isn't my mom, just a birth mom. How many times do I have to relearn that lesson?*

Fina was coming home at the same time Cristal arrived. "What happened to your hair?" Fina looked horrified.

"Ma colored it for me."

"Ma? Rubí?"

Cristal nodded, realizing that Fina never considered their birth mom her real mom. "I wanted a new look for *prepa*."

"Have you looked in the mirror?"

Cristal shook her head and now dreaded going inside. "Cristal, it's bad. Prepare yourself." Fina took her hand and dragged her to their tiny bedroom.

"I can't look," Cristal cried. "What did she do to me?"

Slowly Cristal peeked into the mirror. Her hair was a bleached, orangey-blond, but the worst part was her hair looked like straw, ready to snap like dried twigs. Large tears rolled down Cristal's cheeks. She looked away and fell onto her bed. Fina rubbed her back.

"Pati will fix it," Fina whispered. "She can fix anything."

At that moment, Pati walked in.

"What's the matter?" she said as she saw Cristal in a fetal position.

Fina formed the name Rubí with her mouth, and Pati understood.

"We can fix it, Cristal. It will take a few days, but we can fix it. It won't be like normal, but it will be much better. Don't cry, *mija*."

At the word "*mija*"—"my daughter," Cristal threw herself into Pati's arms and sobbed.

That night after supper and a discreet mention to Miguel not to say anything, Pati mixed up a paste of mayonnaise, avocado, and egg yolk. She plastered Cristal's head and then covered it with a bag from S-Mart. The three of them watched a *novela* together, their nightly soap opera, while Fina covered her new notebooks in plastic sheeting and put her name on them. Afterward, Cristal rinsed out the homemade conditioner and combed through her hair.

"It feels better, maybe not so brittle." Cristal seemed to relax. "Maybe we should cut off the tips?"

"Probably so, but let's wait a few days. Let's condition it again tomorrow. Then maybe go buy a box of coloring at the beauty supply house. They will know what to do. In the meantime, smile, mija. You are beautiful inside and out. Both of you are."

The three hugged into a tight circle just as Pastor Miguel came into the kitchen. "Hey, what's going on in the hen's nest? Nobody worried about the rooster tonight?"

Fina rushed to his side. "How about the last piece of my flan, Papi?"

Chapter 7

2012

Ciudad Juarez
Itzel

THE drafting class lasted three hours. Itzel was exhausted, but she managed to make the walk to the bus stop in time to catch the last express bus home. She still had to change buses at the *Soriana*, the Juarez version of Walmart, but she would make it home before her dad.

As she came in her front door, she could smell her mom's cooking, maybe enchiladas. She was starving. "Hola, Mami," she said as she kissed her on the cheek.

"Hola, *mija*. How was class? Did you have all the things you needed?"

"Yes. The class was so long though—three hours of drawing and measuring and everything so precise—I'm not sure this is my thing."

"It's the first month. Give it a chance."

"I will, but I really just want to help people fix up their homes, make them beautiful like the ones Papi builds."

"You will do that one day, mija. You are young. You have lots of time."

"I met a new boy today."

Carmen looked at her daughter, already worried about what that statement might bring.

"It's okay, Ma, he's a gentleman. He helped pick up this professor's tray and everything."

"Well, if he's a gentleman, then he will want you to concentrate on your studies and not run off with him in his car."

"He only has a motorcycle, Mami." Itzel grinned at her mom. Her mom always worried too much. Itzel knew she had her emotions under control. She could handle school and a cute boy at the same time.

The bell on their door jangled as someone came into the store.

"Itzel, will you take care of them while I finish rolling up these enchiladas?"

Itzel stepped into the store as Adriana came up to the counter.

"Where have you been? I haven't seen you since my first day of school on the bus?" Itzel said.

"We moved to another colonia when Mamá got a new man," Adriana said.

"What happened to Gregorio?"

"Mamá finally kicked him out when she saw him go after me. She didn't believe me when I told her he was trying to watch me change clothes. Anyway, Junior and I are staying with Araceli for now. The new man doesn't want us around. Or maybe Mamá doesn't."

"Are you still working, Adriana?"

"Yes, at the *maquila* Monday through Thursday 6:00 a.m.-6:00 p.m. Then I'm working in the *segundas* selling for a *señora* on Saturday and Sunday. Are you still at UACJ or just working in the store?"

"I'm studying like crazy at UACJ. It's hard, but I like it. Can you believe it?" Itzel grinned at her friend, glad they were nearby again, at least for a while. "What do you need?"

"Nothing, I just came to hang out until Daniel has dinner cooked," Adriana said as they both laughed.

"Araceli's not at home?" Itzel said.

"No, she's always studying, and Daniel is taking care of the house."

"He'll make a good wifey someday," Itzel laughed. "He's really smart though, always reading something."

"Yeah, he reads in English too since he started going across to El Paso to school," said Adriana. "He wants to go to college at UTEP over there too."

"And Memo, happy to be a car salesman," Itzel added laughing. "He's so cute."

The girls enjoyed catching up. They grew up as neighbors and reminisced a little.

"Remember when we made all those mud tortillas in the dump and set up a pretend store?" asked Itzel. "I had some play money. I thought I was so cool."

"You were always cool," said Adriana. "You always had nice things."

Itzel was glad to hear her father's truck pull up. She felt uncomfortable with Adriana's comment. She probably didn't mean anything by it, but she didn't like to think about how other kids didn't have much.

"Time to close up. My dad's home. What did you need?"

"Oh yeah, just a big Coke," said Adriana. She paid and walked back to Araceli's house as Itzel greeted her father.

Itzel didn't want to think about Adriana's string of creepy "step-dads." She knew she had the best dad in the world.

* * *

While at UACJ, Itzel and Javi soon became regular study partners at the student center. Javi was studying engineering, taking advanced calculus and an art class. Itzel was struggling with college algebra. Javi was a good tutor when he could keep his hands off her. They made themselves study at the student center. Itzel didn't dare go to his apartment. She knew she was playing with fire.

"Why don't you stay with some girlfriends near the campus over the weekend? We could go to the *Grito* together." The *Grito* was like a Fourth of July celebration.

"I don't know any girlfriends yet. You take up all my time." Itzel joked with Javi, but inside she knew it was true. She hadn't really tried to make girlfriends since school started. Studying, commuting, and finding time with Javi consumed all her time. She didn't know how other students also found time to work.

"Well, just stay and I will take you home after the celebration."

"On your motorcycle? My parents would die."

"So, I'll let you off a few blocks away."

"It will be at least three o'clock in the morning! It's too dangerous." She hated to sound just like her mom, but she knew about girls who never made it home after a night shift at the maquilas.

"You're right. I'll figure something out."

The next day, Javi came to the student center with a girl. "This is Yoli, my roommate Manuel's girlfriend. Yoli, Itzel."

"Nice to meet you," they said together as they shook hands.

"Are you a student too?" asked Itzel.

"Yes, I'm in education. I want to teach kinder. You?"

"Maybe interior design. This architecture course is kicking my butt."

They sat and visited for nearly an hour. "Javi says you commute nearly an hour. You can always stay over at our place if you need to. Do you have a blow-up mattress?"

"No, but I'm sure my papi can get me one." Itzel blushed as she realized how "little-girl" she sounded. "Javi was talking about us going to the Grito Wednesday night. Would it be okay to stay after?"

The girls made plans, and Yoli explained where they lived. Itzel was glad to get to know another female student on campus. She realized she missed the girl talk she used to have at *prepa*.

That night Itzel talked to her mom about staying with Yoli to go to the Grito with a group of friends. She didn't mention Javi anymore to her parents.

"How's algebra coming?"

"It's good. I have a tutor now." Itzel tried not to blush as she thought about her tutoring time.

"Just don't let this group of friends throw you off balance. I want good grades at Christmas so we can send in the paperwork for scholarships."

* * *

The night of the Grito, Daniel's family picked him up at the bridge. Daniel puffed up as he walked out to meet them. The new school routine made him feel like an adult although he was only sixteen.

He climbed into the backseat and punched Memo in the arm. Memo grabbed Daniel's backpack looking for snacks. Daniel grabbed it back. They were still little boys too.

"Nothing in there, Memo. Anyway, aren't we going to eat somewhere?"

"Probably get some burritos. They should have lots of food by the X."

The X was a well-known landmark, a 200-foot-tall piece of art representing the intersection of the Spanish and the Indigenous people of Mexico. But to the people, it was *la equis*, the main place for festivals, carnivals, and political giveaways.

They parked and walked through the festival grounds smelling the many food offerings– *taquitos, burritos, tamales, elotes,* along with *churros,* candied apples, *raspones,* and *nieves.* So many choices. The music blared reggaeton tunes on top of cumbias. Couples danced, and men hawked their wares of shirts and dresses in the traditional green, white, and red of the Mexican flag. A man made a Pancho Villa puppet dance. Ladies offered face-paint and hair braids in flag colors.

Memo was interested in the tiny cars with big men driving them in tight circles. Daniel watched the new Toltec demonstration of the pole flyers. They bought *elotes,* corn on the cob with *chile,* mayonnaise, cheese, and Valentina hot sauce. Walking down the midway with their *elotes,* they ran into Itzel.

"Itzel, what are you doing here?" Araceli said, giving her a hug.

"I came with my friends from UACJ. This is Javi." She introduced him, and they all shook hands. She didn't introduce the others, and they all moved on. Araceli looked back as the young couple disappeared into the crowd holding hands.

"I wonder if Carmen knows she's here."

"Aw, Ma. She's in college now. She can have a life," Daniel said.

"Just don't you get any ideas. I'm not ready to be an abuela."

"Aw, Ma. I'm only in high school."

The big stage came to life with band after band. Close to midnight the politicians reminded everyone what the party was all about and remembered the fallen soldiers who fought for freedom. Then they all did the Grito, and the fireworks show began.

As they walked to the car, Memo glanced up as a motorcycle whizzed by. "Look, Ma. Isn't that Itzel on the back of that motorcycle?"

"Ay, chihuahua! I'm sure Carmen doesn't know about that."

* * *

September 15th was the first time Itzel remembered lying to her parents. She did go to the *Grito* with the group of girls, but she spent the night at Javi's apartment. Javi made it to work on time the next morning. Itzel missed her first class but caught a bus to campus in time to get the notes from a classmate and make it to her second class.

As she rode the bus home late that afternoon, she struggled to stay awake. Only the memories of her first time with Javi kept her awake. She couldn't stop smiling.

"What are you smiling about?" Adriana was coming down the aisle in her maquila uniform.

"Oh, nothing," Itzel said as she tried to contain herself.

"You have been talking to one of those cute boys, haven't you!?"

"Well, yes," Itzel couldn't hold it in any longer. "He's so cute, and he has a motorcycle. So cool!"

"*Chido,* but your pa will kill you! He better not find out."

The guilt washed over Itzel as she realized the web of lies she had spun for one night. How could she keep up the story?

"But don't tell anybody, Adriana. Please!" She hated the way she sounded—like the little girl in *primaria* again making pinkie promises. She was never a good liar.

* * *

"How was the *Grito* last night?" Carmen said as she smiled at her daughter. Itzel was maturing right before her eyes. "We watched it on TV and tried to find you among the thousands."

"It was fun. Thanks for letting me stay."

"Anything else happen? Where are these girls from? What are they studying?"

Itzel knew she had a guilty look on her face. She tried to change it, but the guilt overcame her. Where were the girls from? What were they studying?

"I think they are all from Chihuahua."

"Why didn't they study at the university there?"

"No, I mean the state of Chihuahua. They live out in small towns." Itzel was stumbling. "I've got a lot of homework. Let me get to it."

"You need to eat first. Go ahead and eat now. Your dad will probably be late. And you can tell me about the boy involved in this before Papi gets home."

Itzel froze, then dropped her head. "How do you know, Ma?"

"I was young once."

Itzel fixed her some melon water from the pitcher in the refrigerator. Why did she think she could hide Javi from her mom?

"He's very nice, Ma. He treats me with respect."

"He respects you so much he encourages you to lie to your parents?"

"It wasn't him. I knew you wouldn't let me stay, and I didn't want him to come here on his motorcycle. I knew you would never let me go anywhere with him then."

"Well, you are right about that, but now we will always have a poor opinion of him. Besides, you could always pay a taxi or ride the bus to see each other."

"Ma, you don't even know him."

"So, let's fix that. If he respects you so much, bring him to dinner tomorrow night."

"Okay, Ma, I'll see, but please don't tell Papi." There was her little girl voice again.

* * *

Javi did come to eat dinner. He paid a taxi instead of using his motorcycle. He used good manners and tried not to tremble when he met her parents.

"Call me Humberto," Itzel's pa said as he squeezed the young man's hand hard. "What does your pa do in Durango?"

"He was a *paquetero*, so he wasn't home a lot. He picked up shipments from a packaging company at the border and drove them down to Michoacan, making stops along the way. He was ambushed and killed five years ago. No one was ever held accountable."

The room got very quiet. No one spoke for several minutes. "I'm sorry, Javi," Itzel said. "I had no idea."

"Do you have siblings?" Carmen said. "Itzel is always sad she is an only child."

"I have an older brother in Zacatecas. He's married and has two little boys. My ma stayed in Durango, and my abuela moved in with us soon after Pa was killed."

"That must have been hard on your mom for you to come all the way here to go to university," Papi said.

"The first year was. I went back home last summer and worked and did a lot of repairs on our house. She has a small store that keeps her busy and provides enough to pay her taxes and eat. I got a scholarship starting last spring, and I have a job for my other expenses."

Papi grunted his approval. "So, what is your plan?"

"I'm studying Arts and Engineering, using my welding skills in art."

"You can make a living with that?"

"I hope so. I learned to weld on my uncle's ranch, so I can always find work. But I hope to make something of art too."

Papi grunted again. Carmen rescued them by bringing out a pan of flan. "Fina made this for us to try. She is hoping to sell it and wants our opinion. It looks delicious."

Papi and Javi didn't have much more to say to each other. Itzel and Carmen chatted about the flan and how Cristal and Fina overcame so much in their lives, but Javi escaped in a taxi as soon as was polite. Itzel breathed out a sigh and looked at Papi.

"You were young once too, Papi." She wrapped her arms around his neck until he finally cracked a smile.

"But an artist, Itzel? Do you want to starve the rest of your life?"

"Papi. I'm not gonna starve. You wouldn't let that happen."

All three laughed as Carmen said, "I always told you, you spoiled her too much."

"My little girl is growing up. Ay, chihuahua."

Chapter 8

2012

Ciudad Juarez
Cristal

CRISTAL'S first day at *prepa* was uneventful. Her hair looked different in a short bob, but the color was almost normal. She rode the bus to the Zaragoza school and was surprised to find Daniel on the early morning ride. She smiled when she saw he was reading on the bus. She sat beside him, and he looked up.

"Oh, Cristal. I didn't recognize you."

Cristal tried to hold her head high. "Yeah, Rubi got hold of it. Pati helped me fix it. Does it look too bad?"

"No, it's nice."

"Thanks, but I know it's a little wild. So much for a new look for *prepa*. But I thought you were going across to school," Cristal said.

"I am. I change busses at Zaragoza and go to the Santa Fe bridge to walk across."

"How long does all that take?"

"I leave home at 6:30 and get to school by 8:00. In the afternoon, I stay for soccer and cross back by 5:00 to get home by about 6:30."

"That's a long day! When did you start?"

"At the end of August. The first day was kinda scary, but I met some guys at the bridge who crossed last year. They showed me the ropes."

"Is it hard? Everything is in English, right?"

"Yes!" Daniel smiled at her for the first time. "I may be in over my head."

"No, you're smart. And you have your family behind you. You'll do fine."

"So why are you going so early today?"

Cristal hesitated, looking down at her notebooks. "I'm going to clean the bathrooms before school each day to help with expenses. There are so many fees for *prepa*."

"Yeah, I know. I'm going to work in the cafeteria at lunch to help with fees not covered by my scholarship."

They sat in silence for a few minutes, each lost in thought of the responsibilities on their shoulders. Finally, Cristal spoke.

"Do you still have visits from Abuelo?"

"He hasn't visited in a while, but we keep in touch. He's helping with my school fees too. I don't think we could manage it without him."

"He was always kind to my ma. I don't know why she never wanted his help. Tell him hello from us when you talk to him."

Daniel smiled again. Cristal smiled back. They both had come a long way.

"Here's our stop," she said. "Maybe I'll see you tomorrow."

"See ya," Daniel said. He crossed to the opposite street corner to await the next bus, and Cristal walked the rest of the way to *prepa*. She realized she was still smiling.

* * *

39

A few days after the *Grito,* Daniel was surprised to see Cristal on his bus again.

"Where have you been? I thought we had the same schedule?" Daniel said.

"I've been working after school at the S-Mart, bagging groceries," Cristal said. "I only make tips, but some people are really nice about it."

"Are you still going early in the morning?"

"Yes, but now my Pa takes me most mornings. Then after school I walk to S-Mart and ride this bus home from there after work."

"You have a lot of homework?"

"No, not really. Remember how in *primaria* one year we would have an organized teacher who gave us homework every night and then the next year we hardly did any at all?"

"Yes. That used to make my mom so mad."

"It did me too. I would finally be making progress and getting the hang of school, and then the next year we would go over the same stuff. There was no challenge at all. I want to be one of those good teachers who challenges the students every day."

"You'll be good at it. You know, they were saying today if a teacher knows English and Spanish, she'll get paid more."

"Yeah, that'd be cool, but I won't be going across."

"You never know. They might have a student exchange or something. I could teach you what I'm learning, and we could practice when we're on the same bus."

"Okay, it'll help pass the time. What do I need to know first?"

"Well, we have this funny teacher who helps those of us who know nothing in English. She makes us sing these baby songs with hand motions. We thought it was really silly at first and didn't want to participate. When we finally got over ourselves, we realized it helps. She said that's the biggest part of learning another language, getting over being embarrassed. I'm still working on that."

"Okay, tell me what to say when I meet somebody new, like when you sat down here, and I didn't know you."

They giggled at each other as they tried new phrases and new sounds. Being the teacher gave Daniel more confidence. Laughing together felt right. Soon the bus stopped for their neighborhood, and they stepped off giggling as they tried to say, "Get out of my way. This is my stop."

"*Hasta luego,*" Daniel said.

"See you tomorrow, dude," Cristal replied in good English. She met his eyes, then ducked around the corner, smiling again as she skipped to her house.

* * *

Daniel surprised himself as he adjusted to the new school routine. English was still hard, but he overcame the initial shock of the first few weeks. Most of the kids he crossed with in the mornings also worked in the cafeteria and stayed for soccer after school.

Daniel and his group of friends from Juarez walked from the bridge toward school. About two blocks in, another group usually joined them, Spanish-speaking students from the El Paso side. They knew more street English than Daniel and his group, so they considered themselves somewhat superior.

"What's up?" the leader of the group with the nickname Chivo called.

Daniel just nodded, and his group kept walking. He remembered his tangles with Toño, his neighborhood bully. He didn't want any problems here.

"Hey," Chivo called again. "You gonna play on our soccer team this year?"

Talk of soccer was an irresistible topic for most of them.

"Yes, I'm planning to," Daniel said. "I'm staying for practice every day."

"Yeah, but you know they don't allow *vatos* like you to get playing time."

Daniel hesitated, hating to ask why. He turned and looked Chivo in the eye.

"Coach seems like a fair judge of our abilities. I think he will let the best players start."

"That's not how it works over here, though. That's the thing. The ones who get to play are the ones whose parents make the biggest donations to the school. Money talks over here, especially in sports."

"Coach doesn't seem like that kind of person." Daniel tried to defend Coach Martinez. He liked the way he coached, always ending on a positive even if he was getting on to a player.

"Yeah, don't be surprised when the season starts. Things will change when homie doesn't get enough game time. You'll see." Chivo swaggered ahead with his uniform pants sagging as much as he could get them to.

Daniel tried to blow off his comments, but still, he worried. What did he know about how people acted on this side?

That afternoon at the end of practice, Coach Martinez called the players in to discuss details of their first game.

"We'll be playing Socorro High School, a much larger school than ours. Seniors, you know how the first game usually begins. I need you all to be the leaders since everyone will be a bundle of nerves." He looked over his group of twelve players. "We'll be on our home field so we should feel comfortable with that. The game starts at 4:00 so I'll ask that you be released at 3:00."

Some of the guys grumbled, hoping to get out of class much sooner. The coach smiled but continued his talk.

"Your parents are welcome to watch, but sometimes the first game is a lot of pressure. You know if you will play better with them or without them watching. I want you to give me one hundred percent. Here is the list of starters for the first game. We'll see how it goes, and I'll try to give you each some playing time. Remember, this is a team sport. No show-boating. Pass the ball, and good sportsmanship all around. That means controlling your temper. You might hear some remarks about where you are from. Self-control is what it's all about. Don't let them control you. You control you! Okay, see you here tomorrow at 3:00."

Daniel was shocked to see his name on the starter list. He wished his parents could come across to watch, but they didn't spend the money for another passport and visa for themselves. Just getting his own paperwork was a struggle. Still, he would make them proud. He was smiling on the ride home when he realized he was hoping Cristal was at the bus stop. His smile faded when she wasn't. Then his thoughts went to Chivo's comments, and he felt his good mood fade as well.

* * *

The opening game against Socorro High didn't post as a win for La Lydia Lions, but the kids were still upbeat. The 2-1 score was a respectable loss against a much bigger school. Daniel made the pass to the player who scored their one goal. Coach Martinez let everyone get some playing time and seemed satisfied with their first competition.

Daniel waited for his friends to walk to the bridge. He wished his pa could see him play. The rest of the kids gathered and began the short walk, discussing the game as they went.

Just before the crossing, Chivo appeared shouting at them. "No win for the Lions today. Too bad. Guess you won't be playing in the next game."

Daniel held his tongue, but one of his group couldn't. "Get lost, Chivo. At least we are out there trying."

"Trying? Is that what you call it?" Chivo taunted.

"Come on, Paco. It's not worth it," Daniel said, pulling his friend along.

"Not worth the time when you could be making cash." Chivo flashed a large wad from his pocket.

"Let's go," Daniel said. "Ignore him."

The group hustled onto the bridge as Chivo laughed. Daniel looked back to see Chivo stuff the cash in his front pocket and saunter off. Daniel thought again of Toño, the bully from his own neighborhood. Toño didn't have cash like that, but the anger was the same. Daniel remembered his ma telling him about Toño's homelife. His ma was gone, and his pa was a drunk who beat him. Daniel bet Chivo had a similar story.

"Paco, do you know anything about Chivo? his family?"

"Yeah, they're all a bunch of drug dealers. I don't know how he got into La Lydia."

When Daniel got home, his ma Araceli was waiting. "How was the game? Did you win?"

"No, but I made a pass that got us a goal. We lost 2-1. I think the coach was happy with us."

"That's good, Daniel. I'm so proud of you for doing all you're doing." Araceli had supper going. Her famous rice and homemade salsa made Daniel's mouth water.

"What's on the stove?" Daniel asked.

"*Carne molida con papas,*" she said. "Your pa should be here any minute so we can all eat together for a change. Memo is at Jairo's. He should be here soon too."

They gathered and prayed, something that always warmed Araceli's heart. Daniel recapped the game, and Lucas beamed with pride.

"I'm glad I went to this school, Pa, but I wish you could see me play."

"I can see you play over here on the weekends. You focus on your studies. That's why you're there."

Daniel felt the warmth leave the room. He knew he had to study, but he would like to hear his pa's pride too. Even in *primaria* and *secundaria*, his pa never praised Daniel for anything, only made sure he always studied and read, even during the summers.

Later that night, Araceli watched as Daniel prepared his things for another day of school and bridge-crossings. "Your pa hardly went to school. He always had to work. He wants you to do better and to be better. He doesn't know how to express it, but he's very proud of you." She hugged her oldest tighter. "I'm so proud of you."

With that hug, Daniel thought of Chivo. How many hugs did he get?

* * *

Daniel and Cristal often rode the bus together during their high school years. They did homework together, Daniel usually helping Cristal with math. He taught her a few English phrases, and she shared some of her snacks from home.

"How's Memo doing?" Cristal asked.

"He's doing good. School is easy for him, but he's not really interested. He still wants to be a car dealer."

45

"Funny, isn't it? I have to work so hard at school, and I really want it. That's why I want to be a teacher. I know there are more kids like me who need an understanding teacher."

"Really? Then you would have students like you or like my pa. You sure you wanna do that?" Daniel raised his eyebrows.

"What do you mean like me? I work hard." Cristal tried to control her voice.

"I didn't mean anything by that, only that you started late without knowing anything. That's a lot of work for a teacher."

"I'm sure it was, but I worked hard too. I think that's what teachers do. They persevere and motivate. Not all kids are like you and your brother with supportive parents. Maybe you don't appreciate what your parents did for you." Cristal didn't understand why his remark bothered her. She knew it would be hard to be a teacher, but she wanted to be there for kids like herself.

Daniel didn't reply.

"Maybe your pa needed a teacher like me. And you're a good teacher too." Cristal wanted him to show more empathy.

"I'll never be a teacher. I'm going to go to college on the other side, to UTEP, and become a lawyer. They make lots of money and work in an office. Pa always told me to learn to lift a pencil because it's a lot easier than lifting a shovel."

"There's nothing wrong with becoming a lawyer, Daniel. Just don't forget where you came from and who got you out. Making money isn't the only reason to work, you know."

The bus stopped, and they both got off. Neither one was smiling today.

Chapter 9

2012

Ciudad Juarez
The *Quinceañera*

THE neighborhood was buzzing with excitement about the *quinceañera* this weekend. Fina's classmate Yaquelín was turning fifteen. She was the youngest in her family. Her older sister celebrated her quince five years ago. The expenses were ridiculous, but everyone pitched in to make it easier for the family.

"What are you gonna wear to the *quince*?" Fina said as Cristal came in from work.

Cristal didn't respond. She was still thinking about her conversation with Daniel.

"Look, Cristal. Ma found this dress at the *segundas* yesterday. What do you think?"

"It's nice, Fina. That color looks good on you."

"What's wrong, Cristal?" Fina could always read her.

"Nothing really. I've been enjoying riding the bus with Daniel some, but I think he's changed. Maybe from going across to school? He doesn't seem the same anymore."

"Really, Cristal? Memo seems the same. He's so funny. He always makes the teachers laugh. They can't help it. What did Daniel say?"

"He seems completely focused on making money. Nothing wrong with that. It's probably nothing, just me. I like the dress, but I don't know if I'm going. I think I'm too old to keep going to those."

"Ay chihuahua, Cristal. All ages go. You know that. Come on. It'll be fun. Let's look at what else Ma has."

The two sisters giggled as Cristal tried on a couple of dresses.

"Okay, maybe we need to go to the *segundas* for you tomorrow," Fina said. "How much do you have saved?"

"Not much. I bought the supplies for Ma's tamales, but I get paid tomorrow. Meet me at the bus stop and we'll see what we can find."

* * *

The night of the quince, Cristal and Fina showed off their new attire to Pastor Miguel and Pastora Pati.

"Wow," said Pastor. "I don't have little girls anymore."

"They're growing up," Pastora said. "Girls, remember our rules. Stay together. Be home before midnight. No Cinderellas live here."

"We will, Ma," they said together.

"We're going to the Catholic church first, the one behind Bodega. Can you give us a ride, Pa?" Fina asked.

"I'd be proud to escort you two. Let me rinse off the truck first. It's not a limo, but I can't have my ladies riding in a dirty truck." He hugged them both tight. "God be with you both."

"Do you need us to pick you up after the mass?" Pastora Pati asked while heating some tortillas for Miguel's supper.

"I think we can get a ride. The party is in front of Yaqui's house so not too far to walk if we have to."

"Okay, you know you can always count on us. Take my cell and call Miguel's number if you need a ride. Have fun!"

The girls giggled again as they each teetered in their high heels.

"Hope we can at least make it to the truck before calling for help," Cristal said.

The mass was very solemn as the priest talked of Yaqui leaving her childhood behind. Cristal didn't really understand that part. She felt she never really experienced a childhood. Afterward, there were lots of photo shoots. Everyone present wanted a picture with Yaqui.

Finally, they all made their way to Yaqui's house for dinner and dancing. The street was blocked off, and lights were strung between the houses. Music blared, and children ran unattended between the tables. Even the dogs joined in. The food tables were loaded with brisket, rice, beans, tortillas, and salsa. One burly uncle supervised the ice chests of beer, and some aunts gave out fruit waters to the children. More photos were taken as Yaqui and her court performed their specially-choreographed dance. Then she waltzed with her papá. Others joined in when the music changed to reggaeton. The night was hot but festive.

Cristal sat alone at the table. She watched Fina begin to dance the cumbia with the others in a circle. She noticed Memo ease into the circle as Fina went by. He must have said something funny because Fina bent over with laughter. They moved gracefully together. Adriana, Memo's aunt, danced very close to her current boyfriend.

"Can I get you something to drink?" Daniel appeared from nowhere.

"No, I've got a Jamaica water. Thanks." Cristal looked at Daniel, trying to get another read on him since their last conversation on the bus.

Daniel sat at her table, hesitated a second, then said, "I didn't intend to come across like I did on the bus. I just don't want to waste my time here. Nobody values education. They just want enough work to supply beer for the weekend."

"Well, I hope to change that," Cristal said.

"I'm sure you'll be a good teacher, but that's not for me."

"When I get to be a teacher, I hope you will come back and speak to my students. Maybe you can put some dreams in their heads. I wouldn't have a dream to be a teacher if it wasn't for Pastora Pati in the *comedor.* Those meals and Bible stories gave me hope. You may not know what that's like, but lots of kids around here do. Just remember to give back, that's all I was saying."

He smiled. "Got it. Wanna dance?"

Cristal smiled, and they joined in with Fina, Memo, and the rest of the young people celebrating Yaqui's big day.

The music got more suggestive as the night went on. Adriana appeared to have been drinking more than the fruit drinks. Some older men made moves on the young teen girls. Cristal decided it was time to go. It was almost midnight anyway. She looked around for Fina and caught a glimpse of Memo giving her a quick kiss before Fina ran back to the table. Cristal was happy for Fina, but was she maybe a little bit jealous? No, she had to concentrate on school. There was no time for boys. She was glad the air was cleared between Daniel and her. He was a good friend. That was all.

"Good night, Cristal," Daniel called to her in English.

"Good night," she tried to mimic. It was like a secret code for them. She felt warm inside, and she and Fina walked home barefoot with high heels dangling from their hands.

Chapter 10

2013
UACJ
Itzel

IT was May, and Itzel was finishing her first year at UACJ. She should have been so happy and proud of herself for finishing and qualifying for a scholarship for next year. But Itzel was not happy or proud. She was in the student clinic. She knew deep inside why she was there. She couldn't deny it any longer. The nurse came in and confirmed her fears.

"It's positive. What did you say was the date of your last period?"

Itzel knew she was three months pregnant. She didn't want to believe she had thrown away all her dreams. Tears leaked out as the reality set in.

"We can help you with prenatal vitamins and care, but you will need to make arrangements for the birth at a hospital. I can give you some brochures for different options of care."

Itzel barely heard the nurse. How could she tell Papi? How would Javi react? What would her mami say?

Itzel wandered in a daze as she left the clinic with the brochures and a follow-up appointment. Vitamin samples poked out of her purse. Javi first, she thought. But how can we manage this? What will he say?

She dragged herself to the student center. Javi was in a corner booth preparing for his last exam.

"Itzel, what's wrong? Did someone die?"

Itzel tried to smile at that. "No, not some one, but some *thing*. "

"What do you mean? What are you talking about?"

"I mean our dreams, or my dream, of finishing college." She took a deep breath. "I'm pregnant."

Javi pulled her onto the bench beside him. "Oh Itzel, I thought someone died. We can handle this. We love each other."

"Love isn't going to pay the bills, Javi, or take care of the baby while I study." She didn't mean to sound so sharp. She felt so lost. What were they thinking?

"It's okay, Itzel. We'll figure it out. I thought you were on birth control."

Itzel began to cry. "I am. I don't know why it didn't work. How am I going to tell Papi?"

"We'll tell him together. We'll get married at the courthouse and then go tell him."

"Is that my proposal?" She stood suddenly, rattling the cup and saucer. She ran out the door leaving Javi open-mouthed. She didn't know why the mention of a courthouse marriage set her off. She didn't know where she was going. She didn't really have any girlfriends. Yoli invited her to a movie once, but Itzel poured all her time and energy into Javi and school. She realized too late that a female friendship would be valuable, especially now. Why did everything become clear to her after the fact? Why didn't she ever heed the warnings?

Itzel slowed her pace as she passed through a covered walkway. The hot dry breeze reminded her of the scorching days of summer to come. How would it feel to be fat and pregnant in August? Her baby wouldn't be born until November. Her baby. She couldn't wrap her brain around that thought.

"Itzel! Itzel!" Javi ran up behind her. "I'm sorry. I was just thinking out loud and said the wrong thing. We'll do whatever you want. I want to marry you. I've wanted to marry you since long before this news." Javi dropped down on one knee. "Itzel, will you let me be your husband?"

Itzel let more tears leak down her cheeks. Was this the right decision? Would this make more problems?

"Yes, Javi. I'll marry you."

Javi held her tight as they both contemplated their future.

"Itzel, my cousin can get us across the border. Let's go across, get married, and work all summer there. Then we can come back and finish school on the money we save."

It sounded like a plan. Money was always better on the other side. She might even be able to send some home to her parents. She wasn't showing. She could work all summer while pregnant.

"But then what?"

Javi pulled her close. "We'll figure it out together."

"I love you, Javi, but my world is spinning too fast. How will this work out?"

"God has a plan for us. He always does."

"Since when have we been including God in anything we do?" There was that sharp tone again. She didn't mean it toward him. She meant it toward herself. When did she ever include God in her day, much less in her life?

"I know, Itzel. I know. We'll do better. We'll do better for our child."

She smiled at him then.

"Our child. I can't believe it, Javi."

He pulled her closer. "Are you feeling okay? Do you need anything?"

"I'm fine. Go take your last exam." She pushed him away, trying to smile.

"I'm going, and then I'll call my cousin. Decide what you want to do about your parents, and let's meet at my apartment at 3:00. Deal?"

"Deal."

"I love you. It's gonna be okay."

Itzel wandered toward Javi's apartment. What was she thinking? How could she make all these decisions in a matter of hours?

Javi's roommates were finishing up today too and leaving for the summer. Javi had to be out by Friday. He planned to stay in Durango again to help his mom. What would he tell her? What should they do?

* * *

Javi arrived right at 3:00. His roommates were gone, and Itzel was alone. They hugged tightly and sat on the tiny patio to talk.

"My cousin said we could leave in the morning. If I could sell my motorcycle this afternoon, I would have enough for both of us to cross with a little to get us started until we find a job."

"Tomorrow? That's so quick."

"I know, Baby. But each day we wait to cross, the price goes higher."

"So, are you gonna tell your mom?"

"After we cross. No sense worrying her now."

"Yeah, my mom wouldn't be able to stand it. Better not to tell. But where are we going? Where will we work?"

"My cousin has all kinds of contacts. Finding a job is the easy part."

"What's the hard part?"

Javi looked down. He didn't really know the details involved in crossing, but he knew people did it all the time.

"I think only a few days of traveling, without much to eat, might be tough."

"Where do we have to go? How do we cross?"

"I didn't ask all that. First, let me see if Yurim is still interested in my bike."

Itzel's head was about to explode. Should she call her parents? Should she just go? She was an adult, but she was still her daddy's girl. Ugh, and look what she'd done. Better to execute a good plan before letting them know anything.

* * *

Javi sold his bike and both their laptops. Together they counted out $3,000. They needed five. Reluctantly, they sold their cell phones and a few other trinkets. Not enough for the $5,000 needed. Itzel put the cellphone money inside her bra.

"My cousin said the coyote will lend us the rest. He'll collect it one month after our arrival."

"You think we can make that much in a month?"

"Yes, my cousin says you can pick up money in buckets along the road."

"Oh, Javi. He's exaggerating. What happens if we don't have that much when the time comes?"

"We'll have it. Don't worry. We'll both be working full-time. Better to go tonight before the price goes up more."

Itzel wished she felt as confident, but what choice did she have? She had to trust her husband-to-be.

At midnight, they took a taxi to a plaza in the isolated area of Loma Blanca. Javi carried his backpack filled with snacks and water bottles. Itzel's backpack carried her make-up and her favorite pair of shoes, a change of clothes for them both, and photos of their families. Javi's cousin told them not to carry any ID, but Itzel wanted her parents to know what happened to her if someone found her body. A grim thought, but she tucked her student identification card into the waist of her panties.

They walked a few blocks toward the safehouse. As they neared the corner, a man grabbed Javi, and a young girl grabbed Itzel covering her mouth with a dirty hand.

"Don't make a sound," the man said. "Gimme $1,000 and walk to the green door."

Itzel and Javi obeyed. The man knocked with a coded rhythm. The door cracked open, and another man demanded the second $1,000. Javi rapidly counted it out and handed it over. Then they were pushed inside.

Their eyes adjusted as they huddled together in the dingy room. Other groups of people with backpacks stood around, and a few children shrank behind adult legs. The air was stuffy and hot, but at least the sun was down. Itzel really needed to go to the bathroom but was afraid to ask.

About an hour later another couple arrived with the same desperate look of fear everyone else had. Itzel wondered about all their stories. Were they fleeing drug gangs and violence? Did they have threats on their lives? Was she taking up space someone more deserving should be using? The others were probably running for their lives. She was only running from shame.

At 3:00 a.m., two men barged in the door giving orders.

"There's a pickup out back. Don't make a sound. Gimme $1,000, and load in the back, however you can do it. When we stop, run down the bank, and wait for instructions. We will be crossing in small groups. Once across the river, run to the fence. Someone will be there to show you the hole and the direction to the safehouse on the other side. No talking."

Itzel's heart pounded in her chest. That was all their money, but what choice did they have now? Life was in motion.

Everyone filed out the back and piled into the pickup. Two men in the group had filthy clothes and scraggly beards. Itzel felt nauseous as their body odor emanated her way. She buried her face in Javi's shirt, and the truck began to pick up speed.

They traveled about thirty minutes down an abandoned road. Itzel saw glimpses of the border fence, but mostly she studied the others. Two young mothers with young children squished together in a pile. How did they decide to make the trip? Were any of the men with them their husbands, or were they making this trip alone? Would she ever be that brave as a mother?

The two smelly men had some scary tattoos on their necks. Were they up to no good or were they asylum seekers? Who knew? The rest were young men, probably going to find work. Itzel counted twenty people in the bed of the pickup. Then the truck stopped. Quickly everyone jumped out and began running down the bank. At the river's edge, a young boy pointed out where they should cross the shallow water.

The water only came to her waist, and they made it across easily. At the top of the hill, Itzel was sweating and out of breath. Another little kid pointed to the hole in the fence. Itzel squatted down and wiggled through. Her backpack caught and ripped down the side spilling her make-up as she ran, but she didn't bother to stop. Why was she so vain to think to bring that?

It was so dark. No moon was out, and there were no street-lights. The group of twenty stayed together as much as possible. No one knew where to go next. Were they good? Were they safe now? A large man with a rifle stepped out from behind a big cactus.

"The safehouse is about a mile down this road. Stay hidden. If a car comes, hide wherever you can. You aren't home-free yet."

No cars passed, *Gloria a Dios*, but the mile seemed much farther. They found the house, and all stumbled inside, gasping for air and water. The two-room house already held about thirty people that Itzel could see. They were huddled in groups on the floor and squeezed closer together as the new group arrived. Javi opened a bottle of water, and they shared a few sips.

"Better save it," a young woman beside Itzel said. "We've been waiting here for two days already."

"Is there a bathroom?" Itzel meant to go while crossing the river, but her adrenaline kept her moving, not thinking about it. She was thinking about it now.

"It's outside. Don't go alone." She pointed to a backdoor.

Javi and Itzel moved to the door. A young man with a gun allowed them to pass but held Javi up at the steps.

"You can guard her from here."

Itzel's eyes widened, but Javi reassured her with his. Itzel stepped into the dark outhouse, praying, "God, please protect me from snakes. Protect us from evil. Forgive us for what we are doing. We don't know what we are doing." Tears dripped into her lap as she positioned herself over a nasty hole. Nausea threatened again, but she made it outside into the early morning air. The sun was beginning to peek over the horizon. "Thank you, Lord."

Javi and Itzel spent the day in the safehouse squished together with the other forty plus refugees, trying to think of ways to help pass the time. They played "twenty questions," and they drew tic-tac-toe with their spit on the floor. Either way, the time dragged on. Even more maddening was not knowing when it would end.

An older lady near Itzel was reading her Bible. When she closed it, Itzel asked if she could borrow it.

"Of course, *mija*. God is with us, just like the Israelites. We will be a blessing in the place we are called to."

"Thank you, *Señora*. I wish I paid more attention at church."

"It's never too late. Do you want a suggestion of what to read?"

"Yes, *por favor.*"

"Start with Deuteronomy 31. Moses is telling his people to cross the river without him. God would be there like He is with us now."

Itzel smiled and used the table of contents to find the book. She read it aloud to Javi, but others began to listen too.

"God, your God, will cross the river ahead of you." Itzel looked at Javi. "He did, didn't he."

She read some more. "Be strong. Take courage. Don't be intimidated. Don't give them a second thought because God, your God, is striding ahead of you. He's right there with you. He won't let you down; he won't leave you."

Itzel heaved a big sigh and handed the Bible back to the lady. "Thank you. I needed to hear that." Then Itzel turned to Javi. "*Esfuérzate,*" she said. "Be strong."

Suddenly, there was a commotion at the door. A large man came through shouting, "We have to leave now. There is a shift change at 4:00, and we need to get around the checkpoint then. There is a large panel truck and a pickup. Load up as soon as I get your final payment."

Itzel looked at Javi. "We don't have any more. Who is supposed to lend us the rest?"

"I don't know. Let's just get in line. I don't wanna be here any longer than we have to."

They were the last in line. As they approached the man with his growing wad of cash, Itzel began to shake. "Help us, Lord."

The man held out his hand. Javi tried to form his words. Finally, he said, "We were told we could get a loan from the coyote for the rest."

The man glared at them both. "Who told you that?"

"My cousin. He arranged everything for us."

"Who is your cousin?" The man barked out his words.

"Jesús Vázquez."

"Where does he work?"

"He does construction for the company Hermanos Sánchez."

"We'll find him if we have to. Or, we will find you. You have one month from today. Call this number in two weeks. We need to know where you are, where you are working, and when we can pick up the cash. By then it will be $3000. I hope you care about your cousin."

"Thank you," Javi groveled. Itzel wanted to cry. How would they ever get that much money so quickly? She remembered the verse she read. They would not be intimidated.

The only space left was along the side of the bed of the pickup. The sun scorched down on them. The metal was too hot to touch. But before Itzel could get seated, the truck lurched and she fell against the side. Javi grabbed her to keep her from rolling off, but not before the metal burned her arm. A blister popped up in minutes, but the truck rolled on.

The checkpoint was about an hour's drive from El Paso, but the pickup made it in forty-five minutes. The driver pulled off about a mile beforehand and covered them with a heavy

tarp, making them lie flat like sardines. It was suffocating un-
derneath, and Itzel's arm throbbed. Then she felt more things
being piled on top of her. She tried to ignore the feeling of
claustrophobia. Sweat soaked her back. She reached for Javi's
hand and squeezed it tight.

"Lord, Lord, Lord. Be with us. Make us invisible. Go
before us. Don't let us down. Don't leave us." She tried to
remember the verses. Then she added, "Don't let us let you
down."

Miraculously, they made it around the checkpoint. The
driver took them to yet another safehouse near Van Horn,
Texas. Itzel thought that was a funny name for a town. Van
meant "they're going" in Spanish and Horn looked like the
word for oven. They were going with God. God was with
them. Like the story of the fiery furnace, God was with them
in the oven.

At the safehouse they were allowed a phone call to arrange
their stay in the United States. Javi called his cousin.

"Jesús, I'm sorry. I had to give him your name. We owe
him $3,000. He'll get it from you if we can't pay."

"Oh, you'll pay. Don't worry. Go to the bus station and
catch a bus to Jackson, Mississippi. From there you'll have to
figure it out. There are lots of jobs near there, but the best
town is either Forest or Morton. Both are less than an hour
from Jackson."

"But we don't have any money, Jesus. Nothing."

"Always look for a church. There are lots of them there.
Somebody will help you. Don't worry, man."

Jesus cut the call short. Javi looked stunned. He turned to
the man in charge. "We need to go to a bus station."

"Those going to the bus station in that corner." He was
directing traffic, not concerned with the lives of the people.
They were only a source of income, not real human beings.

At the bus station, Itzel dug out the cash hidden in her bra. There was just enough for two one-way tickets to Jackson, Mississippi. There were many stops along the route and bus changes in Dallas, but they would be there by tomorrow night. They boarded the bus, swallowed the last of their water, and collapsed into each other for the long cross-country ride.

Chapter 11

2013
Mississippi
Itzel

THE bus arrived at the Greyhound station in Jackson at midnight. They might as well have been on the moon. They had no money and knew no one. The dingy smell of Lysol and feet filled the air of the station. Itzel went to the ladies restroom while Javi stood guard outside the door. Inside Itzel found some bilingual fliers with information about shelters. She picked one up but regretted again the decision to sell their cell phones.

They left the station and saw that the city seemed to still be alive. They were near some type of market area. A carnival still had lights on the *rueda de la fortuna,* a giant Ferris wheel. They walked that way, not knowing what else to do, and were surprised to hear lots of Spanish. A husband-and-wife team was packing up an *elote* stand, working in sync as they packed up the rest of the corn-on-the-cob. Javi stopped.

"*Disculpe.* Do you know where we could find a shelter for the night?"

"*Buenas noches.* Where are you from?"

"We just arrived from Ciudad Juarez."

"Wow, that's a long way. How did you pick Mississippi?"

"My cousin told us there are lots of jobs here."

"There are, but it's not easy work. And here in Jackson, the cost of living is higher than in smaller towns. What are you hoping to do?"

"My wife is expecting. We need to make enough to pay for the birth."

"What can you do?"

"I can weld."

"That's a good start, but probably you should have stayed in Texas for that. The easiest places to get on without papers are the chicken plants. There are some near here in Canton, Morton, Forest."

"I think that's what my cousin was talking about."

"You can both get on there if you don't mind the blood and guts." He grinned at them. "I'm Matías. This is my wife, Ana. We are from Michoacán. *Bienvenidos.*"

"I'm Javi, and this is my, well, she's my wife-to-be. We want to get married here."

"Are you believers?" Ana stopped working to join the conversation.

"We are, but we haven't been very faithful," Itzel said. "We promised God we would put our faith in Him for this crazy plan."

"That's a good place to start," Ana said.

"There's a Catholic Charities office across the interstate," Matías said. "They help a lot of recent arrivals, but for tonight, there are only the homeless shelters. I don't think I would recommend them. Plus, you'd be separated."

"Itzel, how far along are you?" Ana asked.

"Only three months. I think I'm finally over the nausea part."

"Mati, let's call Pastor Reynaldo and see if they can stay at our church tonight." She looked at Javi. "Tomorrow, we can take you to Morton to apply for jobs."

"*Dios les bendiga.* Surely God put you in our path."

Javi and Itzel helped the couple finish up. Then they all drove to the church. The Pastor and his wife welcomed them into the small fellowship hall.

"There's a shower in the bathroom," the Pastor's wife said. "We made sure to put one in for this exact need. We brought some clothes too that might fit. And there are snacks in the refrigerator. We will be here at 8:00 to take you to Morton tomorrow. Rest. God is in control."

"Thank you so much, all of you," Itzel said. "I don't know how we can ever thank you enough or repay all you are doing."

"You can pay it forward, *mija*." The Pastora smiled at her. "God has a plan. Now, take this cell phone. It has some paid minutes on it. I'm sure you want to let your family know you are okay."

Tears rolled down her cheeks as Itzel hugged the Pastora. "Thank you."

When everyone left, Javi took Itzel's hand. "Let's start keeping that promise right now. Let's ask God to stay in this crazy plan with us."

They bowed their heads together. "Lord, thank you for safe travel to this place, for putting good people in our path, for having a plan for us even when we didn't consult you first. Now, give us the words to tell our families. Amen."

Itzel began to giggle before the amen. The giggles turned to tears. "What are we going to say?"

"Just dial. God will give you the words."

Itzel took a deep breath and dialed. It took her a few times to figure out the international calling. Finally, she heard the familiar ringing and then her papi's voice. She panicked at first and then jumped in.

"Papi, I'm fine. We're fine. I'm sorry Papi, but I made a decision without telling you. I'm on the other side with Javi. We are going to get married and make some money before we come back. I love you, Papi." She blurted it all out at once. Well, almost all of it.

"Itzel, where are you?"

"We are in Mississippi. Javi's cousin told us where to go for jobs."

"Itzel, where are you staying? Where did you get the money?"

"Papi, we are at a church. The Pastors are very nice and helpful. They are taking us to get jobs tomorrow."

"But Itzel, where did you get the money? How did that boy convince you to run away?"

"He didn't convince me, Papi. We decided this was the quickest way to make some money."

"Why did you suddenly need so much money? Don't I give you everything you need?"

"Papi," Itzel cried, "I'm sorry. I'm pregnant. We didn't want to tell you like this, but we didn't want you to worry."

"*¡Ay, chihuahua,* Itzel! Now you think I won't worry? Here's your mama."

"Itzel, are you okay? Are you taking care of yourself? Oh, Itzel, why didn't you tell us?"

"I know, Mami. It happened so fast. We had to cross when they called, or we would miss the chance. I'm sorry, Ma. We'll be home soon."

"That's what they all say. Here's your pa."

"Itzel, let me speak to Javi."

"Okay, Papi, but be nice."

"Javi, where did you get the money?"

"I'm sorry, sir. We wanted to come tell you, but the ship was sailing."

"Just tell me where you got the money."

"I sold my bike and our cell phones. The coyote lent us the rest."

"The coyote! When is he expecting the rest?"

"In a month. We have plenty of time."

"Javi, you don't know that. You don't realize you have sold your soul to the devil and my daughter with it. How much do you owe?"

"It should be $2,000, but with interest I guess, it will be $3,000."

"If you are lucky. You can't play with these guys. They'll take everything you have. They don't play nice. They don't play. Get a job and send my daughter back. I don't want her to have any part of this trafficking business."

"I can't send her back. We are getting married. She's my wife. I'll take care of her."

Itzel grabbed the phone. "I'm going to be working too, Papi. You've taught me how. Now let me show you. I know you've spoiled me, but I was always watching. I'll call you when we have jobs. Everything will be fine, Papi. I love you."

She ended the call and looked at Javi. "That's done. The worst part is over."

Javi grabbed two water bottles from the refrigerator. "To our new life in America."

"To our new life together with God."

Chapter 12

2013
El Paso and Ciudad Juarez
Daniel and Cristal

THE first year of *prepa,* or high school, flew by for Cristal and Daniel. Occasionally their schedules coincided, and they rode the bus together. Daniel became more confident in his English and taught Cristal more phrases. He also told her about the tough guy Chivo who was eventually expelled from La Lydia for dealing drugs in the boys' restroom.

"I'm sorry about Chivo," Cristal said as they returned by bus from downtown together. "I know you tried to talk to him."

"Yeah, it's too bad. He was very smart. Why wouldn't he use his smarts to make good money the legal way instead of trying to make it the quick way?"

"Well, I hope the school will still try to help him, maybe sending his lessons to the juvenile facility. If he could realize the school did him a favor, he might turn out okay."

"Yeah, but he'll probably end up being another statistic."

"Are there really lots of kids using drugs on the other side?" Cristal wanted to understand how kids with everything could still want to do drugs.

"Yeah, I don't see it too much at our school, but kids over there have access to so much more money. They don't realize the chain of violence they perpetuate by using."

"No, I'm sure kids here don't realize it either. They think it's only a little marijuana. They don't think about the chain of command and the cartels," Cristal said. "Hey, but changing the subject, did you know about Itzel? Did you hear what she did?"

"Itzel from the store? Carmen's daughter?"

"Yes. She and her boyfriend crossed to the other side to go to work. She didn't even tell her ma until they were both across and safe. I heard Pastora Pati talking to Carmen this morning. She was really upset."

"Wow, that was really stupid. It's dangerous crossing that way. Especially for a girl." Daniel thought about all his crossings. The razor wire, the drug dogs, the Border Patrol vehicles, and the automatic weapons on both sides. All of that was crossing legally. He looked down often as he crossed and wondered what it would be like down there at night.

"Yeah, her ma was so angry, but Pastora just kept telling her to be thankful her daughter made it safely across, that God was looking after her. She's thankful, but she's also mad at that boyfriend Javi for putting her at risk."

"Yeah, he should have gone alone. He could have sent her money."

"Well, I think they are getting married there. Itzel is pregnant."

"Oh, I guess that changes things, but not really. Why didn't he just go by himself? How's she gonna work?"

"Ma said they both already have jobs. I guess pregnant women can work over there. I don't think the maquilas let you work pregnant here."

"I wouldn't know about that. That's why I'm gonna be a lawyer. Probably an immigration lawyer. To help people like Itzel and Javi. They should have had better advice."

"Well, it's kinda romantic though. He sold his motorcycle to fund their trip, and she sold her laptop and their cell phones. Off on a new adventure together."

"A romantic adventure that could've gotten them killed," Daniel said, blowing out a big breath.

"Well, it's more romantic on television." Cristal grinned at Daniel, but he didn't seem to think it was funny.

"Adriana is smoking marijuana. She's probably gonna lose her job. Ma's all upset about her, but Adriana won't listen. Sometimes girls are so hardheaded."

"You're so right, and boys always use their common sense," Cristal said as she poked Daniel in the ribs.

Daniel finally grinned at her. "Okay. Not all girls are hardheaded, but not all boys are idiots either."

"Agreed," Cristal said as she held out her hand for a shake. Then she slid out of the seat and made her way home. Daniel was a neat guy. She felt like she could talk to him about anything. She hoped they would always be good friends.

Chapter 13

2013
Mississippi
Itzel

Within two weeks, Javi and Itzel rented a room, got jobs at the poultry processing plant, and found a church home. Doña Elia owned a large house a few blocks from the plant and rented rooms to recent arrivals. Her children were grown, but she kept many grandchildren and neighborhood children during the week.

Itzel and Javi worked from 6:00 to 6:00 five days a week. On Saturdays, Javi worked with a yard crew while Itzel helped Doña Elia with laundry, grocery shopping, and cooking. On Sundays, they all went to church together.

"Javi, God has been so good to us. How can we ever thank him?" Itzel smiled in the mirror at him as they readied for church.

"He has, and I want us to pay it forward as soon as we are able."

Itzel smiled again at him. "Remember, we get to stay after service to meet with the Pastor and his wife today."

"I didn't forget. I want to get married as soon as we can." He grabbed her around the waist. "I love you, baby. And I can't wait to be your husband and the father of our baby."

* * *

The church music was lively with tambourines and drums. Itzel attended an evangelical church in Juarez, but Javi only went to Catholic mass and then only on special occasions. The singing and preaching were all new to him.

During the sermon, Javi looked over at Itzel several times, but she was concentrating. He wondered what it all meant. He rarely listened to the priest. He kneeled and crossed himself when everyone else did. He never felt this much energy at mass before, and the Pastor talked of real-life situations. He seemed to understand the struggles of his people and pointed them to a better way of life.

"Not every problem will be solved by more money," he preached. "The love of money is the root of evil. We must guard our hearts and minds. There is so much temptation to believe that more stuff in this world will make you happy. It might make you more comfortable, but true happiness only comes from the joy of the Lord."

Javi thought about their growing savings stashed under the mattress. In two weeks, they saved $2,500 from their jobs. It was nasty work, but it was worth it. He couldn't imagine how long he would have to work back home to accumulate that much savings. He made the call to the coyote as promised. There were two more weeks to save for the $3,000 owed. They would be fine.

After church, Javi and Itzel met with Pastor Cesar and his wife Maribel. They lived behind the church in a two-bedroom home. Maribel hurried to get lunch ready for them and to control their two active boys.

"Junior, Alex, change your clothes before you go outside." Maribel began heating tortillas on an old *comal*, a flat cast iron skillet. The smells of her kitchen brought Itzel to sudden tears. "*Mija,* what's wrong?" Maribel stopped what she was doing and hugged Itzel.

"Everything makes me cry. Don't worry. The smells of your cooking brought me to my mamá's kitchen. She is such a good cook, and I never really appreciated her or showed her any gratitude. I was so selfish."

"It's never too late to show gratitude, *mija.* When did you last call her?"

"We made a quick call when we got here and another one when we both started working. She's so worried."

"Call her now while I finish here. Tell her what you just told me. Mamas like to hear that they are remembered."

Itzel went out on the porch to talk while Javi and the Pastor went to the small shop out back.

"Itzel?" Her mama answered on the first ring.

"Ma, I miss you." Itzel said. "I smelled your cooking from here."

"Oh, *mija.* I miss you too. How are you feeling? Have you been to a doctor?"

"No, Ma. I'm fine. We're paying off the coyote first, but I feel fine."

"Itzel," her pa grabbed the phone. "Are you saving every dime? That coyote will add on more than you expect, and you can't tell him no. Tell Javi not to fool around with that."

"I love you, Pa. I have to go. We have our marriage class after lunch."

"¡*Ay, chihuahua!*" her pa said.

Itzel walked back to the kitchen.

"All better?" the Pastora asked.

"All better."

After a delicious lunch of tostadas made with beans, lettuce, tomatoes, avocados, and salsa, the two couples began to talk about God's plan for marriage. At first Itzel felt ashamed as she realized she was already out of God's plan.

"Itzel, Javi, don't feel ashamed. Our culture doesn't like to talk about sex. Not many cultures do. We watch all kinds of things on YouTube and in our *novelas,* but we never think about what God's plan for marriage and sex is. And He invented it all. I wish our parents talked to us more. We didn't know any more than you two. Let's look at what the Bible teaches us."

Together they read in Ephesians about job descriptions for husbands and wives. Then they read about the job description for love in First Corinthians 13.

"We men, especially Mexican men, think we are the rooster." The Pastor began to explain as he looked at Javi. "We like to strut around and have the women wait on us. But that is not love. Love serves. It's a big mind shift, Javi, and you can't do it alone. You have to have the Holy Spirit in you. Do you know what that means?"

"I'll be honest, Pastor. I don't. I haven't read the Bible. I go to mass when my family goes. I don't know what it all means. I cross myself when I make a goal or when I almost get hit on my motorcycle. But why? I don't know."

"Javi, God can use any church to show you the way. If your heart is open, God will come in and lead the way. That's the first step to a solid marriage. Are you ready to trust God by taking that first step?"

"I am."

"Itzel, do you want to dedicate yourself to learning more of God's word?"

"I do."

"Let's pray."

Together the four prayed and asked God to lead their marriage. Javi prayed for God to enter his heart. They planned to meet again Wednesday night. Itzel helped the Pastora wash dishes, and Javi helped the Pastor get his lawnmower running. Then Javi and Itzel walked back to Doña Elia's house hand-in-hand. It was a good day.

* * *

On Wednesday, Itzel and Javi rushed home to shower before going to church. The bloody aprons soaked in the sink, and yesterday's aprons hung on the line outside, ready for tomorrow. Itzel couldn't believe the work she was doing now compared to the little chores she used to complain about at home. When her ma would tell her about wringing a chicken's neck to make dinner, Itzel would cover her ears. Now she was the one gutting the carcasses. But, she was getting paid. And, the money was adding up. She and Javi were a good team.

After the prayer meeting, Javi and Itzel met with the Pastor and his wife again.

"How has your week been, Javi? Everything okay?"

"Yes, Pastor. I got moved to a different position Monday, and it pays a little bit more. God is good."

"Yes, he is. But be on guard. The devil is always roaming, looking for ways to trip us up. He really likes new Christians. God didn't promise us a smooth ride, but He will be with us every step of the way. We have to remember to call on Him."

"I'll remember. We've been praying together morning and night."

"That's a great start. The Bible also tells us to pray without ceasing. Sometimes that's hard to wrap our minds around, but it doesn't have to be a formal prayer. Just ask Him to help you make wise choices, remembering him before you make a choice."

"We know about that for sure," Itzel said.

"That's great," the Pastora said. "Now, when do you plan to marry, and how can we help?"

It was exciting to talk about wedding plans and a marriage license. Itzel happily jumped in with the Pastora on the details as the Pastor made plans to take them to the courthouse. Afterward, they walked home hand-in-hand again.

* * *

Thursday after work, Javi didn't come straight home. Itzel thought he must be working overtime. She helped Doña Elia finish cooking and washed the big pot she used. Two grandchildren were still there, and Itzel helped them with some math homework. Her English was still not very good, but she could explain the long division in Spanish. Math was math.

Suddenly they heard a horn honk. They all rushed outside to see Javi standing beside a small, red Mitsubishi with one gray door.

"It's ours, Itzel. We own a car!" Javi was smiling, but Itzel was not.

"Javi, we have to pay the coyote! How could you do this without talking to me first?"

Javi's face fell. Then anger filled his eyes. "I did it for us. You know we need transportation. We aren't going to always live within walking distance of the plant."

"Kids, let's get inside." Doña Elia herded her grandchildren to the kitchen to give the couple some space.

"Javi, the coyote will be here next week."

"I still have $1500 left. I didn't spend it all."

"But what if he demands more like Pa said."

"Your pa! I'm your husband now. I make the decisions."

"You're not yet." Itzel ran up to their room and slammed the door. *What was he thinking? He knew how anxious I was about this payment. I wanted that part behind us. I didn't want to worry about a stranger showing up as we left work on payday. Does he think we are immune to the violence we saw in Juarez just because we're a thousand miles away?*

"Itzel," Javi called through the door. "Let's talk. I'm sorry. I should have talked to you first. It was such a good deal. I was afraid to pass it up."

Itzel opened the door. "Javi, you know how scared I am about this payment. And have you not listened to anything the Pastor's been saying?"

"I know, Itzel. I know. I didn't think. I let the devil tempt me, just like he warned. I'm sorry. We'll be okay. I've got that extra pay, and we'll get a bigger check next week. I'm working all day Saturday too. We'll have enough."

But Friday after work, Itzel's nightmare came true. As they left the plant together, a stranger approached them. "Let's have the cash. All $3000 of it."

"We only have $1500. We'll have the rest by next Friday. I promise," Javi said.

"That's only half. By next Friday, it will be $4000. Give me the $1500, and we will get the $2500 on Friday."

"I can't make that much by then." Javi tried not to whine, but his voice was shaking, and his hands were sweating.

"Together we only make $1800 before taxes," Itzel said, trying to help.

"Shut up, woman," he said to Itzel, then turned to Javi. "Go get the money. She stays here with me." Then they saw the knife.

"Go, Javi! Please, go!" Itzel pleaded as Javi ran. She kept her eyes on Javi even as the smelly man pushed her into a stand of trees. "Why, Lord?" She prayed out loud as she felt the knife pressing into her side. "Protect us, Lord. Help us, Lord. Forgive us, Lord."

Finally, she saw Javi returning with the envelope of money. He handed the envelope to the man, but he grunted at Javi.

"You count it."

Javi counted as Itzel gritted her teeth and tried not to breathe. Suddenly, she couldn't hold back anymore.

"Javi," Itzel began to cry. "Why did you buy that car? Why?"

"Car? Where's the car?" the man said. "Why didn't you say so?"

The man pushed them both to the house, demanded the keys, and cranked the engine. "Okay, where's the title and we're good."

"It's in the glove compartment. I haven't changed it to my name yet."

But Javi didn't finish the sentence before the man sped off with their car and their money. Itzel collapsed on the curb. "Javi, we have nothing. Nothing to show for all our blood and guts work."

He sat down beside her and held her tight. "We're alive, and we have each other."

Itzel could feel his heart pounding harder than her own.

"I learned a lesson, but I could have learned it a very hard way," Javi said. "I could have lost you and our baby. That would really be losing it all. I love you, Itzel. I'm sorry. We're a team. I won't forget that again. The three of us are a team. With God, we will recover."

Itzel wanted to believe him. Her whole life was in his hands. Now she realized she should have put her whole life into God's hands. God, forgive me. Help us. We can't be a team without you.

At that moment, Doña Elia stuck her head out the screen door. "Is everyone okay?"

The smell of tamales wafted from her tiny kitchen. The locusts were beginning their summer song. The sun was painting a beautiful sunset across the western sky, the direction they had come from only a few weeks earlier.

Itzel looked up. "We're fine, Doña Elia. We had a terrible scare, but we'll be fine."

Javi stood, pulled Itzel to her feet, and turned to Doña Elia.

"We might be here longer than we planned. I'm still learning," Javi said.

She smiled at the young couple. "Aren't we all?"

* * *

Sunday after church, Javi and Itzel met with the Pastors again. The rice and beans were just like Itzel's mom cooked, and the carne asada was just like her dad's.

"I miss my family so much," Itzel confided in the Pastora. "I didn't think I would."

"I know, mija. I haven't seen mine for nine years. I can't tell you it gets easier, but with God we can be there for each other. It's not the same, but we can be family."

"Gracias, Pastora. You know our plan was to make enough money to pay for the hospital and have some to live on when we went back to school in the fall. Now we are starting over again. I don't know if we will make that goal."

"Sometimes God changes our goals. Draw close to Him, and He will direct your path."

Javi and the Pastor brought the meat in. It smelled delicious. The Pastor asked Javi about the car.

"So, what was it?"

"A 1995 Mitsubishi."

The Pastor tried not to laugh. "How many miles?"

"I don't know. Maybe about 210,000."

The Pastor couldn't hold his laughter in any longer. "You are lucky the guy could drive it away. Do you know how hard it is to get parts to keep that thing running? God did you a favor, young man. That car was going to be a terrible investment."

Javi ducked his head. "I didn't know. I bought the first thing I saw. I didn't listen to any of your advice from last week. You warned me."

"It's okay, *mijo*. You learned something, not just about cars, but about how marriage works."

"Let's pray and eat first, Papi," the Pastora said. She grinned at Itzel. "Then we can plan the wedding.

Chapter 14

2013
Ciudad Juarez
Daniel and Cristal

SCHOOL was over for Daniel at the end of May. He liked that part of the American school calendar. Cristal, Fina, and Memo didn't finish until the end of June.

Daniel decided to work with his pa for the summer. He was not good at stucco, but he was a good helper. The trouble was that his pa never found steady work. After a couple of weeks of hit-or-miss work, Daniel decided to see what else he could do. There were several maquilas with openings, but he had to be eighteen.

"Why don't you apply to work in the cafeteria at my maquila?" Adriana offered. "I think they will hire you at sixteen there."

"What would I be doing?"

"Cleaning up after me," she teased.

"I do that now!" Daniel said.

Adriana and Junior had lived with them for about a year now. Junior went to the same school as Memo. They were so close in age that they felt more like cousins than aunts and uncles and nephews.

"For real, what would I be doing?"

"Probably busing tables, sweeping, mopping, refilling. Nothing too complicated for a teenage brain like you."

"Okay, I'll go tomorrow. Thanks."

"But no spying on me. I didn't think about that," Adriana said. She tried to smile like she was joking, but she didn't quite pull it off.

Daniel wondered about that for a second, but he moved on, happy to have a new option.

The cafeteria manager was happy to hire Daniel. He put him straight to the tasks Adriana described, and Daniel did his best to shine. He occasionally saw Adriana when she was on break, but she usually sat at a faraway table with a rough-looking group.

One day a group of executives from El Paso came to tour the plant. They were from the main headquarters and were looking at ways to reduce costs. Daniel heard them discussing the benefits and costs of having on-site food for the workers. One guy was sure it was a waste of money and wanted to close the cafeteria. Daniel tried not to react as he eavesdropped on their conversation.

"On the other side, we have a lot of food trucks that park outside our plants at break time. That way, we have no over-head."

"What do you do about security?" the manager from the Juarez plant asked.

"What do you mean? We have a security guard who patrols the grounds."

"One guy? Do you have a gated compound?"

"No, it's a large open-air parking lot. There are some shade trees and picnic tables and some tables inside."

"But how do you know who is coming and going?"

"We let anyone with a food truck come in. There's never been a problem."

"We have a sealed entrance. We couldn't let anyone and everyone come and go through our parking lot. That's asking for trouble. We like having our employees here for the entire shift and no one else from outside interrupting that flow."

The men argued on, but Daniel could tell that they didn't understand each other's different problems. After the men left, Daniel approached his manager.

"Did you know they were thinking about closing the cafeteria?"

"What? What are you talking about?"

"Those men from the other side who were touring, they were talking about closing us down to cut costs."

"You speak English?"

Daniel blushed a little. "Yes, I go to *prepa* on the other side."

"Why didn't you say so? Let me find you a better job."

Soon Daniel was on the catering team. He helped serve meals when visitors came from the other side. He made complicated orders for guests with special dietary needs. He kept the office coffee areas stocked and delivered pastries to the executives during their breaks. But the main thing he did for his manager was listen. His English skills and some snooping helped save the cafeteria.

Daniel received a nice raise and worked there all summer. However, he also discovered more about Adriana's life than he wished to know. Most days, they rode the maquila route bus together. But on the days there was a special banquet, Daniel's hours would change.

One day Daniel clocked in at the same time Adriana was having her morning break. She was with her usual group, who slipped out a side door. Daniel imagined they had to smoke. He didn't think Adriana smoked since he never smelled it on her clothes like he did sometimes on his pa.

"Daniel, can you help me with these garbage bags? Alvaro didn't show this morning," his manager said.

"Sure," Daniel said and dragged the heavy bags to the same side door. As he approached the dumpsters, he smelled a different smell, something smoky but sweet. He immediately recognized it from Chivo's friends. Then he saw Adriana. And she saw him.

"Get outa here, nephew."

"I've gotta get to those dumpsters."

The group hurriedly stubbed out their cigarettes and went inside.

"It's just a smoke break," Adriana said.

"Yeah, Adriana. I know."

"Give me a break," she said.

"Your break was getting to live with us. Why do you wanna throw all that away?"

"I'm not throwing that away if you don't snitch."

"It's not about whether they know or not, Adriana. It's about your choices for your life."

"Oh, look at my little nephew trying to preach to his auntie."

"Adriana, think about what you're doing with your life. We've both seen how this ends. It's not good."

"Get back to your little cafeteria job, nephew. It's just some pot." She rolled her eyes and went back to work.

Daniel sighed and finished his task. He knew if his ma knew about this, she would be so sad.

That night, Daniel went to Carmen's store for some tortillas.

"How's my favorite gringo?" She teased Daniel like he was her son.

"I'm okay. I need some tortillas."

"You don't look okay," Carmen said as she rang him up.

"It's Adriana. She's making bad decisions."

"How your ma made it out of that house, I don't know. I don't want to talk bad about your *abuela*, but she was not a good mamá to your mamá, and not to Adriana either. What's Adriana up to?"

Daniel didn't hesitate. "She's smoking marijuana on her break."

"On the premises?"

"Yes, and she always throws the 'little nephew card' at me if I try to say anything to her."

"Adriana and my Itzel ran together. I know how stubborn they both can be. What does your ma say?"

"She doesn't know yet," Daniel said, groaning.

"I get it, Daniel. You don't wanna be the little snitch, but you know your ma needs to know. You are *entre la espada y la pared*."

"Yes, in English they say between a rock and a hard place. Either way is not good."

"Just tell her, Daniel. She needs to confront Adriana. It's a slippery slope."

Daniel walked home, looking down at his feet. He didn't see Cristal coming toward him.

"Hey, why the long face? School's out!" Cristal punched him in the arm and tried out her latest English phrase, "What's the big deal, man?"

Daniel smiled at that and told her about Adriana.

"I hate to say it, but I'm not surprised."

Daniel's eyes got big. Then he scowled at her.

"I'm sorry. I know you don't want to hear it, but I saw her last weekend with my ma, Rubi. At first, I thought Ma was buying something from Adriana's stand, but then I saw the quick exchange and the immediate exit. It was a drug deal, Daniel. I'm not sure what it was, but Rubi was dealing something."

"I wish you'd told me, but I guess that's what my ma would say too. I need to tell her."

"I'm sorry."

"So, what are you doing this summer?" Daniel wanted to change the subject. "Memo's working with Ivan."

"Fina and I are bagging groceries at the S-Mart. It's only tips, but they add up."

"That's too bad. You're smarter than that."

"Yeah, well, I'm an underaged girl, so there's not much else. At least it's air-conditioned."

"Yeah, I don't know how my pa works all day in this heat, lugging buckets of stucco."

"So, are you still planning to go back across when school starts again?"

"Yes, and we need to work on your English. I got a better job at the maquila because of my English."

"That's great, and I'd like that too. Let me know how it goes with Adriana and your ma. I'll be praying for all of you."

"Thanks," Daniel said and turned toward his house. He believed in God, and he believed God helped people, but he wasn't sure about prayers solving a drug problem. It seemed like drug problems continued to get worse instead of better. He took a deep breath and tried to plan his first words to his ma. She was studying now. She wanted so much to get her diploma. Adriana better not mess that up.

* * *

"Ma, I need to tell you something."

"What is it, *mijo?*"

"Adriana is smoking marijuana at work."

Araceli pushed back her notes and sighed. "I hoped she wasn't going down that path. I'll have to get her attention. Your pa won't stand for that going on while she lives here."

Daniel understood. His pa smoked a cigarette or two outside at night, but he would not tolerate drugs. "There's a little bit more, Ma. She's buying from Rubi."

"*Ay Dios mío,*" she said. "What is that girl thinking? She's watched Rubi's life. Why does she think she is gonna be different? Thank you, Daniel. You did the right thing telling me."

That night there was a discussion with Adriana, as Lucas and Araceli tried to convince her of the error of her ways. She was stubborn though, just like Carmen said. She tried to turn it on Daniel being a snitch, but they held firm. Finally, she promised that was the end of it, but Daniel had his doubts. How could she escape the crowd she was running with at work?

The rest of the week was calm. Daniel did not see Adriana at break times, and he concentrated on his job. He hoped to save enough to eventually buy a car, but that was probably a long way in the future. Right now, every peso went into his school costs.

The following weekend, Memo suggested they go to the carnival. "All work and no play make sad little boys. Come on, Daniel. Spend some of your money. Let's invite Cristal and Fina."

Daniel tried to act nonchalant when he said, "Sure, if you want to."

"Come on, bro. You know you've got a crush on her."

"Yeah, and you sneaked a kiss with Fina at the quince."

"I'm not denying that. Let's go!"

* * *

At the carnival, the four of them walked around as they ate *mangoneadas* with *chamoy*, a frozen treat made from mangoes and hot sauce. The girls were dressed casually in jeans, but Memo was dressed like a vaquero in his cowboy boots and hat.

"Hey, Memo. Remember when Abuelo brought you some boots, and you wore them night and day until they got too tight?"

"Yeah, I still kept trying to wear them. But I left them out front one day, and someone stole them. Remember?"

"Yeah, and Carmen hollered at the kid to bring them back. He dropped 'em and took off. You were so glad to get your boots back."

"I remember Abuelo," Cristal said. "He tried to help us so many times. Ma would blow him off, but he always showed up with something. Once, when I was so hungry, he brought us burritos, nice and hot. He's the best."

"He is," Daniel said. "I keep hoping he will visit again, but Ma said he hasn't recovered from a recent surgery."

They walked along, reminiscing, past the usual rides and games. A *lucha libre* show of local wrestlers they all wanted to see was scheduled for eight o'clock. They rode the *rueda de la fortuna,* a rickety Ferris wheel, and Daniel caught a glimpse of Memo stealing another kiss as they went over the top. His brother was something else.

Then it was time for the match. They bought tickets and squeezed into seats. The smell of popcorn mixed with body sweat was overwhelming. The different wrestlers were introduced, and the crowd went wild. Memo couldn't control his laughter at the stunts and moves of the crazy wrestlers, and soon all their sides were hurting from laughing so hard.

It was a fun night, and they walked toward the bus stop, Memo and Fina hand in hand. Daniel was conflicted about

Cristal. He wouldn't mind holding her hand, but she seemed to only want to be friends, and he didn't want to ruin their friendship.

Suddenly a man stumbled from a side street trying to call for help.

"There's—there's a woman down," he stuttered. "She n-n-needs help."

Daniel stepped forward, but Memo pulled him back. "What are you thinking, man? Don't go down there. Let's call the cops."

"It might be too late if we do that," Daniel said. He turned down the street and immediately saw the woman face down. "Call an ambulance."

Daniel and Cristal ran to the woman and eased her onto her back. Cristal gasped, and Fina screamed. Then another person appeared from the shadows. Adriana was barely able to stand, and she reeked of some kind of inhalant.

"Oh, God, Adriana. What's going on here?" Daniel said.

"Daniel," Cristal said in a low voice. "It's our ma. It's Rubi. Is she breathing? Does she have a pulse?"

Daniel tried to remember the CPR course he took during health class. He couldn't feel a breath and couldn't feel a pulse. He started compressions to the beat of "The Macarena," and tried to ignore the crying of the girls. Finally, the ambulance arrived, and the paramedics took over. They loaded her into the ambulance while continuing compressions. Another paramedic attended to Adriana.

"Tell us what you consumed so we can help you."

"I was just huffing thinner," Adriana said.

"You were just frying your brain cells," the paramedic responded impatiently. "You're lucky you didn't die from an immediate heart attack. Is that what your friend was doing too?"

"No. I don't know. Maybe."

"I'm afraid your friend isn't going to make it."

"What? She just smoked a little pot and took a huff of thinner," Adriana said, suddenly more awake.

"Excuse me," Cristal stepped in. "That's my ma in there. Is she gonna make it?"

"They'll give her a good twenty minutes before they call it. I'm sorry. That's what makes inhalants so dangerous. They can kill in an instant."

"Can I use your phone?"

Pastor Miguel and Pastora Pati, along with Lucas and Araceli, arrived quickly. The girls flew into the arms of their foster parents as Adriana stumbled into her sister's arms.

"I'm sorry, ladies. There is no response. They are ready to call time of death."

Cristal and Fina held on to Pastora Pati for all they were worth. Everyone knew this day would come. The church had paid for several admissions to rehab programs already, but Rubi always returned to the only life she knew. Pastor Miguel held his three women close and prayed for peace and comfort. Drugs were a slow road to suicide.

Chapter 15

2013
Ciudad Juarez
Rubi's Wake

A RACELI was furious with her sister. Every time she tried to say something to her, she only managed to lash out.

"How could you? What were you thinking?"

"It was just something cool to do with the guys after work," Adriana said. She appeared to be coming out of her stupor.

"It sounds like you don't have enough responsibilities to keep you busy. There's always something that needs doing here. And what in the world were you doing with Rubi? You know who she is. Why did you go with her?"

"I just went to get a little weed. She said she was cleaning up her act, that she didn't have any more weed to sell, but she wanted to go out one more time to celebrate her getting clean. She asked me to go with her."

"Why wouldn't she wait to celebrate after she was clean a while, and celebrate with her own family?"

"Rubí said they all cut her off. All she used was that can of thinner. She was so pitiful, not having anyone to hang out with. So, I decided to be her friend." Adriana took a shuddering breath. "I'm sorry, *hija,* I didn't know it could kill you."

Araceli wrapped her arms around her sister. That nickname *hija* they used for each other really meant daughter. How could she turn her back on her sister now.

"Adriana, I can't be your mother. I can't watch you all the time. And I can't let you be a bad example for my boys. Plus, I don't think Lucas will allow you to stay anymore after tonight. What can you do? Where can you go?"

"I don't know, hija. I don't know."

"Let's get to bed. Maybe God will give us a plan in the morning."

Araceli didn't see Adriana roll her eyes at the mention of God.

Meanwhile Cristal and Fina stood in their kitchen in stunned silence. Pastor Miguel made arrangements with the funeral home to have their mother's body delivered the next afternoon for the wake. She would be on their patio until ten o'clock the following morning. Then the funeral home would transport her to the cemetery on the edge of town for a graveside service.

"Let me fix you two some hot chocolate," Pati said.

"For me too," Pastor Miguel said as he ended the call. "I know we can't believe it. We are all still in shock. But girls, I want you to understand something. Sit down. Let's talk."

They moved as robots to the table, huddling close to each other as they did all those years when they were left alone by Rubi. And now she was really gone. She wasn't coming back.

"Your ma made lots of mistakes and chose drugs many times over God and over you, but we don't know about the last minutes of her life. We don't know her heart. Only God knows. And our God is merciful. He gives grace after grace if only we will ask. Adriana said your ma decided to get clean, that this was her last night out. I know she's said that before, but again, only God knows her heart. I'm sure you have many conflicting feelings. It's okay to be mad at her and mad at God. She was your mom no matter what, and that bond will always be there. Grief may hit you at different times and in different ways even from each other, but know this: Pati and I are here for you for life. We love you, and we hurt for you. God loves you, and God hurts for you. I promise He will use this loss for good. We may not ever understand it all from this side, but God is in control."

"Well, if He is in control, why did she have to die? Why didn't prayers work?" Cristal cried out.

Pati wrapped her arms around her as she placed the hot chocolate on the table. "*Mija*, our ways are not His ways. We get to make free choices, and Rubi made hers. God placed many people in her path to help her, but she chose drugs. Or maybe the drugs chose her. That's the scary part about drugs. One person can do it once and walk away, but for others the drugs are their captor. In her lucid moments, she told me she believed. I have to believe that she meant it, and God knows Rubi's heart."

"I guess I was still holding on to a hope she would become the mom we never had."

"I know, *mija*, but she was a good mom in that she gave you both to us. After her initial protests, she realized placing you here was the most loving thing she could do for you."

"We need to tell Ivan," Fina said, always the stoic, practical one.

"Yes, we do," Miguel said. "I can go now."

"No, let's all go," Cristal said. "We should be together now."

* * *

At five o'clock the next afternoon, Rubi's body arrived in a simple coffin with a plexiglass covering. Flowers arrived from florists, and neighbors brought food and coffee. Chairs were arranged around the patio, and soft music played from the speakers brought from the church. An offering box sat by the entrance for donations to help with funeral expenses; it was expensive to die in any country. Young children played, and the inevitable dogs slept under chairs occasionally waking to grab a fallen crumb. The whole neighborhood turned out, it seemed.

Daniel and Memo came with their parents, but Adriana stayed home. Even distant relatives of Rubi came to pay their respects. About ten o'clock that night, an obviously inebriated visitor came. He wobbled to the coffin to peer for a few minutes, then raised his head to look around.

"Where are her kids?" he shouted. "Where are they?"

Everyone stared at him, not knowing what to say. Ivan was the first to speak.

"Pa?"

The man stared back. His expression didn't change.

"Who are you, sir?" Pastor Miguel said.

"I'm Rubi's husband."

"I'm sorry for your loss, but we didn't think she had a husband."

"Well, we never married officially, but we had kids together. Doesn't that count for something?"

"Yes, you're right about that. It counts in that you should have been supporting these kids all this time, and I don't mean only with money."

"Yeah, well, they did okay without me."

"Sir, why are you here?"

"Someone told me Rubi died. I wanted to see for myself."

"Well, you've seen," Ivan said in a loud voice. "Time to go."

"Look here, son. You don't talk to your pa in that voice." The man stumbled toward Ivan.

"You don't have any right to call me son." Ivan threw a punch before anyone could stop him, and with one punch the man collapsed.

Jairo pulled Ivan back. "Take it easy, Ivan. He's not worth it."

Pastor Miguel turned the man over and lifted his head. He was conscious. The alcohol probably kept him from feeling any pain. "Sir, where do you live? Let us get you home."

Officer Chuy helped Miguel lift him and walk him away from the patio.

"I don't want to arrest you, but you need to go home and not come back. You aren't welcome here."

Pastor Miguel, ever the optimist, said, "If you can sober up, we'll be glad to help you get to know your children. You have two beautiful girls also."

"Oh no, those aren't mine, only the boy."

Pastor Miguel was glad the girls did not hear that last statement. They put him on a bus and hoped he made it to his home. God really had his hands full in this neighborhood.

* * *

At the cemetery many neighbors circled the grave and prayed. Pastor Miguel offered a short message about God being in control even when we didn't understand. He talked about Rubi's last moments and how drugs can rule even when we try hard to break free. He hoped some young people were listening.

Then they lowered the coffin, covered the grave, and walked by, leaving flowers on top. Everyone hugged the children and thanked Pati, Miguel, and Jairo for filling the gap for them as parents. As everyone was loading into cars and backs of pickups, a couple arrived, also very inebriated. They staggered to the lead car asking for Rubi.

Pastor Miguel once again stepped forward. "I'm Pastor Miguel. May I help you?"

"What have you done with our daughter? Where is she?"

"Rubi passed away Monday night. We just finished the interment."

"Rubi is gone?" The woman suddenly burst into uncontrollable tears. "She's our only daughter," she wailed between sobs.

Pastor Miguel took some deep breaths. *Why do people wait until now to step forward?* He had looked everywhere when Rubi was at her worst and the children needed family so badly. Where were they then?

"I'm sorry for your loss. When you are sober, you may come to our house to see your grandchildren."

"Sober? What business is that of yours? Where are our grandchildren? We have a right to them."

Pastor Miguel returned quickly to the car and drove home. He didn't want the children exposed to any more of their drunk relatives than necessary. They had legal documents for them. The grandparents were AWOL for eight years. The children were old enough to decide if they wanted contact or not. *Lord, give us wisdom. We know you are a gracious and loving God even unto these difficult relatives, but we also know we have a responsibility for these kids. Help us handle this situation correctly.*

During his silent prayer, Cristal suddenly spoke. "I know these people are our blood relatives and God's children. But you two are our true ma and pa. You two have shown us what love is. We can pray for them and love them from afar, but we don't have to let them in. I get it now. Thank you for all you two have done."

"Thank you, *mija*. God be with us."

Chapter 16

2013
Mississippi
Itzel

THE wedding would be in two weeks. Itzel had to get a dress. So, the Saturday before, Itzel went to the thrift store beside the pantry where they received help when they first arrived in town. The lady in charge of the pantry was Frida, and the lady in charge of the clothing was Tootie. The ladies didn't speak any Spanish, but somehow, they all communicated just fine.

"I need dress for wedding," Itzel said in her halting English.

"We have some nicer dresses on this rack," Tootie said. "When is it? Will it be outside? It's awful hot now and you never know when it's gonna rain." Tootie kept talking and pulling out dresses until she noticed Itzel's expression.

"I need dress for me wedding."

"Ooh, you're getting married! Congratulations! We have two dresses in this corner. Come see,"" Tootie said. "I bet this one's just your size. You're so slim and trim."

Itzel followed Tootie and tried to understand her rapid-fire English.

"We have this one that would probably fit you, but it has long sleeves. Is your wedding outside? It would be too hot. When is your wedding? Where will it be?"

"My wedding next Saturday. My wedding in chapel Iglesia de Alabanza."

"I know where that is. Pastor Cesar and his wife, Maribel, are big supporters of our pantry. Is he doing the ceremony?"

"Yes, Pastor Cesar. He marry me."

"Well, he's married, but I got it. He's doing the service. But next Saturday! Girl, that's quick. You got a bun in the oven?" Tootie laughed loudly so Itzel did too.

"This dress will be cooler but might need some alterations." Tootie talked louder as she went instead of slower.

Itzel tried to understand her. "I like dress. I test?"

"Yes, here's the dressing room. I'll pin it up for you so you can see what needs to be done."

Later at home, Doña Elia helped her hem and alter. It was perfect.

"Now go change and bring it to me before Javi gets home."

"Thank you, Doña Elia. I..." Itzel couldn't finish. Tears ran down her cheeks. Her throat tightened. "I only wish my parents could be here. What was I thinking?"

"You were thinking in your teenaged brain, just like Javi with the car. Now you'll begin to think in a grown-up brain. God is giving you a new family now. Keep Him at the center of your marriage."

The two women hugged, and Itzel straightened to go upstairs. "Thank you," she whispered.

* * *

Itzel was a beautiful bride. Javi stood in awe as she made her way down the aisle of the small church. Pastor Cesar asked the traditional questions and draped the couple with decorated rope binding them together. Then he pronounced them husband and wife.

Their church family turned out for the special event, and everyone helped with food and drinks for the reception. The church yard was decorated with tiny white lights. Doña Elia arranged wildflowers from the roadside into gorgeous bouquets. Phones were snapping photos and shooting videos that would soon be flying through the internet to Ciudad Juarez and Durango thanks to WhatsApp and the expanding Wi-Fi in Mexico. Itzel and Javi received many congratulatory messages from friends at UACJ and friends and family at home.

"*Señora*," Javi said to Itzel. "You are beautiful!"

"Gracias, *Señor*." She laughed at their new titles. "I don't feel any older, but when I think back to our first days at *uni*, I realize how young we were."

"We still are. But thanks to all these friends, we can learn from their experiences, God willing."

"We've got to learn fast. We've only got a few months to get our act together."

"You will be a great mother."

"And you will be a great dad."

Everyone toasted the new couple with *"Dios les bendiga"* and *"Felicidades."* The music started up, and the couple danced their first dance as husband and wife. Later a money dance brought in some much-needed cash as each dance partner pinned bills to Itzel's dress. Children and dogs ran around just like at home.

Pastor Cesar handed Javi the keys to his truck. "Only one night." He grinned at Javi. "Be back tomorrow night. You both have work on Monday morning. You have a reservation at the Hampton Inn in Pearl, past the Jackson airport exit. Breakfast is included."

"Thank you, Pastor," they said together.

"Pastora," Itzel said, "thank you for everything. If my mom and dad couldn't be here, you two were great substitutes. We love you"

The couple drove away under a hail of birdseed and confetti to their one-night honeymoon destination. Real life would crash back in Monday morning, but for now they were living most of the dream.

* * *

Itzel and Javi returned from their honeymoon ready to work. They realized their dream of returning home with buckets of money was just that, a dream. They needed to save for hospital bills, a car, and enough to live on while Itzel wasn't working.

One day when Itzel was waiting for her first check-up at the community health clinic, she met Sandra.

"Where are you from?" she asked Itzel.

"We came from Juarez, Mexico, about three months ago. You?"

"We came from Guatemala about three years ago. My girls were both born here, at the hospital in Jackson."

"This is my first visit. I didn't know I had to go to Jackson to deliver."

"Yes, but have you signed up for WIC?"

"What's that?" Itzel had no idea.

"It's a program to help feed the baby. It also helps you eat well while pregnant."

"Won't I need papers?" Itzel was always wary of anything related to her immigration status.

"No, only a positive pregnancy test. The site is near the Dollar General," Sandra said.

"But will it put me on the radar for I.C.E.? I don't wanna call attention to myself to the immigration officials."

"No, not at all. They want healthy mamas and babies, so they provide us with good nutrition."

"Who is 'they?'" Itzel asked.

"The government, I guess," Sandra said, shrugging her shoulders.

"Well, the government doesn't just have money to give away. They get it from somewhere. I remember that much from school."

"Yeah, probably from taxes or something, but they have plenty to share."

Something didn't seem right about that, but Itzel knew the program would help them through the tight times.

"Be sure to ask for a referral when you see the nurse. I'm Sandra. Where do you live?"

"I'm Itzel. We live in a boarding house until we can afford our own place."

"Doña Elia's? We stayed with her for two months when we first came. She's my second mama."

"Mine too. She might be this one's abuela too." Itzel felt a pain in her heart as she realized she was depriving her mom of the joys of being a grandmother.

"I see that face. I know how it is to be far from your real mom when you need her most. But you'll make it. Doña Elia will be there. I can be too. If you need anything or have questions about how to navigate the maternity care here, call me." They swapped cell numbers, and Itzel was called to the back. She held her head higher. She had a friend who had been there.

When Itzel arrived home, Doña Elia was helping a man unload a large live turkey from a cage in the back of his truck. Itzel watched with mouth wide open as they led the turkey by a rope around his leg to the large dog pen in back. Doña Elia paid the man in cash and filled a water bucket for the turkey.

"What in the world?" Itzel said.

"That's for our Thanksgiving feast. In November we take a whole day just to give thanks to God for our blessings. We also eat way too much food."

"This is a custom for your family?"

"No, *mija.* It's a great American tradition, a national holiday. And turkey is the main dish." She turned to address the turkey, "Sorry, Tom."

"When is it? Do we get off work that day?"

"Yes, even the poultry plants shut down. When's your due date? I want you around to help me cook."

"November 25th," Itzel said.

"Well, it's the 28th. With it being your first baby, you might make it. When do you find out if it's a boy or girl?"

"I can find out before it's born?"

"Yes, mija. When do you have an ultrasound?"

"My next visit I have to go to Jackson. Javi is asking off for both of us that day."

"I think it will be a girl. I'm usually right, you know?" Doña Elia grinned at her and gave her a hug. "I'll be here to help you. You won't be alone. It won't be your mama, but you will have enough help."

"Thank you," Itzel said. There was still so much to do.

Chapter 17

2013
Mississippi, The First Thanksgiving
Itzel

Poor Tom was butchered, and the large turkey was in the oven. Itzel tried not to think about it, or nausea would overcome her. She helped all she could in the kitchen, always conscious of how much room she occupied now. The baby was low and could come anytime. Her last visit was Monday. Her bag was packed, and Javi knew the way to the hospital.

"Just try to hold off until Friday, please," her doctor said smiling. "Every doctor I know will be watching the Egg Bowl Thanksgiving night."

"Egg Bowl?" Itzel said.

"A big Mississippi football game. It's more important than your World Cup."

"Oh, okay. I understand. Javi not take me to hospital if watching World Cup." She smiled, proud of her English. Would her baby speak English? Would she forget how to speak Spanish? Would her little girl not be able to talk to her *abuela*? Itzel determined that day that her child would be completely bilingual. Teaching her Spanish would be one gift she could give her.

"Are you daydreaming over there?" Doña Elia smiled at her. "Or are you having some twinges?"

"Twinges?"

"Little pains."

"No, no twinges yet, but I can't believe it's finally time." She finished chopping the apples for the fruit salad and stirred in the *crema* just like her ma used to do. A tear slid down her cheek.

"Aw, mija, let the tears fall. I promise we will get your ma on the phone and keep her there during the whole event. She will be a part of this experience. It won't be in person, but it'll be the next best thing." Doña Elia squeezed her shoulders. "You're gonna be a great mom because you obviously have a great one."

"But why didn't I realize that when I was home?"

"That's the circle of life, *mija*. Now you get to show her you really were listening all those years you tried to block her out. You will make her proud, and one day she'll witness it all in person."

"Thank you," Itzel said. "Now show me how to make this pumpkin pie. I've never heard of that before."

The meal was a success. Doña Elia's extended family filled the house. Some of the men went deer hunting that morning, and Javi wanted to know more. He only shot rabbits on his uncle's ranch.

"You better wait 'til next season, Javi. A new baby and deer hunting don't make a happy marriage," Elia's son said. "It's kinda addictive."

"Just enjoy the meat. I always give Ma my second deer," Elia's other son said. "In fact, you've probably been eating some since you came."

"Oh, I thought it was better beef!" Javi said. "It's always delicious whatever she cooks."

"Yeah, we know," the sons said in unison as they patted their oversized bellies.

Itzel brought out plates of pumpkin pie, and the grand-children fought over who got to squirt the whipped cream. As they all contentedly stuffed in their dessert, Itzel thought of her parents and the life she was creating in Mississippi. She never paid attention to individual states in her studies at school. She never dreamed of living in Mississippi. She really thought it was only a river. But, here she was. Did God lead them here or did she and Javi force a path?

"We have lots to be thankful for," Doña Elia said. "Let's live thankfully every day."

"Amen," said Javi as he gave her his seat and put his arm around Itzel. "Thank you for showing us a new custom. Anyone want a game of soccer?"

Elia's sons groaned with full bellies, but the children all ran to join Javi. He was a natural organizing them into teams and calling rules. Itzel had never seen him in this role before, but she wasn't surprised. When they finally tired of soccer, Javi and Itzel strolled through the deserted downtown. God led them to a place that honored God. She hoped their lives would honor Him in this new place.

And just like that, the pains began. "Oh, Javi. I think it's time. That's more than a twinge."

They rushed back to the house and loaded Doña Elia and Itzel's bag. The daughters-in-law promised to finish the clean-up, and everyone waved them off.

"Call your mom now," Javi said as he drove. "Let her know to be on stand-by for the phone call."

Itzel dialed, her hands shaking. "Ma, it's time. We're on the way to Jackson."

"Oh, Itzel. I so wanted to be there. Pa will be home in about an hour. We want to be there all the way through."

"You will be, Ma. Doña Elia will keep my phone when I go into delivery. She'll keep you updated. We may be able to have you "*en vivo*" in the delivery room. I love you."

"I love you too, *mija. Dios te cuide y te guarde.*"

About midnight, after the Mississippi State Bulldogs captured the Egg Bowl Trophy, the on-call doctor arrived in maroon and white scrubs to deliver baby Carmela Elia to the world. She weighed eight pounds and was completely healthy. Javi held her up to the camera as her grandparents in Mexico cried with delight.

Itzel held the little bundle close as tears streamed down her cheeks.

"God is so good to us. God is so good. Thank you, Lord."

Chapter 18

June 2015
Ciudad Juarez
Cristal

C RISTAL straightened her cap and zipped her robe. She couldn't believe she was graduating from *prepa*.

"Cristal, you look amazing," her ma said. "I'm so proud of you."

"Thanks, Ma. I'm kinda proud of myself too," Cristal said. The word "ma" came more easily since the death of Rubi. And, after starting school three years behind her peers, Cristal was graduating *prepa*. She had come so far. She hugged her parents Pastor Miguel and Pastora Pati. "Thank you both. Thank you for loving us."

Fina came in and joined the group hug. "Let's get going or we'll be late," she said. "I've got the whole meal ready for when we get back. Cristal, you can invite Daniel to come too if you see him. Memo is coming."

Fina and Memo were inseparable the last few years. They shared most of the same classes and helped with the younger kids at the *comedor* on Saturdays. Cristal rarely saw Daniel as he seemed to spend more and more time on the other side.

"I'll see, but he's still in El Paso, I think," Cristal said. "Would it be okay to invite his parents? and maybe Carmen? Carmen and Araceli have always supported me through school."

"And Chuy, our first soccer coach."

"Yeah, and I wish *Abuelo* could be here."

They rode to the school in the pickup, Ma insisting Cristal ride in front for her big day. As they exited the vehicle, Carmen and Araceli walked up with a big bouquet of flowers.

"We are so proud of you, Cristal," Carmen said.

"Congratulations, *mija*," Araceli said. "You have come so far. You are amazing!"

"We can't wait to see what God has planned for her," Pastor Miguel said.

"Cristal has some news," Pastora Pati said. "Tell them, mija."

"Well, I got a partial scholarship to UACJ. If I keep up my grades, I can get a full one in January."

"That's wonderful," Carmen and Araceli said together. "Congratulations!"

"Maybe my Itzel can give you some tips. She would be graduating next year if she'd stayed."

Pati gave Carmen a hug. "Your grandbaby is beautiful, Carmen. One day you will see them in person."

"Thanks, Pati. She's pregnant again. I wish I could be there to help her."

The ceremony was a long-winded affair with speeches from several staff members, photos with the principal, and a long line to a photo booth for families. Everyone was hot and tired when they finally made it home for Fina's banquet.

"You'll be graduating in another year?" Araceli asked Fina.

"Yes. I can't believe how fast the time passed."

"Will you be going on to university too?" Carmen asked.

"Maybe, but I'm not sure what I'll study. I'm also looking at a culinary school."

"That sounds like a plan. You're already a great cook. Memo talks about your cooking all the time."

"Ma, stop," Memo said. "A boy's gotta eat."

"Yes, and a boy's got to study. Memo knows he has to graduate, but after that it's his decision," Araceli said. "I've told him he should at least go to some technical automotive trainings."

"I've been telling him that too," Fina said. "That's why I'm thinking about culinary school. There's so much more to it than cooking, and a certificate would help me get in the door. Same for a mechanic, I think."

"Hey, why are you all talking about me?" Memo interrupted. "Tonight's all about Cristal."

Pastor Miguel called everyone together for the blessing.

"Dear Lord, we give thanks for this momentous occasion, for all you have provided for Cristal. Be with her now as she takes her next steps. Guide her and protect her. Show her where you would like her to serve. Bless this food, and as always we ask that you give us more hunger for you."

Everyone said "Amen" and quickly filled their plates. Cristal looked around the kitchen with a full heart. So many people stepped up to walk beside her and Fina when Rubi wouldn't or couldn't. She hoped to pay that great gift forward one day, maybe as a teacher. She was ready for next steps.

* * *

The next week a similar scene occurred at Daniel's house, but with a twist. Araceli finally got a passport and a tourist visa. She and Daniel crossed the bridge together for Daniel's graduation. Thanks to technology, Memo and the neighbors watched Facebook Live as Daniel received his diploma. Everyone on both sides cheered as his name was called. Even

Abuelo tuned in from Dallas. Lucas sat in his truck at the bridge watching from his cellphone and waiting to bring the bilingual high school graduate home.

When they all returned, Araceli and Lucas cooked a big *discada,* a mix of meats cooked outside on a large disc. Carmen provided the sodas, and Fina brought a *tres leches* cake.

"We're so proud of you too, Daniel," Pastora Pati said. "You've come a long way from the little boy at our *comedor.* But that's not a surprise. I remember your standing up to a bully for Cristal. May God continue to guide your steps."

"I think his next steps are going to be on the other side too," Araceli said. "He got a scholarship to UTEP."

"That's wonderful, Daniel," Pastor Miguel said. "What do you think you want to study?"

"I'm not sure, but I'm thinking about being a lawyer."

"I thought you were gonna be a doctor," Memo said.

"No, I got enough of hospitals hanging with you all your life. You go be the doctor."

"I'm a doctor already. I'm a doctor of cars. That might even be the name of my shop one day, Dr. Memo's Car Clinic."

"That's my boy," Lucas said as everyone laughed.

Fina served her cake which was delicious as always. Daniel looked around at all who supported his family and how they all lived so close to the other side. He wanted to do better. He wanted to have nice things. He wanted what the other side had, and becoming a lawyer seemed the fastest way to achieve that goal.

Part II

College Days and Beyond
2015-2020

Chapter 19

2015
UTEP
Daniel

DANIEL entered his freshman year at the University of Texas at El Paso along with almost 23,000 other students. Although it was a big campus compared to his high school in El Paso, UTEP was not as big as the Universidad Autónoma de Ciudad Juarez, or UACJ, with 33, 000 students. Still, he was easily overwhelmed by the economic status of the students. Everyone had his own car and was eating out or buying new clothes or shoes without a second thought.

All the opulence around him made Daniel feel fairly certain of his major in pre-law and going to law school. He was glad for his scholarships and part-time jobs, but he was ready to get out and make a big salary. He was tired of working all the time only to be able to buy a beat-up, old car. He wore decent, mostly second-hand clothes, but he had to watch every penny to make ends meet. He always ate the meal plan in the cafeteria and only drove his car when he went back to visit his family.

His first day on campus Daniel settled into his dorm as his roommate came in with a big duffel bag.

"Hi, I'm Kevin," he said as they shook hands.

"Daniel. Where are you from?"

"Las Cruces. You?"

"Juarez," Daniel said, pronouncing it the gringo way and not putting "Ciudad" in front.

"Cool, so you speak Spanish." Kevin said.

"Yeah. I learned English in high school on this side."

"Cool. I only know a little Spanish, but I've been trying to learn more because my church group goes across a lot to do some kids' programs."

"That's good. What church?"

"Catholic. You?"

"I go to my neighborhood church when I'm home, but I never really go here. I went to chapel during high school, and I went home on the weekends, so I didn't go to a church on this side."

"Come with me tonight to the Newman Center. It's a cool place to hang out and meet some more people."

"Yeah, I guess. Is that on campus?"

"Yeah. That's the good thing about UTEP. We can walk most places. You got a car?"

"Yeah. You?"

"Yeah, I got it for graduation. It's a Jeep. What do you drive?"

"Oh, man, you don't wanna know." Daniel grinned. He needed to get over always being the poor kid. "Let's go see what's to eat in the cafeteria for lunch today."

"No, man, gross. I'm going to pick up Taco Bell or something. Let me get unpacked. I told my mom I'd send a pic of my bed if she wouldn't come move me in."

"No, I better use my meal plan. Thanks, though."

Daniel walked to the cafeteria thinking about his own mom. She would love to be here too. She did finally have a tourist visa to cross, but transportation back home from the bridge was too complicated. He'd have to bring her one day to see the campus.

He decided to give his mom a call while he walked around the campus. She'd be surprised that he called her first.

"Daniel, what's wrong?" She answered on the first ring.

"Nothing, Ma. I'm walking around campus on the way to the cafeteria."

"I hope it's good food. You need to eat more."

"I'm sure it's fine, Ma, but it won't be like yours."

"Did you meet your roommate?"

"Yes. He's cool. He's from Las Cruces, and he's actually been to Ciudad Juarez."

"I hope you can find a church to serve in now that you will be gone so much longer than when you were in high school. Did you know Cristal is going to UACJ? Riding the bus all the way downtown by herself like Itzel used to do."

"She'll be fine, Ma. She's been on the streets before."

"I wish you wouldn't say that so casually. Plus, it's different for a girl. I don't think you really realize that since you don't have any sisters."

"I didn't mean it casually. I meant that she's tough. She knows how to be alert and pay attention to her surroundings. She did fine going to *prepa*."

"Yes, she did, but all the way to the center of the city is a big deal."

"Don't worry, Ma. I'm sure she'll be fine. Pastor Miguel wouldn't let her go if he didn't think she was prepared."

"I know you're right, Daniel, but I worry about you too. I hope you know I pray for you every day. Will you pray for Cristal too?"

"Yeah, Ma. I will."

They hung up, and Daniel felt a guilty twinge. He prayed, sort of. He'd try to do better.

That night he did go to Newman Hall and met more guys to hang out with. They served free hamburgers plus brownies for dessert. That was one thing he'd learned to like on this side, desserts. They rarely ate dessert at home unless it was a birthday or a very special occasion.

Classes started right away, and Daniel dug in, trying to keep up with so much reading in English. Social English was beginning to feel natural to him, but reading textbooks was much harder. He kept his translator app open all the time.

Saturday, Daniel started his part-time job in the athletic department, sorting uniforms and cleaning the locker room. He considered being a walk-on to the soccer team but decided to play intramurals and focus on class instead. One of the football players came in from lifting weights.

"Hey, man," he said. "How's it going?"

"Slow day. I guess everyone's gone home for the weekend."

"Yeah, last weekend before our kick-off game. I'm Burly."

"Daniel." They shook hands.

"There a few of us around though. We're planning to hang out at Buffalo Wild Wings tonight to watch some pre-season games. Come hang with us."

Daniel always hesitated. He hated that he had to always count the costs. Finally, he agreed. "Yeah, thanks. See ya there."

After work, he showered at the dorm. He'd heard the guys complaining about having to walk down the hall to the shower. He was glad he didn't have to go outside to light the water heater and wait thirty minutes for it to heat up. And even that was a luxury back home. Most people in his neighborhood heated hot water in a bucket with a dangerous hot iron plugged into the wall and dropped into the water. He remembered how happy his ma was when Abuelo helped them buy the hot water heater.

Daniel came into Buffalo Wild Wings and found the group of athletes, well into their pitchers of beer. He ordered a Coke and some wings, a big splurge for him. He always thought of Abuelo when he ate wings. Funny how Abuelo popped up in almost every situation. Daniel hadn't realized how much Abuelo was a part of his life, even though Abuelo visited only twice a year.

"Daniel, pour you a glass," Burly from the locker room said.

"I'm good," Daniel said. He was glad his wings arrived then.

"Everybody knows wings are better with beer." Burly poured him a glass anyway.

Daniel didn't make a big deal about it. He toasted the other guys and sipped, then went back to his wings and Coke.

"Where are you from, Daniel?" one of the jocks nick-named Geezer asked as he grabbed another pitcher.

Daniel answered, and the usual questions ensued. He responded until they finally turned back to the game. Relieved, Daniel finished his wings and tried to watch too. He still didn't quite get American football, but he knew to yell at big hits, long completed passes, and touchdowns. He relaxed and enjoyed the game.

As they made their way to the parking lot, Geezer said, "Hey, Daniel. Give me a ride back. I probably don't need to drive."

"Sure," Daniel said, and they got in.

They pulled onto the interstate to head back to campus when Geezer said, "Hey, I hear there's some sweet weed in Juarez. I bet no one would check a clean-cut college boy like you coming across."

Daniel stared at Geezer a second then quickly returned his eyes to the road. He didn't respond.

"You could make some quick money that way, get you a decent set of wheels."

Daniel still didn't respond.

"This piece of junk isn't gonna last you through college, you know."

Daniel turned on the radio, thankful for some loud reggaeton.

"Think about it, man. You wouldn't have to distribute it. I'd take it off your hands immediately. I've got a large base here already."

Daniel couldn't wait to dump this guy. He should have known this guy wasn't trying to be a responsible drinker. He just wanted Daniel alone.

"Which dorm, man?" Daniel asked.

"The jock dorm, where else? Think about it, dude. We'll be in touch."

Geezer got out, and Daniel watched as he immediately flagged down another friend to presumably get a ride back to his car. Daniel went back to his dorm. Tomorrow was Sunday. Maybe he should find a church.

* * *

Sunday morning, Daniel ventured out to a Methodist church near campus. He wasn't sure what to expect. He visited this one once during high school for a special program, but never went to a regular service. He hoped to slip in the back but was surprised to see Burly handing out programs.

Burly looked a little embarrassed as he said, "Hey, man! Glad you came."

"You're from here, Burly?"

"Yeah, this is my home church. My grandparents, parents, and siblings all go here. There's no escape for me."

"That's kinda cool though. Family is nice to have around. Where do you sit?"

"Back row, to the right. I'll be there in about ten minutes."

"Thanks, man."

After church, Burly invited Daniel to have lunch at his grandparents' home.

"They live up past the Franklin Mountains State Park. Do you know where that is?"

"Yes," Daniel said hesitating. "But, I probably don't have enough gas to get up there and back."

"You can ride with me. We live in town. I'll bring you back."

Daniel and Burly did the usual back and forth. Burly went to the local high school and was a stand-out on the football team. His grades were average, but he managed to get a scholarship to UTEP and would be a starter on this year's team.

"So, you live at home or in the athletic dorm?" Daniel asked.

"Oh, I live in the dorm, but I go home every weekend for home cooking and laundry service." He grinned. "Can't you go home on the weekends?"

"Yeah, I can, but it's easier not to. I'll probably go once a month, but I didn't realize the campus would be so empty on the weekends."

"It'll be better once football games start. Do you like fried chicken? My grandma makes the best."

"Sure, it's probably different though. My pa cooks it outside on a disc. We even ate fried rabbit at my uncle's ranch."

"Yep, us too, and rattlesnake."

"Yeah, my *tío* Hernan cooked that for us on the ranch, but I never got the guts to try it."

"Aw, you shoulda. Tastes just like chicken!"

"Yeah, that's what he said too, but I remembered a picture in a National Geographic magazine my Abuelo showed me one time. A lady was trying to sell an iguana on the side of the road saying, 'four-legged chicken.' That's all I could think about."

They both laughed at that. Then Burly asked, "Who's Abuelo?"

"He's kinda like an adopted grandpa. He lives in Dallas and used to come about twice a year to our neighborhood to help. He always ate meals at our house. He and my ma have a tight relationship. He helped us buy our first car. He helped me be able to go to La Lydia." Daniel stopped, afraid he talked too much, but Burly didn't say anything.

Burly's family was welcoming and relaxed. Daniel enjoyed the meal and the visit. Then Burly drove them back to campus.

"Thanks, man. You have a great family. I appreciate it." Daniel meant it.

"Sure, man. Anytime, but once football season starts, I won't be as regular at church. Those road trips are killers."

Daniel returned to the dorm to catch up on his reading, but the fried chicken dinner was too powerful. He was fast asleep when Kevin came in.

"Man, whatcha doing in bed at this time of day? You have a big night out last night?"

"No, man. I ate too much lunch. It was worth it though. Now I've got to finish this homework."

"Well, hurry up so you can go back to Newman with me."

Daniel finished his readings, and they got ready to leave. But, in the hall, Geezer was waiting for Daniel.

"Hey, man. I was just coming to hang out. Where are you going?"

"To church, man," Daniel said as he kept walking.

"I'll walk with you. You can go ahead, Dude. Daniel will catch up," Geezer said to Kevin.

"No, man. I told you last night, I'm not interested. See you around."

Daniel and Kevin walked on. When they were far away from Geezer, Kevin said, "Good move, man. He's bad news. It's only a matter of time before he's caught. Everyone knows he's dealing all over campus. One of the guys at Newman warned me about him."

"It's still hard for me to understand why people on this side need drugs. Y'all have everything."

"Well, we have everything that doesn't fill us up. More stuff isn't always the answer."

"Yeah, but it sure makes life easier."

"Yeah, easier, but not fuller."

They walked in silence to Newman Hall, contemplating. Daniel was sure Kevin was wrong. He was still sure that becoming a lawyer was his goal and his solution for himself and his family. What would Abuelo say? Abuelo again. Maybe he should give him a call.

Chapter 20

2015
UACJ
Cristal

Cristal watched Pastor Miguel drive away from the bus stop with Fina in route to *prepa* for her senior year. Cristal waited for the bus downtown to begin her freshman year of college. Carmen, Itzel's ma, had tried to warn Pastora Pati about the dangers for Cristal, but to no avail.

"I trust Cristal to make wise decisions. I think she is prepared. God will be with her," Pastora Pati told Carmen.

"I thought the same thing about my Itzel."

"I know you did, but God has been with her too. Our plans are not always His plans, but He will be with us."

Carmen turned to Cristal then. "*Mija,* focus on your studies. You have a long life ahead of you." She gave Cristal a hug. "I just miss my girl so much. I'm sorry. Go have fun, just not too much!" Everyone laughed then as the tension broke.

With that memory in her mind, Cristal stepped onto the bus for the city center and the university. Butterflies flitted in her stomach, but she was ready. She was going to be a teacher.

Cristal's first class that day was Human Growth and Development. She was fascinated. She hung on every word of the professor and rushed to the bookstore to get her book. There was an hour before her next class, so she bought a coffee and settled in to read.

At the next table, a girl was also reading. She looked up and smiled as Cristal settled in. Noticing Cristal's cross necklace, she leaned in to ask, "Are you a Christian?"

Cristal answered hesitantly, "Yes."

"Freshman?"

"Yes. You?"

"*Yes* to both questions. What are you reading?"

"It's the text for my Human Growth and Development class. It's all so interesting. I didn't know that those first years of life were so important."

"Oh yeah. Babies know a lot more than we realize. My mom's a pediatrician."

"Oh," Cristal said. She shrank back a little in her seat.

"You're cool. That's why we're here at university, to learn new stuff. I bet there's a lot of stuff you know that I don't. What does your mom do?"

Cristal never knew how to answer that question. Maybe she should skip to Pastora Pati and forget the whole Rubí part of her life. "My mom's a pastor's wife. She is also a good cook and sells food during the week."

"There, see? My mom was rarely home to cook so I don't know much around the kitchen, and I bet you know a lot of behind-the-scenes church stuff too."

They smiled at each other and introduced themselves. Yarely was from Ciudad Juárez but lived in a dorm on campus.

"There's a Christian student meeting tonight down the hall at 6:00. Wanna go?" Yarely asked.

"Thanks, but I have to catch the bus at 2:00 when my last class is over. I go to work at 3:00 at an S-Mart near my neighborhood."

"That's cool. If you ever wanna go, you can stay overnight in my dorm room. So far, I don't have a roommate, but if she shows, we can get a blow-up mattress."

"Thanks. I appreciate it. What are you studying?"

"Right now, I'm in pre-med, just like my mom always wanted. She's not pressuring me, but I do like science, so I'll probably stick it out."

"Wow, a doctor. That's a lot of studying."

"What about you?"

"I'm going to be a teacher. I've never wanted to do anything else."

"That's great that you are so certain. Anyway, I'll be here tomorrow about the same time. See you then."

Cristal was glad to make a friend on the first day, but their worlds were so different. Would she still be her friend when she realized where Cristal came from?

Cristal went to her College Algebra class with a slight knot in her stomach. Math had never been her friend.

The professor met them at the door, handing each one a Hershey bar.

"Don't open it yet," he said. "Show me your maturity."

Cristal smiled as she took hers to her seat. So far, this was the best math class she ever attended.

"Now," the professor said, "you can open the bar and divide it into the marked sections. No eating yet."

The students followed his directions as he had them divide the sections into groups and asked them questions. The first ones were easy, demonstrating division.

"Now the fun part. You may eat a few pieces, but write down how many. Just a few!"

Everyone giggled as they ate.

"In front of the number you wrote down, I want you to write "X equals." So, some of you may have X=3, or some of you greedier ones may have X=9."

Again, everyone laughed. Cristal was really enjoying this math class.

"Now, do you remember how many pieces you had at the beginning?"

"Twelve," several students said at the same time.

"Okay, I want you to make an equation. Don't panic. An equation is just a fancy word for a math sentence. There are different ways to write your sentence. Who has one?"

As different students gave varied answers, the professor explained how the X was used as the part they didn't know. Cristal was amazed that she actually understood algebra. She also felt confident she could teach math as well as she could reading. As the students left the classroom that day, the professor shook hands with each student.

"Thank you, professor. I've always been terrified of math."

The professor beamed at her. "Then my lesson today was just for you. I knew there was one in here. What's your name?"

And so began a great college semester for Cristal.

Chapter 21

2015
UTEP
Daniel

Daniel fell into his routine of college classes, work, and study. His roommate Kevin was a good influence on his study time, and his new friend Burly helped him with his social life. Since Burly was an athlete, he didn't go too far on the partying. He also ran interference for Daniel whenever Geezer was around, and Kevin kept dragging Daniel to Newman house for meals and hanging out.

Daniel's hardest class was Government. The instructor was from India, and Daniel could barely understand him. Plus, the readings were long and intense. After the first week, Daniel went to the tutoring center and met Mr. Acosta.

"Hi, Daniel. How can I help you? *¿Prefieres español?*" Mr. Acosta greeted him.

Daniel's grin said it all.

"*Está bien. No te preocupes,*" Mr. Acosta said. "We'll figure it out. Don't worry. When I saw your name on the list today, I looked up your records and saw you went to *La Lydia*. Students from there have a great success record. Coming for help is a good sign. I'm glad you didn't wait until the end of the semester."

Daniel's shoulders relaxed as he exhaled a big breath. "*Gracias,* I have to keep my scholarship."

"Well, that's important, no doubt, but learning is the main thing. First, come on back, and let's set up this vocabulary app for you. I want to see where you are on some of these government terms."

Every day Daniel practiced some of the apps and tips from Mr. Acosta, and soon he noticed an improvement in his understanding in class. He stopped by at least once a week to visit, often talking about life more than study skills.

"How about helping me coach a little soccer, Daniel," Mr. Acosta asked one day. "I coach a youth team from the neighborhood around *La Lidia.* You would be a good example for them."

"I don't know. I'm pretty busy with school and my job in the athletic department."

"We practice Thursday afternoons and have games on Saturday mornings."

"I'll think about it," Daniel said as he remembered his games in his old neighborhood. "No, I'll come. When and where?"

The next Thursday, Daniel arrived ready for practice. The boys were kicking soccer balls, waiting for their coach.

"I'm helping Mr. Acosta coach today," Daniel said. "He'll be here in a few minutes. What do you usually do first?"

The boys eyed him warily. The smallest one spoke up. "We do passing drills."

"Okay. Let's go," Daniel said.

"You aren't our coach," the largest of the group said. "We'll wait for our coach." He turned, and most of the group followed him.

"Well," Daniel said to the small one, "let's start those drills. I've got a dollar if you can pass me the ball every time without overshooting me. When they came to the last pass, the little one put out his hand. Daniel gave him the promised dollar, and more players came back.

"What's your name?"

"Paco."

"Paco, who's the best player on the team?"

"Abel, but Coach says he's lazy." Paco grinned, then ducked his head.

"Where's Abel?" Daniel asked.

Everyone pointed to the boy who wouldn't take instruction from Daniel.

"Abel," Daniel called. "Come over here. Let's have a shootout. Best three out of four gets a dollar."

"With who? With Paco?" Abel snorted.

"With me," Daniel said.

Abel straightened up. "You're on."

The whole team gathered then, each one hoping to see the new coach get beat. At 3-3, Coach Acosta arrived.

"What's going on?"

Daniel grinned. "I'm trying to build some team spirit, Coach. Your guys are good, but they said you thought Abel was lazy."

"I guess he wasn't being challenged enough," Coach Acosta said. "Finish it! Let's see what he's really got."

Paco threw the ball into the middle, and Abel got to it first. He dribbled to the left of Daniel, then cut right unexpectedly. Daniel recovered and blocked his shot, but Abel beat him to the ball and scored. The team exploded in cheers. Daniel high-fived Abel and pulled out his last dollar.

"Good move, Abel. We can work on setting you up for that as a team."

"Yeah, I've been having a hard time getting him to realize he needs his team," Coach Acosta said. "Maybe you can help him see it. Okay, boys, let's start with our passing drills."

The moans from all the boys were expected, but they quickly followed Coach Acosta onto the field as he gave balls to each group. They knew what to do and went through all their drills without instruction.

"You've got a well-disciplined team," Daniel said.

"Yes, they are good kids. I'm just waiting on Abel to step up as a leader instead of a show-off."

"What's his homelife like?"

"I haven't been able to get him to open up yet. Maybe he'll talk to you."

The practice continued, and Daniel enjoyed the workout. At the end of practice, Coach Acosta called the boys into a huddle.

"Coach Daniel will be helping us on Saturday. Daniel is studying at UTEP now, but he also went to *La Lydia*. He crossed the bridge every day to come study. That's a big commitment. I want to see the same commitment from each of you, not just on Saturday. I want to see your first report cards. I think they come out next week. Your studies are as important as your playing skills. Our game is at 10:00, so be there by 9:30. 'Chihuahuas' on three. *Uno, dos, tres...*"

"Chihuahuas!" all the boys shouted, and then they ran from the field. They picked up bookbags and walked home in several different directions. Abel seemed to be the only one going out the south entrance.

"Abel," Daniel called. "You need a ride?"

But Abel waved him off and kept walking.

"Maybe next time," Coach Acosta said. "I'm glad you came. You are a great addition to the team."

"Thanks, Coach. It was fun."

Chapter 22

2015
Cristal
UACJ

CRISTAL met Yarely most days between classes for a coffee, reading, studying, and girl talk. Yarely was enjoying her science classes, especially the labs. Cristal was surprised to enjoy her math classes.

"I might become a math teacher. I always thought I would like reading and writing the most, but I love finding the right answer," Cristal said as she drank coffee with her friend. "I never would have believed it. What's your favorite class this semester?"

"I love dissecting this cat. I know that sounds gross, but I'm learning so much from doing it. Not about cats, but about the human body."

"Wow, I don't know if I could do that, but I never thought I could do math either."

"The more I study the human body, and even the body of this cat, the more I am amazed at God's design. Science doesn't leave God out. To me, it proves there is a God."

They finished their coffees and their homework. When it was time for the next class, Cristal said, "When's the next Christian students meeting? I might like to go."

"Tomorrow night at 6:00. Can you get off work?"

"I'll ask this afternoon. I think it will be fine."

"Want to spend the night so you don't have to go home after dark?"

"Yes. I'll check with my ma about that too."

After work that night, Cristal rode the bus home. Pastora Pati had supper waiting for her. Fina and Pastor Miguel had already started.

"You must be tired. How was class this morning?"

"It was good, Ma. I can't believe I'm enjoying math."

"I'm not surprised. You're a smart girl, Cristal. You just had a late start. Now you are catching up. Did you see your friend, Yarely?"

"Yes, and she invited me to stay tomorrow for the Christian students meeting and spend the night in her dorm. Would that be okay?"

Pastora Pati hesitated, but then she said, "I think that will be fine. I was just hearing Carmen in my head. You know, that's what Itzel told her ma when she stayed overnight on campus."

"I know, Ma. Thank you for trusting me."

"I do trust you, *Mija*. Just remember that broken trust is hard to restore."

"I will, Ma. I will."

"Hey, Cristal. Maybe you can help me with my math homework tonight," Fina said.

"Okay, I will, as long as you really mean 'help me do it' and not 'do it for me.'" Cristal grinned at her sister. "You've been hanging around Memo a lot lately. Daniel tells me how he is."

"Aw, Cristal. I would never do that! But if you worked the problems, I could cook you some brownies."

"See! You and Memo are two of a kind."

The girls laughed as they washed up the dishes and got out their homework. Cristal felt warm inside. Pati and Miguel had allowed them to have a secure, stable environment to grow up in, to explore their strengths, and to see more of their small world. Where would they be without them?

Chapter 23

Spring 2016
UTEP
Daniel

THE spring semester for Daniel was a little smoother than his first. Thanks to Mr. Acosta, his grades were maintaining an acceptable average and his extracurricular soccer coaching was turning into the highlight of his week.

"Coach, I think I need to go to Abel's house. I can't seem to get close to him."

Mr. Acosta sighed. "He's really coming along as a player, just not a team player like we want."

"Who would know his story?"

"Maybe a teacher."

"Do you know where he lives?"

"I think one of the apartments on the other side of the interstate. He never lets us see which way he goes home," Mr. Acosta said.

"Can I say a parent has to sign a form or something and take him to his house?"

"I don't want to lie to the boy. Let's both take him home today."

But when practice began, Abel was a no-show. After practice, Daniel asked some of the other boys about Abel.

"Is Abel in your class?"

"He was last year, but he got held back. He's in fifth again. We're in sixth," one player said.

"Do you know where he lives?"

"I think he stays with an uncle now," said another player. "His ma is a meth-head."

The guys laughed nervously at that. Another spoke up, "I heard his pa is in prison."

"Thanks, guys. I appreciate your telling me. We are a team, but not just on the field. If you know anything else that might help, I need to know."

Paco spoke up next. "I think he got suspended yesterday. He was caught breaking into the school cafeteria the night before."

"Thanks, Paco. Who at the school is easy for you to talk to? Who would talk to us about Abel?"

"Officer Riley," they all answered at once.

"Alright then. Thanks, guys. See you on Saturday." Daniel turned to Mr. Acosta. "Do you know him?"

"Yes, he's the truancy officer. I'll give him a call and see what he can tell us."

"Thanks, Coach."

"No, thank you! You're making a real difference here, Daniel."

On his drive back to campus, Daniel thought about his soccer team. Most of the parents rarely came to their games. He knew that most of them were working two jobs to be able to give their children more than they had growing up. But, giving time was also important. These boys were so hungry for attention. Abel was too, but he showed it in a different way.

Daniel was glad he was able to give them a little of the attention they craved. When he became a lawyer, he could sponsor a team, buy them the best-looking uniforms and latest cleats. But, he wanted to spend time with the team as well. Time to these boys, maybe to everybody, equaled love.

Suddenly Daniel's conversations with Cristal came flooding back. She wanted him to come back to spend time with her students when she became a teacher. Now he got it. How was she so wise?

Chapter 24

Spring 2016
UACJ
Cristal

CRISTAL and Yarely became close friends. Every Wednesday, Cristal stayed at the dorm after attending the Christian students meeting. The group was planning a mission trip during Holy Week. They would stay in a church in the south of Ciudad Juarez doing Bible school with the kids and working with other teams building houses. Both girls planned to go.

"My ma said she may bring a team from her clinic for a half-day to do some diabetes screening and education. She said we could help check immunization records on the kids and height and weight. Does that interest you?" Yarely said.

"Yes. I remember teams coming to our neighborhood," Cristal said, then added, "They built our first house."

Yarely's eyes widened, then dropped. "I didn't realize that. What did you live in before?"

Cristal took a deep breath. "It was just a hut made of pallets. It had a tarp for a roof and a dirt floor. We went outside to a hole in the ground for the bathroom."

Yarely was quiet for a long time. Then she said, "I had no idea. When did you get a better house?"

"The team built us a block house when I was about eight. My sister and I went to live with our foster parents when I was about ten. That's really when I started school. And that's when I realized what love is."

Yarely hugged her. "You've come so far! I'm so spoiled. I complain when Ma won't buy me a new iPhone. Help me open my eyes on this trip. It's not about me, but I want to see where I can help. I think I still want to be a pediatrician like my ma, but maybe I won't be in a practice like her. Maybe I'll serve in a clinic in a neighborhood like yours."

"Well, you won't make any money, but you will be paid to overflowing with love," Cristal said. She was glad she shared a little more of herself with her friend. Maybe her experiences could be helpful to others.

Chapter 25

Summers
Ciudad Juarez

THE extreme climate of the Chihuahuan desert surprises visitors. Spring and fall may have mild temperatures, but the vicious sandstorms are brutal. The huts barely have a chance to remain standing, and the block houses cannot keep the ever-present dust out of the many cracks and crevices. The poorly-insulated constructions are no match for the summers which often see many consecutive days over one hundred degrees with swamp coolers the only source of relief. The few swimming pools are so packed with people that no one can swim. The patrons just stand in the water to stay cool.

Each summer as classes ended for Cristal and Daniel, the dilemma of summer employment arrived. Finding a temporary job was not easy. Cristal usually returned to S-Mart. She realized she should be making more money, but she and Fina could both work the same schedules and ride the bus together. Safety was more important.

Daniel weighed the differences between staying in El Paso or returning home for the summer. He earned more in El Paso, but his expenses were higher. Living at home was free, but he earned substantially less at a maquila. Minimum wage at a maquila was about the same per day as it was per hour in El Paso. But his ma's cooking won the argument, and the manager of the maquila cafeteria gladly welcomed Daniel back. He rode the maquila bus to save money on transportation, only using his car to take his ma to buy groceries.

One evening when returning from his shift, the bus was rocked by what seemed like an explosion. Everyone screamed and pushed for the doors as the bus pulled over. On the other corner, a bus was on fire. Shots rang out as people scrambled to find cover. Daniel made it to a pharmacy and ducked inside with several others. They watched in horror as their bus was also set on fire. Then two men dressed all in black torched the store beside the bus. People came streaming out of the store. More shots rang out.

"*¡Ay Dios mío!*"

"*¡Válgame, Dios!*"

Prayers were going up, stranger clutching stranger. Then Daniel saw Cristal and Fina running for their lives from the burning store. He had to help. He jumped to the door of the pharmacy to open it, but a large man blocked him.

"We aren't opening this door," the man shouted.

"Yes, we are," Daniel said and charged forward shouting Cristal's name. The door opened enough for Cristal to recognize Daniel. She and Fina ducked inside. They all fell in a heap under the glare of the large man.

"What's going on?" Daniel said.

"We heard there was an uprising in the Cerezo prison. The two gangs are fighting, but it spilled into the streets. Someone said they are trying to free the leader of the Mexicles cartel."

"Were you two on that bus?" another lady asked.

"Yes. We were sitting in the front. I'm not sure everyone got off. The cocktail came in through the back window."

The smell of smoke clung to their clothes. Firemen were slow to respond, preferring to wait safely in the station rather than risk being shot. As the fires burned out, the people got antsy.

"Anybody seen any reports? Is it safe to go out yet?"

"I just saw there were three other buses torched at the same time."

"Here's a Facebook Live report from the intersection near the bridge."

The reporter said what they already knew. An uprising at the prison started the violence, local officials were investigating, they would follow up on leads, but everyone knew the perpetrators would not be caught. An uneasy peace would settle for a while, until the next wave hit without notice. Daniel, Cristal, and Fina walked the rest of the way home, pausing at each corner before cautiously continuing. Such was the normal life in Ciudad Juarez. Happy summer vacation.

When Cristal and Fina got home, Pati and Miguel were waiting for them in the street.

"We were so worried," Pati cried as she hugged both girls to her.

"We were too, Ma, but Daniel was there. He pulled us into a safe space," Fina said.

"God was with us, Ma," Cristal said.

"Aleluia," Pastor Miguel said. "You girls are our life." He tried to hide his tears as he hugged them close.

Later, Cristal returned the many missed calls from Yarely. "I'm fine, Yarely."

"But you were on one of the buses," Yarely insisted.

"Yes. It was close this time, but it happens a lot. God was with us."

"Aren't you afraid to go to work tomorrow?"

"Not really. The streets were all deserted tonight. Our parents were outside waiting on us, but most everyone was locked inside their homes. We didn't have any cell service for a while, but by tomorrow, everything will be back to normal. Don't worry. Thanks for checking on us."

Cristal hung up and wondered how people made it without a little bit of faith. Without her faith, without that constant comfort of God with her, she would be overwhelmed with anxiety. *Thank you, Lord, for walking with us each and every day.*

Chapter 26

August 4, 2019
El Paso, Texas
Daniel

DANIEL stepped out of his car in the Walmart parking lot. He needed a few school supplies for the start of his senior year. But as he turned towards the store, he heard the unmistakable sound of gunshots. He ducked beside his car, confused that the shots sounded so close. It was broad daylight on a Saturday morning in El Paso, Texas. He never heard gunshots on this side of the border. Should he get back in his car or stay crouched beside it? Someone probably needed help, but was it gang stuff? Drug cartel stuff? Daniel knew he should help, but where was the gunman? His heart pounded and sweat ran down his face. What should he do?

Suddenly a surge of people ran from the garden center exit with their hands up, screaming, crying. "Don't shoot!" they shouted. An older woman fell, was nearly trampled in the crush, then rose again to escape. Two little girls with matching Frozen t-shirts were holding hands as they ran, no parent in sight. A young man in camo ran toward the crowd.

The screaming horde ran to the closest cars in the lot, some ducking down to continue running, some stumbling together into piles of hysteria, hugging and sobbing. The sirens of police and ambulances added to the confusion. The older woman limped past Daniel's car.

"Señora, let me help you," he said. "Where is your car? Are you alone?" Daniel rushed to support her.

She looked at him in a daze, trying to form words. "They're shooting." She gasped, trying to force air into her lungs. "Somebody is killing people in there. I just heard the bangs and everyone screaming." She pointed to an older model, gray Lincoln. "And I just ran with the crowd. I should have stayed. I used to be a nurse. Why did I turn away?"

Daniel helped her to the car, but then realized she didn't have her purse or keys.

"Is there someone I can call? Will you come sit in my car where it's cooler?"

She nodded and walked slowly with him to the car. Tears ran down her wrinkled cheeks.

More people ran from the store. Police and emergency medical technicians ran inside. Helicopters whirred above in the blazing August sky.

Daniel started his car and turned the air conditioner on high. He wished he had a bottle of water for her. He pulled out his cell phone and asked, "Do you know the number?"

She nodded and took the phone. She dialed with trembling hands.

"Clara, I'm at Walmart." Her voice cracked, but she tried valiantly to hold it together. "I'm okay. Can you come get me?"

Daniel couldn't hear the words at the other end of the line, only the frantic tone of Clara's voice.

"I'm fine," the elderly lady said in a composed voice, "but I lost my purse while I was running out. I'm sitting in a car by the garden entrance." She tried to smile at Daniel.

Clara spoke some more, and then the *señora* said, "Okay. I'll try to find you."

She turned to Daniel. "My daughter said I should meet her near the entrance to Sears. Can you take me there?"

"Yes, Señora, if they will let me out of this parking lot."

"Thank you, *mijo*." The lady stared out the windshield. "I only wanted to buy a new garden hose. I was reaching for one when I heard everyone screaming and saw them running out the garden exit. I tried to go too, but I got knocked down. I guess that's when I lost my purse. Why would anybody do this? Why was he shooting?"

"I've never seen anything like this, even in Juarez." Daniel eased the car to the exit and crossed over to Sears. "Let's try to find Clara."

"What's your name, *mijo*?"

"I'm Daniel, Señora." He smiled at her bravery and warmed to the word "*mijo*," "my son," the word his mama used for him. "I'm glad you made it out."

Before the day was over, Daniel would hear the news that twenty-three mostly Hispanic customers were killed with at least twenty-three more injured. That day was supposed to be the last back-to-school shopping day. And for some, it was.

* * *

Daniel drove from the Sears parking lot toward the University of Texas El Paso campus. He couldn't remember why he went to Walmart in the first place. He felt like a robot. Clara had thanked him profusely for helping her mama and tried to pay him. He refused.

He listened to the news on the radio and could make no sense of what he heard. What if he had hit a few more green lights on his way to the store? What if he had gotten up earlier that day? So many what-ifs.

His cell phone rang as he drove, but he couldn't answer it. He knew it would be his ma, but he also knew he would cry like a baby if he answered now.

Instead of going to his dorm, Daniel made a detour to the Franklin Mountains State Park. The park was a beautiful natural space inside the city limits. He parked the car, grabbed his phone, and hiked to his favorite spot. August was not a popular hiking season in this part of Texas. He found a bench in the shade and called home.

"Daniel, are you okay?" his mom Araceli said. Her voice was shaky.

"Ma, I was so scared." Daniel choked out his words. "Why would anyone do that?"

"Evil, evil world. I always worried about you facing violence here on our side or going to the bridge each day to cross for school. I never considered that evil is on that side too."

"Ma, I could have been inside."

"God was with you, Daniel."

"But why wasn't God with the rest of them? Our world is so messed up."

"It is, Daniel, it is. But God is in control."

"But Ma, so many died, and I could have been one of them."

"*Mijo*, will you come home for a few days? Just come home. Don't try to go through this by yourself."

"No, Ma. I need to be here, to know things firsthand."

"Tomorrow, Daniel. Come home."

"No, Ma. I'll be fine. I'm going to take a walk and then go back to my dorm. I've got to get ready for my trip next week."

"I wish you would come home before you go."

"I'm okay, Ma, but I can't stop thinking about those schoolkids, so full of hope and excitement for the new school year. I always loved getting my new backpack full of fresh notebooks, pencils, crayons. They were just cut down, Ma. Cut down."

"I think the little kids are gonna make it," Araceli said. "I'm watching the report right now."

"Thank God, but, Ma, so many dead. Dead, Ma. The end."

"No, *mijo*. It's not the end. We know that. Don't lose your faith, Daniel."

"I'm trying, Ma. I'll call you later. Don't worry about me. Pray for the others."

"*Te amo, mijo.*"

Daniel walked until his clothes were soaked. Then he returned to his car and drove. After a couple of miles, he turned on the radio. "Twenty-three dead, twenty-three injured." The youngest victim was fifteen, the oldest, eighty-two. A suspect has been arrested. A twenty-one-year-old white male was taken into custody and charged with twenty-three counts of capital murder with further charges pending. First reports indicate the man traveled from Dallas, Texas, to 'kill invaders' as they prepared for their return to school.

Daniel turned it off. He couldn't fathom the evil. The randomness. The uncertainty. Why make plans? Why study? Why work? He felt himself spiraling into a black hole. Then he heard a voice say, "Grab my hand."

Daniel stopped at the next traffic light. He was dropping further into the blackness. He heard the voice again. "Grab my hand." He raised his head and reached up. The dam of tears broke, and he pulled to the curb.

"Oh, God, why?" Daniel raged at God, questioning all he ever believed.

"Just grab my hand."

And Daniel did.

Chapter 27

August 2019
Four Days Later in Morton, Mississippi
Itzel

THE helicopters whirred overhead as the exit doors to the factory slammed shut. Production came to a halt, and the screaming began. The work crew was mostly young women, tears dripping on their bloody aprons, resignation in their slumped shoulders. The day had arrived. There was no escape.

The main door opened, and Immigration and Customs Enforcement officials moved in. The word I.C.E. caused ice to run in an immigrant's veins even if he or she never did anything wrong. Most officers spoke basic Spanish, telling the women to stay in their places and lay down their knives, the tools they used every day to prepare chickens for sale. Evisceration was not a job many wanted, but a job that supported their families.

One by one, each woman was questioned and asked to show identification. One by one, each was led to a waiting bus. The bus filled, and the women began to whisper among each other. "What will happen to my kids?" "Who will cook?" "How long until we see our families again?" The questions and the low sounds of crying floated through the air of the bus. The bus began to move, and the wailing began in earnest.

Itzel tried not to cry, looking down at her steel-toed work boots, but a few tears hit the dirty floor anyway. *What have I done? What about my precious little girls? Will I ever see them again? Will they grow up without me? Did I give them over to greed? Was I greedy to want a better life for my family?*

The bus pulled into an armory of the local National Guard unit. They were unloaded and processed, each woman giving her real name, country of origin, and the name she was working under. Other groups arrived soon after, some from towns thirty miles away. Most of the 'detainees,' as they would all be called, wore the same work boots, hairnet, and bloody aprons.

As the day wore on, ICE officers offered water bottles and apples. Later, they allowed the detainees to go to the bathroom one at a time. A few lucky workers were released after proving they had a work permit, that precious piece of paper that meant the difference between freedom and deportation. Others left with a GPS ankle bracelet and paperwork for a future court date. The rest loaded onto the buses again and disappeared into the night.

Itzel had an ankle bracelet. It wasn't the jewelry she envied in the many catalogs that arrived in her mailbox, but it was beautiful. Beautiful for the temporary freedom it gave her. She would see her girls tonight.

She breathed in the night air, appreciating the freedom but uncertain of her world. Just that morning she got up at her usual 5:00 a.m. to have everything ready for her daughters' first day of school. She packed them each a special burrito with a juice box and the yogurt they loved. The backpacks were ready with new school supplies, had been for days. *Where will I find my girls now? The school day ended seven or eight hours ago.*

Itzel walked the two miles back to town, sweating and exhausted from the march in work boots. Her mobile home was in the back of a small trailer park. A few dogs barked as she walked by. A mosquito hummed in her ear. Most of the trailers still had lights on, but her trailer was dark. She knocked on the door of her neighbor and immediately heard the squeal of her own girls running to open the door.

"Mami, Mami," the two girls cried. "Where were you? Where's Papi?"

Itzel hugged them to her, not wanting to let go, not wanting to answer those questions. Where to begin?

* * *

Itzel's two beautiful daughters slept soundly, curled up next to her in her bed. The oldest, Carmela, should be going to her second day of first grade. The youngest, Monse, was in pre-K. Itzel had no intention of waking them. She was terrified they would all be separated again.

Itzel didn't sleep much. Sometime about 3:00 a.m., her husband, Javier, called. She snatched the phone crying, "Javi, are you okay?"

"I'm in a jail in Natchez, but I'm going to be moved to Louisiana. Get something to write this down." He gave her an A number. Then the call was cut short. Itzel had an A number too, "A" for "Alien." That's how they would find each other. That's how they would be found, numbered people in a broken system.

She looked through her bedroom doorway into the kitchen of her mobile home. She could see a case of boxed milk and two boxes of cereal, all that was left from Monse's last WIC appointment. She would no longer be eligible for the additional food from the Women, Infants, and Children program now that Monse turned five. Itzel tried to do a mental inventory of other groceries. She always had rice and beans in the cabinet, some chiles and bouillon. There was some meat left from the deer Javi killed last December still in the freezer and the chicken packs that she bought from the company store. They would be okay for a few days.

But then she remembered they were out of toilet paper and toothpaste. They could make do with baking soda for the toothpaste, but the toilet paper would be trickier. She remembered growing up in Juarez, many times having to use newspaper in their latrine. But nobody bought newspapers these days.

Gently sliding from the bed, Itzel went to the kitchen to make coffee. She had half a jar of Nescafe, milk, and sugar. There were some *conchas* from the Mexican bakery on the counter. She turned on the TV to the news from Univision. The first thing she saw was an aerial photo of her chicken plant. How was this story on national news? How was this her story?

Itzel flashed back to six years earlier. One harrowing day, she and Javi crammed into the bed of a truck so hot from the sun she still had a scar from burning her arm on the fender. They spent the night before at a safehouse waiting their turn to cross the river and then the desert. They were so unprepared. Not enough water, not enough money, nothing to eat, and she three months pregnant. What was she thinking? But God was good. They made it.

Crossing today would be a different story. Maybe $15,000-$20,000 each, along with the risk of being a mule for drugs or her being raped. The realization hit her. *If Javi is sent back to Mexico, he won't be coming back for us.*

Itzel wanted to call her own papi. He always knew what to do. She missed him so much. Six years was too long. But,

she thought, she was twenty-six years old. She should be able
to figure life out by now. Why did she still need her papi?

Chapter 28

August 7, 2019
El Paso
Daniel

M ONDAY morning, Daniel checked his messages before rolling out of bed. Classes were not scheduled to start for another week, but there was a message from the Law School Preparation Institute concerning the internships for his final two semesters. The text was to remind him of the email he received last week with the attached packet of required reading. He was pretty sure he wanted to be a lawyer, but studying recent judicial opinions on immigration law did not excite him. The thought of all that reading to get prepared was overwhelming. Daniel was ready for hands-on work. That was why he returned early to campus. He wanted a jump-start on his internship.

Later at the student coffee shop, Daniel put five packets of sugar in his coffee along with five packets of creamer and settled in to read. Other students were beginning to return to campus, but it was quiet for the moment. After twenty minutes, Daniel realized he couldn't recall a thing he read. He couldn't get the images of the Walmart scene out of his mind. He opened his phone and looked for more information on the shooting. Some of the victims were Mexican nationals, just like him. He wondered if he knew any of them. That thought gave him a brief smile when he remembered a gringo asking him if he knew his friend Maria in Mexico. Daniel was surprised to learn that even gringos living this close to the border had no knowledge of the vast country of Mexico. He learned not to take it personally. They lived in their own bubble.

From Facebook, Daniel saw there was a memorial service planned for that night. Flowers and photos were forming a makeshift memorial at the edge of the Walmart parking lot. Stories of bravery were blowing up social media. A young couple was killed as they shielded their infant son. A grandfather died protecting his wife and granddaughter. A dad who was helping his daughter's soccer team with a lemonade stand was in critical condition. It went on and on. How do people keep going after something like this?

Daniel had to get out. He went to his car and drove to the Cielo Vista Walmart. He parked at Sears and walked over. Most of the parking lot was roped off, but the memorial area was overflowing with trinkets, plaques, and teddy bears. Media was everywhere too. Each reporter wanted the next best story. Daniel waved them away. He didn't know why he was here. He only knew he should be. Then he heard his name.

"Daniel, Daniel. I'm Clara. You saved my mom."

Daniel smiled and recognized Clara and her mother. "Are you all right, Señora?"

"Yes, *mijo,* thanks to you." She hugged him tight. "I still can't believe it."

"Me either." Daniel didn't know what else to say, but being together with those experiencing the same shock was comforting. "Did you know anyone?"

"Yes, my neighbor."

"I'm so sorry." What else was there to say?

Two ladies came by giving out rosaries. Daniel accepted one and tried to put it over his head, but it was too tight. Clara smiled at him. "You aren't Catholic, are you? It's not a cross necklace. It's a rosary. You keep it in your pocket. It's a good reminder for us to pray without ceasing."

Daniel smiled. "Thanks. That's a good thing for all of us to remember."

The señora smiled at Daniel. "Would you come over for carnitas Wednesday night? My son is cooking."

"*Sí, Señora. Muy amable.* That's very kind."

Clara gave him the address. "Any time after 5:00. You know, *hora hispana.*"

Daniel returned to UTEP and went to the library. He spent the afternoon reading the required information. Immigration law was so confusing. There were so many different categories and steps for each type of visa. How would he ever learn it all? He knew there had to be a gate and some rules, but who made them so complicated?

He tried to maintain focus, but when a library worker accidentally dropped a large reference book on the tile floor, Daniel jumped under his table. He looked around and tried to take a few slow breaths. Then he stood, closed his laptop, and returned to his dorm room.

* * *

About 6:00 p.m. on Wednesday, Daniel parked in front of the family home of Señora Claribel Ochoa. She was a widow of five years. Clara and her husband, Royder, lived with her. Clara's brother Julio was cooking outside. Julio's five children and various cousins and neighbors played on the trampoline.

"*Oye, Gordo, ven a brincar,*" one little boy shouted to another.

"No, *no puedo. Voy al* convenience store *con mi tío.* I'll jump *cuando regreso.*"

Daniel always marveled at the ease the kids switched from Spanish to English and back. He didn't start learning English until his tenth-grade year. He still struggled at times, but Pastor Miguel in Juarez told him not to worry, that people always prayed and counted in their native language. And that was true for Daniel. He knew God spoke Spanish to him. He had heard his voice.

The women were in the kitchen as Daniel entered the house. He was hit with the smells of rice and beans and salsas that swirled in the kitchen. His mouth watered. He had only been away from his mama's cooking for two weeks, but he missed that aroma. Fast food and cafeteria fare got old quick.

"*Buenas tardes, Daniel.*" La Señora greeted him and began to introduce him all around. He politely shook hands with each one, but he would never remember the names, much less the relationship. "Daniel saved me in the parking lot."

"*Dios le bendiga*" filled the air. Daniel felt like a returning soldier must feel except he didn't really do anything compared to those who were inside.

"Did anyone see the news?" Clara interrupted. "About the big *redada de* ICE *en* Mississippi? More than 700 people were rounded up at the chicken plants there."

They switched the big-screen TV from soccer to the news on Univision. "*Ay Dios mío,* those poor people. They must be so scared."

A notification hit Daniel's phone. A quick glance showed a text from the law center again, but this time 'change of plans' was in the subject line. Daniel opened it.

"Because of the events today in Mississippi concerning ICE, our trip next week is canceled. Instead, we would like to take as many students as possible to Mississippi to assist with the legal needs of the recently detained. Please meet at 8:00 a.m. Thursday morning for more details. Make every effort to attend."

"Looks like I'm going there to help," Daniel said.

"That's great, *mijo*," la Señora said. "I know you'll be needed. *Dios te guarde.*"

The carnitas and the fellowship of family made Daniel feel at home, but he also felt excitement. Finally, he would get to do something hands-on. He needed to look at a map to see how far this trip was. Coming to El Paso was a big deal for him. He believed he was ready for the next step. But where exactly was Mississippi?

Driving back to the dorm, he called his mom.

"*Bueno, Ma.*" He tried to hurry through the usual greetings and obligatory questions about each family member. "*Oye,* I'm going to Mississippi Friday, I think. We were supposed to do a tour in Austin, but something big happened. Lots of people are in jail and probably being deported. Did you see anything about it?"

"*Sí, mijo*, and poor Carmen says it is the town where Itzel lives. She hasn't heard from her yet. She's so worried."

"Do you think she got picked up?"

"I don't know, *mijo*, but she and her husband are both *mojados*. Looks like they are getting everyone without papers."

"Okay. Let me know if you hear anything. I have a meeting in the morning about the trip. I'm pretty pumped about helping. I feel like I've been preparing for the Olympics. Now's my chance."

"*Mijo*, be a blessing to all you meet. God is sending you there for a reason. *Cuídate.*"

Cuídate. His mom always told him to take care of himself. He did. He could. He was ready. But that Walmart event shook something loose in him. And that night he felt God move into those empty places and fill him with a new strength. He would take care of himself, but he also felt God taking care of him, being in him, for the first time.

Chapter 29

August 8, 2019
Mississippi
Itzel

ITZEL refocused on the news feed from their television. "The ICE raid was the largest workplace roundup in history with nearly 700 workers taken into custody. The word this morning from ICE is that about 300 of the workers initially detained have been released to care for their children. ICE officials stated they do not believe there are any children left home alone."

Itzel smiled, thanking God that she was one of those released. But what now? She was told she couldn't work with an ankle bracelet. Her husband was in detention, she had two little mouths to feed, and there were always bills to pay. *Lord God, help us all. We only want to take care of our families.*

"Mami, why aren't we getting ready for school?" Carmela asked as she and Monse stumbled in from the bedroom still in pajamas.

"It's a holiday," Itzel said, hating to lie but hating to explain.

"Already?" asked Carmela, ever the sharp one. "We just started yesterday."

"Well, some things have changed, *mija.*" Itzel so wanted her own mamá now. And her papá.

"Itzel!" A pounding on the door made her jump. "Itzel, open up. We need to go sign up for help."

Itzel opened her door to her neighbor, Sandra, a Guatemalan lady who befriended Itzel at the doctor's office years ago when Itzel was pregnant with Carmela.

"What is it, Sandra? Where are your girls?"

"I sent them to school. You didn't?"

"No. The holiday, remember?" Itzel tried to make Sandra understand with her eyes.

"Okay. So you are staying in for now? I'll see what I can do."

"You aren't worried? Oh, wait. I didn't see you yesterday. Did they not come to your area?"

"I asked for the morning off for a dentist appointment. I took the girls to school for their first day and was driving to the dental office when I saw the helicopters and the ICE vans circling the plant. I came back home and cried as I watched it all unfold on TV."

"But your husband? Where was he?"

"He switched to night shift for this week so another worker could be available for his kids when they got off the bus. Javi?"

Itzel shook her head.

"Oh, no, Itzel. I'm so sorry." Sandra grabbed her friend into a big abrazo. "But listen. They are saying on Univision that the mission center will have free lawyers and groceries. Come on. Let's go get signed up."

"Not today, Sandra. I'm afraid to go out. If you find out more, maybe I'll go tomorrow."

Itzel closed the door. She knew they broke some laws to get here and to work, but the companies were practically advertising to come work. And they didn't break any more laws once they got here. They filed taxes, bought cars with tags and insurance, paid the hospital bills after both girls were born.

They opened a small savings account and never used a credit card. They were faithful members of the evangelical Hispanic church. She didn't feel like a criminal.

"Mami, we're hungry," said Monse, obviously being sent by her older sister to get something to eat.

"Of course, *mija*. Let me get to cooking." She would have to stretch what she had until she felt brave enough to venture out. She turned off the news and tried to think of something to fix for the girls.

But another knock at the door brought another surprise. Itzel opened the door to her girls' two teachers, each with a school lunch and a few groceries.

"We're so sorry your family has been split apart. We want your girls to return to school. They will be safe. When you are ready, we still have a place for them in our classrooms."

The girls ran to hug their teachers. Even though they were only with them one day, their faces reminded them of normalcy.

"Thank you, Mrs. Cummings," said Carmela.

"Thank you," said Monse, not sure of her teacher's name.

"Thank you. Thank you both so much," said Itzel as she closed the door. *There are good people in the world. Thank you, God.*

* * *

Itzel and her girls stayed inside the rest of the day, blinds closed, a/c running. When she got the girls to nap briefly in the afternoon, Itzel turned on the news. The same story repeated continuously with a helicopter view of her chicken plant. One new story caught her attention. A lady with five children took in her brother's four children and her niece's three. Their parents were all caught in the raid.

Itzel gasped. "One woman and twelve kids!"

She continued to listen to the reporter. "The Mississippi Diocese of the Episcopal Church has stepped up to adopt this extended family. Reverend Brian Seage, currently the state's bishop, is encouraging his parishioners to donate through the Jackson office of the diocese. Reverend, can you tell us how else your churches will be helping this rather large family?"

"We are meeting with the matriarch this afternoon to find out the main needs. We anticipate providing food for sure, and we understand there are some family members who may need transportation to medical visits and therapies. We are not here for this week only. We intend to walk beside this family for the long haul."

Itzel sat down with a notebook and made a list. A box of food was great, but no one was talking about the light and water bills, gas for the car, or the cellphone. She had to keep in touch with Javi.

Late that night, Javier called home. The girls were still awake and squealed when they heard his voice. *"Papi, Papi. Te quiero. ¿Cuándo vienes? Te extraño."* They talked on top of each other until Itzel shooed them to their room.

"How are you really, *cariño*?"

"I'm in Louisiana. I don't have a court date until February. I could get out to wait for the hearing if I had a lawyer. Can you find me one?"

"Yes, Javi, yes! February is so far away. But how will we pay for one?"

"Can your family send us something? We've been sending to them all this time. Can't they step up?"

"Oh, Javi, you know they barely make it with what we send. Your family is in the same boat."

"I'm sorry. I didn't mean that. But I can't stay here until February."

"Sandra told me there are free lawyers here. I'll go tomorrow and find out."

"Free might not be good. We may have to get a loan."

"No, Javi. Not like we did when we crossed. No, that's too scary."

"I'll figure something out. We're going to be okay. Be strong for me and the girls. We will get through this. But I need a lawyer. I can't stay here."

"I love you, Javi, but I'm so scared. I can't live if they separate me from our girls again."

The line went dead as Itzel sagged to the floor. How much would a lawyer cost? Would a free lawyer be any good? She Googled immigration lawyers on her phone. Most were located in New Orleans, but there were two in Jackson. She wrote down their numbers. She didn't want to think about the thug who came to their place the month after they arrived in Mississippi.

* * *

The next day Carmela was begging to go back to school. "Please, Mamí. I don't want to get behind. You heard my teacher. She said she'd take care of me. Please let me go."

"Okay," Itzel said. "Let's get dressed. I'll fix some breakfast and run you both to school. It's too late for the bus."

Monse began to cry. "No, Mamí, no. I don't want to go. Please let me stay with you." Itzel wanted to cry too.

"Okay, Monse. You can stay with me today. I might need a helper." Itzel did not know if she was making the right decision, but Monse was only in Pre-K. It wasn't mandatory.

Itzel and Monse walked Carmela to her classroom door. The teacher smiled and said, "Carmela, I'm so glad you came. We're still missing several students. Come on in and sit on the carpet." Then, glancing at Itzel, she said, "We'll be all right, Mama."

* * *

Itzel drove carefully to the mission center in Forest, the next town down the highway. She didn't want to get stopped for any reason. She was never stopped before, but things had changed. She rolled her shoulders and popped in a Frozen music CD. Monse joined in as always singing in perfect English.

Trinity Mission Center was ground zero for the displaced, fractured families of the raid. Donations of food and diapers were pouring in. Sunday school rooms were turned into interview rooms as lines formed to the street. Several different groups were offering free legal help, some from union organizers, others from immigrant rights groups, and some from Catholic Charities. It was a circus on a hot and humid Mississippi day. Temps rose to 97 degrees, and tempers rose even higher. News crews were everywhere, every reporter and photographer hoping to get a big break with this crisis. One woman who seemed to be in charge vainly tried to keep the photographers away, especially from the children.

Itzel got in line for legal help with Monse on her hip. Many of her friends from Morton lined up with the same dazed expression and trickles of sweat. As the wait time grew longer, Monse grew tired. She got down from her mother's sweaty arms and played along the sidewalk. She walked along the curb, balanced like a tightrope walker, and skipped back. But then she slipped and skinned her knee. Blood ran down her leg, and she howled. Suddenly, a crowd of photographers rushed in. No one was trying to help Monse. They only wanted a photo of a crying child. The next Pulitzer Prize swung in the balance.

The woman in charge came running. "Get back. I told y'all to stay behind the yellow tape and not to photograph anyone without permission, especially children." She chased them away and offered Itzel wipes and Band-Aids.

"I'm sorry," she said. "We're trying to keep things moving and give you some confidential legal advice. I'm Shannon. What else can I get you?"

"Thank you," Itzel said. "We really appreciate everything you are doing."

Finally, Itzel reached the intake table. After giving some basic details of her situation, she was sent to another line to wait. When she finally made it to the legal table, she was told that the tables represented lawyers who would be in contact with her in a few days. She could not sit and wait for days for a lawyer to call. She had to take charge. Javi would do that for her. Itzel grabbed the donation box of food and personal hygiene items and drove back to Morton. It was time to pick up Carmela.

She swung by the school in time for pick-up. Carmela was waiting with her teacher.

"How was school, Carmela?" Itzel asked as they drove home.

"It was good, but a lot of kids were absent. Bobby said their parents got picked up by ICE. Everyone was talking about it. Did you know that Giselle's dad got picked up too? He might be with Papi."

Itzel's heart hurt listening to her little girl talk of such horrific topics with ease. Would these events traumatize her in the future? Or did the parents' attitude and tone set the reaction of the children? She hoped she was setting a good example for her girls.

* * *

That night Itzel received two hard phone calls, one from Javi begging her again to get a lawyer and bail money, and the other from her parents.

"Mami, Papi, I wish you were here." Itzel let her tears roll and her voice crack. "I'm so sorry. I wasn't thinking clearly when I left. I never dreamed something like this could happen. I always thought we would come back as soon as we had enough. I miss you so much." Itzel cried into the phone letting out all her emotions of the last two days, plus the last six years.

"Mija, we saw the news. Even all the way from here we knew it was your town and your plant. Tell us what's going on," said her papi.

"Javi's in jail in Louisiana, another state. I have an ankle bracelet and can't work. The churches are helping us with food and maybe a lawyer, but I don't know what to do about Javi. He needs a lawyer and bail money now. I may have to sell our car, but who's going to buy it? Everybody is in the same boat." Itzel knew she sounded like a child again, but she was so glad to talk to them. She didn't realize how big the ICE story was.

"Don't make any quick decisions," her wise father told her. "Do you and the girls have enough to eat?"

"Yes, Papi. God is faithful."

"One day at a time, mija. God will provide. Tell us what happened."

As Itzel told them the story of that horrific day, she realized again how good God was. She and her girls were together. They had food, a place to live, and a good school with caring teachers for the girls. Plus, there were people trying to help. She took a deep breath. "Thank you, Mami, Papi. I miss you so much. I want you to know your granddaughters in person. One day we will all be able to meet."

"*Sí, mija.* That is our dream too. *Primero Dios.*"

God willing. How many times did she say that line a day?

Itzel hung up, grateful for technology to connect with her parents so easily, but sad at the thought of maybe never seeing them again. She could go home, of course, but she would lose all they gained.

Life was hard enough. Why did she have to choose between her children and her parents?

Chapter 30

2019
Mississippi
Itzel

THAT night another meeting took place. The Pastors and some lay people from the Methodist, Pentecostal, Baptist, and Catholic churches together with some of the immigrant rights leaders met to coordinate a plan. They came from Morton, Forest, Canton, Carthage, and Sebastopol, small towns nearby, all affected by the raids.

After opening with a prayer for wisdom, the Pastor from the Pentecostal church said, "We can continue to man our food pantry here in Morton. Our director, Glenda, will open it more days if we can get more donations. Our congregation is on board for packing boxes and manning the distribution. We have an old warehouse we can use to store the donations separately from our regular pantry offerings in case anybody questions us."

"We can continue to run our Baptist mission center in Forest," Brother John said, "but we want to know who these people are. We can't just give to anybody and everybody. Our donors want to know we are being good stewards."

"We can't ask for information, or we'll scare them all off," said Mildred. "Our funds are to be given with no strings attached."

"The food is a great first step," Pastor Shannon said, "but they'll also be needing to pay bills soon. Then what?"

"We're stepping up with legal help and funds," said Sister Pat. "We will have a counselor in each community starting tomorrow night in Morton, then rotating to Forest, Carthage, and Canton."

They brainstormed and argued and talked on top of each other, but soon came to a rough plan. The pantry in Morton was already a known source of help as was the Trinity Mission Center in Forest. Each community would designate a central place for signing up for help and would encourage the families to go only to the center in their own community. The main source of contention was from MIRA, Mississippi Immigrants' Rights Association, and the Union organizers who did not want anyone asking questions in order to give help.

Glenda had several years' experience running the food pantry and clothes closet in Morton. "Let's help anyone and everyone the first two weeks as long as the food and funds hold out," she said. "After that, let's meet again and see how it's going. Right now, they're all scared and in shock, just like us. There might be a few who take advantage of us, but for the most part, I believe they will be honest. Let's help everyone get over the shock and learn to trust us for the long haul."

"I agree," said Pastor Shannon. "Let's work by community, but let's try to be consistent. May God rain down the blessings of donations on our communities."

And God did. Large orders from Amazon, Costco, and Walmart were delivered to the centers, sometimes from anonymous donors. Local donors purchased from the local grocers who had lost a huge percentage of customers to the raid. Churches from many states sent large checks while some churches sent teams of volunteers to assist in the distribution. Local Hispanic neighbors stepped up to translate and to deliver to friends who were still too scared to leave their homes. Many of the chicken plant employees who were not picked up in the raid stepped up to help their former coworkers. All races and nationalities and denominations became the hands and feet of Jesus in a common goal.

Chapter 31

August 9, 2019
Texas
Daniel

THE UTEP van rolled east along I-10 just as the sun rose. The five other students were already asleep with earbuds in place, but Daniel was wide awake. He was glad Burly was going on the trip. He almost missed out because of football, but exceptions were made. One teacher, Mr. Acosta, drove and another navigated. The navigator, Ms. Coronado, was his teacher last year and encouraged him to apply for Law School Prep.

Ms. Coronado turned in her seat to Daniel. "Have you ever traveled this far in the United States?"

Daniel shook his head. "Not even in Mexico. One summer my whole family rode the bus to Torreon, a 24-hour bus ride. But looking at the map now on my phone, I realize the trip really wasn't that far. The routes and stops made it longer."

"Is Torreon a vacation destination? I've never heard of it."

"No. That trip we went to meet my grandfather and my uncle for the first time. My uncle Hernán is my mama's older brother. They didn't grow up together because their parents divorced and separated the two children when they were little."

"Oh, that's an interesting custody arrangement. So, your mother didn't know her dad either?"

"No. Her mama remarried, actually remarried several times. I have six or seven aunts and uncles on my mama's side."

"Well, tell me about that trip. All travel is good. It helps us appreciate what we have and see what else is possible."

"It was very different. They live in a tiny town, about 300 people, I think. They have electricity but haul water from a lake. No Wi-Fi for sure." Daniel smiled as he remembered. "Memo, my little brother, has always been sickly, but he ran around from field to field meeting all the animals. Our girl cousins laughed and giggled at everything he did. He even caught a tarantula in a jar and nearly stepped on a rattlesnake. I've never seen either one before. It was pretty scary."

"I don't care for snakes myself. Did your mother get along with her father and brother?"

"Yes. It was kinda neat. My mama was getting to know this part of her family too. She was communicating with her brother on WhatsApp. Tío Hernán called her once a month when he came out of the mines. But in person, I couldn't believe how much mama is like her brother and her father, even though they barely knew each other. Tio Hernán is a hard worker in the mines and takes care of his family when he's home. My *abuelo* gets up before sunrise to tend the animals, his corn field, and his vegetable garden. He doesn't stop moving all day.

"My mama is the same way at home. She doesn't work outside the home except for flea market sales and helping my pa with his business, but she never stops moving—cooking, washing, cleaning—and makes sure we help with chores and do our homework. When she does stop, it's to read something to improve our lives, not to get on social media."

"She sounds like a great mom. I hope to meet her someday. Has she ever thought of going to college herself?"

"She always wanted to, but her mom wouldn't even let her go on to junior high. Ma always wanted to do more, but I've never seen my grandmother hold a job for more than about three days. I wonder, what makes the difference? What gave Ma and Hernán that extra umph?"

His teacher looked far away as if the answer were in the mountains they were passing through. "I think more government programs need to help people like your grandmother to get ahead. She probably didn't have the opportunities."

"I don't know about that. The government helped her add onto her house, but then she recently ran off with another husband. She sold what the government built for her and bought the guy a car. Now my younger aunt and uncle don't have anywhere to live."

Daniel laughed when he saw his teacher's expression. "My family's a little crazy. I'm older than my aunt and uncle."

His teacher attempted to smile and turned back to consult the map. "So, twenty-four hours on a bus. That must be exhausting."

"It was long, especially on the way home. But one scary thing happened. We got stopped by someone like Highway Patrol. Two men got on our bus with machine guns and started checking for papers. There were two men traveling on our bus, each with a child. I thought that was strange because men don't usually do that back home. The officers took them off the bus and put them in their patrol car. I don't know what happened to them. Ma said she thought they were from Guatemala trying to make it to the United States to work. She heard on the news they would let families with children in, so they were carrying those kids with them."

"Oh, how scary," Ms. Coronado said. "But surely that's not what's happening. There are single dads in Guatemala as in any area of the world. They were just looking for a better life."

"But why take a child with you? How can they work with a child to care for? And it's dangerous crossing without papers."

"I guess I don't really know about all that. Anyway, I'm glad you got to know the rest of your family."

Daniel watched the empty desert of West Texas change colors as the sun beamed stronger through the windows. He knew no one understood his family. He didn't either. His ma was proud of him going on this trip though. He was sure his pa was too, but he didn't always express it like his ma.

* * *

"Daniel, whatcha listening to?" Jennifer waved from across the aisle. She was in many of his classes last year.

"I'm not. I'm just thinking."

"You ever been outside of Texas?"

"No. I've never been farther than El Paso. It's a long way to Mississippi."

"Yeah, we shoulda flown. I can't believe they're making us take a bus."

"I've never flown either."

Jennifer glanced at him wide-eyed. "Well, I have family in Atlanta, and we always fly to visit them. We also fly to Colorado every Christmas to go skiing."

Daniel tried to think of a response. Sometimes it was hard to explain his life and his background. He didn't want the others to pity him, but he was always surprised by how much the other students took for granted. Finally, he said, "Have you been to Mississippi? What do you think this work will be like?"

"Oh, you know, a bunch of poor people who work in factories, kids running around barefoot, nothing to do. It'll be sad and all, but we'll get to use some of our interviewing skills. It'll look good on our resumes." Jennifer adjusted her Ray-Bans and sipped from her Yeti cup. Her blond hair was sleek, and her fancy nails flashed as she ran them through her tresses. Her expensive-looking bag bulged with who knew what. "Maybe we can make our own entertainment tonight." She returned her earbuds to her ears and slouched back, knees pressing into the seat ahead of her.

Did she wink? Was she flirting with him? Daniel felt the heat inch up his neck. Jennifer was pretty and always nice to him, but was she really on this trip only for her resume?

Daniel thought about how far he had come and who made that possible. He remembered Abuelo, his pretend gringo grandpa, who visited his family often in Juarez. He first arrived with a group of missionaries building houses in Daniel's neighborhood when Daniel was still in elementary school. Abuelo quickly became part of the family.

Later, Abuelo bought his parents a used car to help rush Memo to the hospital when he had a breathing attack. And when Daniel was ready for *Prepa*, Abuelo paid the tuition for him to go to a bilingual high school. He always showed up in a crisis. But Abuelo stopped visiting a few years ago. His health was failing, and he couldn't make the long drive.

Thinking of Abuelo, Daniel got an idea. He pulled up his maps app again and saw they would pass near Dallas. He tapped his teacher on the shoulder. "Do you think we will stop around Dallas?"

"We're a long way from there, Daniel. Didn't you go before we left?"

Daniel smiled. "Yes, ma'am. I was wondering if I could ask a friend in Dallas to meet us somewhere if we stopped."

"Well, we have at least eight hours to Dallas and then eight or nine more to Morton. So, Dallas will probably be a good place for a longer break. But we are going to be on the interstate, not downtown."

"Okay. I'll see if he can meet us somewhere then."

Jennifer nosed in, "There's a Buccee's on I-20 east of Dallas. That would be a cool place to stop. It's like a convenience store, mall, and food court all in one. They have everything."

"We're not shopping, Jennifer. We are only stopping for gas and a break. I'll let you know where we will be stopping, Daniel, when we get closer."

"Thank you."

Daniel looked up Abuelo on WhatsApp and sent him a text. He hoped Abuelo would feel like getting out to meet him. He missed the old man. But somewhere around Van Horn, Daniel drifted off, and Abuelo didn't respond.

* * *

Daniel felt the van slow, and he tried to straighten his stiff neck to look at his map. They were in Odessa.

"We will take a break here for gas and to walk around for a few minutes. The next stop will be close to Dallas, so plan your eating and bathroom accordingly." Ms. Coronado was an immigration lawyer for an agency known as JFON, Justice for Our Neighbors. She told lots of good stories in class that made the dry readings come to life.

"Daniel, were you able to get with your friend?"

"He hasn't answered, but I'll text him again. So, maybe about 2:00?"

"Yes, I think so. Mr. Acosta is a little more conservative than I am. I'll be driving the next shift."

Daniel smiled at that. His mama was very cautious, but his dad was like a racecar driver no matter how old he got.

"You probably drive more like my dad. We never wear seat-belts when he drives. None of our vehicles even have seatbelts anyway. I had to learn lots of new traffic rules when I first got a car in El Paso."

They continued talking as the group entered the convenience store.

"Have you been driving long?" Ms. Coronado said.

"No. I got my first car last year. Rules are rarely enforced in Juarez, unless a traffic cop needs a pair of shoes for his kid." But then Daniel remembered his neighbor who was still a cop and regretted saying that. He protected Daniel when he was beat up by a bully when he was only eight. Daniel felt bad painting him with a broad brush. "Not all cops. There's always good and bad in every group."

Jennifer came up beside him slipping her hand under his arm and pulling him to the counter.

"Daniel, let's get some breakfast burritos. You're in another world today."

"I am. I can't believe I'm going to see so much of the United States on this trip."

"Mainly just Texas. Nothing new here."

"It's all new to me." Daniel knew she would never understand. Even this convenience store with spotless bathrooms and shower facilities for truck drivers was a marvel to him. He thought about buying a very real-looking rattlesnake for Memo but decided to send him a photo instead. Burly bought the extra grande burrito and an energy drink. Daniel got a chorizo with egg burrito and a coffee. Then everyone reloaded into the same seats as before.

The teachers' plan was to alternate driving so they could arrive that night. Mr. Acosta was a lay preacher in the Methodist church who taught in the education department. He made arrangements for the group to stay in Sunday School rooms at the Methodist church in Morton, Mississippi. Daniel didn't have classes yet with Mr. Acosta, but he spoke Spanish, so Daniel often asked for explanations as he adjusted to life on this side of the border. His translator app was helpful, but cultural differences and idioms were confusing.

As they drove past refineries, man camps, and wind farms, Daniel started to realize how vast "this side" was too. *Out of all the families in Mexico, how did God arrange for Abuelo to find our family? Incredible!*

"Daniel, are you planning to go to law school?" Jennifer was back in the seat across from him. "I'm going to SMU. I've already taken the LSAT and have been accepted for next fall. I can't wait to be in Dallas."

"I don't know yet. I'm not sure I'm cut out for it. I'm hoping this trip will help me make some decisions. I'm supposed to work at JFON this fall too."

"Oh, you'll be a good lawyer. You read all the time. That's the hardest part for me. I'd rather be arguing all the time."

The van swerved suddenly, and Jennifer's big bag tumbled into the aisle. "My Michael Kors!"

Daniel picked it up along with a few things that spilled. "I don't understand. I thought Coors was beer."

"Oh, Daniel. You're so cute and naive. He's a designer." She rolled her eyes and put in her earbuds.

Daniel still didn't get it, but it didn't seem important. He was used to being in a fog, but now he was thinking again about law school. He wanted to help his people with immigration, but was there another way to help besides law school? He looked out his window to marvel at the giant wind turbines along the highway. Who worked on those motors? Who climbed that high for service work? He thought about his pa and knew he could fix anything up there. But since he couldn't read, his pa never dreamed of coming across the border.

He texted Abuelo again and this time got a quick response.

"Let me know when you get close to Fort Worth. I'll meet you. You can tell your mama you did what she said to do."

"No, Abuelo. I really want to see you. It wasn't her idea."

Abuelo was always kidding, but Daniel knew he didn't like getting old. He didn't want pity visits. He didn't want to sit at their house for the neighbors to come and look at him. "I don't want to feel like an exhibit in an old folks' home," he always said when they asked him to come back.

The miles ticked by, and Ms. Coronado zipped down the interstate as promised. They passed through Big Spring and Sweetwater, then Abilene and Weatherford. Daniel didn't recognize any of those towns. When they neared Fort Worth, Daniel again tapped his teacher's shoulder. "Where do you think you'll stop?"

"I'm almost on empty. I think I'm gonna need to stop in Fort Worth. The gauge says I've got fifty more miles. What's the next big gas station?"

Before Daniel could open his phone, Jennifer butted in. "There's a mall right on I-20. That's a good place to take a break. I'm sure you can find gas there too."

Ms. Coronado smiled. "Okay, Jennifer. But remember we don't have a lot of room on this van for extra bags."

Daniel texted Abuelo the name of the mall and they agreed to meet at the Dillard's entrance in an hour. Daniel felt something like butterflies in his stomach. He was excited to see Abuelo. It had been too long.

* * *

As soon as they entered the mall parking lot, Daniel recognized the big old Suburban Abuelo always drove around

Juarez. He couldn't believe it was still running. Ms. Coronado parked, and Daniel was the first to exit. He raced to the entrance and soon was in a bear hug from Abuelo.

"I missed you," Daniel said.

"I missed you too, *mijo*. How long have you got? Let me buy you a decent meal."

"Only thirty minutes."

"Okay. How about we sit in my car and eat Vienna sausage?"

"Abuelo, you know I always think of you when I see those. The dogs are still coming around watching for you to throw them some."

"I'm kiddin'. What do you want? Pizza? A big hamburger?"

"How about that China buffet?"

"Well, get what you like. Here's a twenty. I'll meet you back at this table."

Daniel ran to fill his plate while Abuelo grabbed some wings and a Diet Coke.

"So, tell me what you're studying. Whatcha gonna be when you grow up?"

"I'm in Pre-Law, but I'm kinda doubting my choice. I hope this trip will help me see the need."

"Well, my daddy was a West Texas lawyer, and he was an S.O.B."

Chapter 32

2019
Ciudad Juarez
Cristal and Fina

CRISTAL and Fina ran to the corner as the route bus pulled up. They dropped their pesos in the box and hurried to the back. Adjusting their backpacks, they settled into their seats for the long ride downtown.

"I can't believe I'm almost done with school." Cristal was in her last year at UACJ, but she felt the same as when she started her first day of elementary school. She was nine years old when she entered first grade with her sister Fina, the first time for either of them to attend school. Now, she was a student teacher. "I can't wait."

Fina couldn't wait either. She was starting her third year at the university. She still could not believe there was enough money for her to attend the university at the same time as her sister.

"I'm getting off at the Primaria," Cristal said. "Remember where your first class is?"

Fina nodded with a trace of fear in her eyes.

"You'll be fine," Cristal said. "Teachers always love you."

Fina tried to smile. She never went anywhere without Cristal. Cristal was always taking care of her—finding scrap to trade for something to eat, holding her close when they were in the children's shelter together, helping her adjust when they went to live with *Pastora* Pati and Pastor Miguel. But now, even though Fina knew the campus, she would be alone. What if she got lost? What if someone tried to bully her? What if…and then they were at Cristal's stop.

"You'll be fine, Fina. I'll see you tonight."

Cristal stepped off the bus in her professional dress. She already looked like a teacher. She would be fine too. She was tough. Now it was time for both sisters to fly solo.

Cristal walked crisply into the principal's office, her shoulders back and head high. She exuded a confidence she didn't fully feel yet. "Good morning, Maestro."

"Good morning, Cristal. Maestra Beatriz is waiting for you. You don't have to check in here. Do you remember her room?"

"Yes, thank you. Thank you for this opportunity."

Cristal weaved her way through the many students playing in the courtyard of the busy *primaria*. The school held first grade through sixth and had at least three rooms of thirty-five students in each grade. Moms with strollers and various dogs careened through the crowd as well, but Cristal managed to find her classroom.

"Buenos días, Maestra. ¿Cómo está?"

"I'm a little frazzled this morning, Cristal, but so glad you are here. Most of these kids went to kindergarten last year, but there will still be some first-timers, crying their way through the morning. I'll need extra hands to keep everything under control." She looked up at Cristal. "Are you ready?"

Cristal smiled. "I think so."

The bell sounded, and the children poured into the room. Cristal didn't have a chance to ask questions. She helped the students find their seats to get started on a coloring page and collected some of the classroom supplies the students brought from the supply list. Not everyone contributed, she noticed, but there was enough to start the first semester. Toilet tissue, paper towels, hand sanitizer, PineSol, and Fabuloso piled onto a table. The parents supplied janitorial supplies as well as typical classroom supplies. Some parents signed up for the cleaning days.

One little girl didn't have her uniform and cried silent tears at her desk. She had no supplies in her backpack and no parent brought her in. Cristal tried to engage her, but the little girl made no eye contact.

The biggest boy in the class was having the hardest time letting go of his mom.

"I'll take his backpack, Señora," Cristal said as she slid the straps from his arm. But at that moment, the boy let out a howl and bit down on Cristal's wrist. She tried not to howl herself as she let the bookbag fall to the floor.

"Benito, tell the lady you're sorry. Tell her." But Benito had no intention of talking to the teacher.

Maestra Beatriz deftly detached the boy from his mom and shooed her out the door.

"Benito, you are a big boy. Let's go." Maestra Beatriz took charge in her teacher voice.

Cristal straightened and rubbed her wrist. She knew she had that teacher voice too, but she only used hers to survive on the streets. She didn't realize it would come in handy in the classroom.

"Come with me, Benito." Cristal grabbed his hand, taking him from Beatriz and leading him to his desk. "Here's your first paper for first grade. Let's make a better first impression. Get busy."

The other students glanced at Benito and smiled. They seemed glad Benito was put in his place.

The rest of the morning was still chaos, but when the principal finally locked the main gate, the teachers got busy. With only a four-hour shift of school, they didn't have a moment to waste.

The little girl with the big tears was Quetzali. Cristal worked with her and four others on writing their names.

"Quetzali is a beautiful name. Did you know it is a greenish-blue bird from Central America?"

Quetzali stared at her paper. A tear dropped in the middle.

"Don't cry, Quetzali. Here, let me show you a picture of it. It's as beautiful as you are."

Cristal pulled out her phone and found a stunning picture of the bird with an extremely long tail. The other girls leaned in and commented, "Ooh, it's so pretty."

"Do we have those here?"

"I've never seen one of those."

Cristal closed her phone. "No. They live in the rain forest. They wouldn't like our desert climate. It's too dry."

The other girls continued their interest, but Quetzali never said a word.

"Quetzali, your name starts with a letter with a long tail like the bird. Let's see if we can make the letter and color it like the bird."

"I wanna make a bird. Can I draw the bird too?" Soon all the girls in the group were drawing quetzals and making the letter Q. All except Quetzali.

At the recreation break, Beatriz and Cristal supervised the children as they zoomed around the courtyard, burning off steam. All were happy to be there, even Benito. But Quetzali stood behind a post.

"Do you know anything about Quetzali?" Cristal asked Beatriz.

"No, I don't. She might be from some of the squatter families who moved onto the lots behind the S-Mart. I didn't notice who brought her in. We'll need to watch who picks her up." But, at pick-up time, Quetzali was picked up by an older sibling. The big brother showed no emotion as he grabbed Quetzali's arm and dragged her toward home.

Cristal felt a familiar knot in her stomach. She knew what these children were suffering. She was like them.

"Can I follow them home?" Cristal asked Beatriz.

"No, not by yourself. We can plan a home visit on one of our teacher meeting days. Now, let's get the room picked up for tomorrow."

* * *

Cristal and Fina both worked shifts at S-Mart now. Cristal was a night cashier. Fina worked in the pharmacy. The pay was poor, but they could help with their own personal expenses. As they took the bus back to their neighborhood one night, they both saw the fliers. A young girl about their age was missing.

"That's why you aren't going to ride the bus home alone at night anymore," Fina said. "If we don't have the same shift, we either get the manager to change it or Pa will pick you up."

"I know, but I hate having to ask for anything special at work, and Pa will already be asleep when we get home. I hate to ask him to do that when he gets up so early for his work."

"He won't mind at all. You know that, Cristal."

"I know, but maybe I'll try that new Uber thing. That should be safe."

"Safer in a car alone with a man than on a bus with other people around?"

"Yeah, okay, but why do women have to be so much more careful?"

"I agree, it's not fair. But God gave us that extra sense to know when a situation is not safe. Promise me you will listen to it."

Cristal smiled at her younger sister. When did she become so wise?

* * *

Cristal loved being a teacher. She woke up alive and on fire for each new day. School had been a struggle for her, but now she knew she was where God had called her to be.

"Buenos días, Miss Cristal," the students greeted her, many wanting a hug at the door. But each morning as she reached to hug Quetzali, she felt the little girl stiffen. Cristal remembered that defensive move she used when Pastora Pati first stepped into her own life.

"Buenos días, Quetzali," Cristal said as she hugged the fragile statue. "I'm so glad you're here today."

But Quetzali slipped into her desk without a word, without a backpack, without any sign of a snack for later. Her disheveled hair and dirty fingernails told more of her story, a story without any love.

Cristal's heart broke again. Many of her students lived in extreme poverty, but they arrived with love. She could see it in their faces and in their neat hair and clean uniforms. Someone cared about them.

After school, Cristal asked teacher Beatriz about visiting Quetzali's home. Beatriz agreed to accompany Cristal the next day after school.

But the next day, Quetzali was not at school, and neither was her brother.

"Well, I guess that gives us a good opening for being at her house," Beatriz said. "Don't expect this mama to welcome us in for coffee."

"I know. My mama was that way," Cristal said tentatively.

Beatriz looked at her with raised eyebrows. "Really? I figured you were a teacher's kid. You are a natural helper and teacher."

Cristal reddened at the unexpected praise. "Thank you, Maestra. My foster mother is a Pastor's wife and teaches Sunday school. I learned a lot watching her, but in my early years, I was a lot like Quetzali."

"I had no idea. I'm sorry. I should've tried to get to know you better. The university sends these student teachers out each year with so little experience. I guess I've grown tired of doing the university's job."

"I'm learning so much from you. Thank you for accepting me into your classroom."

"Tell me about your early years, Cristal. I'd love to hear your story."

As they walked to the poorest area of their school district, Cristal shared some of what it was like growing up in the pitiful huts they were coming to, shacks made of pallets and tarps with dirt floors.

"I mainly remember being cold and hungry all the time. Our mom didn't know how to be a mom. She had my brother when she was thirteen. He got out as soon as he could, and I took care of my younger sister. We roamed the neighborhood looking for scrap to sell to get a few tortillas."

Beatriz looked at Cristal with new eyes. "I knew there were some children who lived that way, but I didn't realize they were right here next to my school. I'm sorry."

"It's not your fault. It's too overwhelming sometimes even for me to think about. But when I see Quetzali, I see myself. I can't let her slip through the cracks like I almost did."

Beatriz gave Cristal an unexpected hug. "Thank you for making me a better teacher. Let's see what we can do for Quetzali."

They finally found the little hut where Quetzali lived with her brother and mother. The ever-present wind picked up the dirt and trash from the yard and carried it through the open windows. A big dog was chained at the door, so Cristal picked up a rock to tap at the bed springs that formed part of the fenced patio. A small head peeked out of the curtain hanging at the door.

"Quetzali, is your mama home?"

She darted back inside. The dog gave a low growl, and the smell of tortillas heating on a comal drifted through the neighborhood. Finally, a young woman parted the curtain.

"Miss, we are Quetzali's teachers. We were concerned about her missing school today."

"I had an appointment."

"We wanted to see if Quetzali needed anything we could help with." Beatriz was treading lightly, not wanting to offend.

"I take care of her. She doesn't need anything." The mother already had a defiant tone.

"Can you tell us about yourself? Are you working? Is Quetzali's father here?"

"I work at a maquila at night. Their father comes to check on them most nights. We're fine. We don't need any help."

Cristal remembered those same words from her own mother's lips. Why? Cristal took a deep breath and said, "Sometimes pride keeps us from a greater blessing." Should she continue? "I would love to help Quetzali with her homework. I imagine you are tired from long shifts when you get home."

"We brought some crayons, pencils and paper for Quetzali and her brother to have at home," Beatriz said, offering the small bag. "She is a beautiful child, just like the bird. Cristal showed her the picture she was named for."

"She wasn't named for a bird—Quetzali's the girl on Instagram." The mama snatched the bag and let the curtain close.

Beatriz and Cristal looked at each other. What was there to say?

Chapter 33

2019
Mississippi
The volunteers

Pastor Shannon met with her church board. She updated them on the community response to the raid and her hopes for the church's participation. "I'm taking our youth group to shop for groceries at Walmart tonight," Shannon told them. She had pastored a church on the coast during hurricane Katrina and had a good idea of the urgent response required. "We've been given a large donation from the Wesley group at Ole Miss. The youth are going to add to that from their own pockets."

"Is that a good idea?" asked board member and banker Greg Tollison. Greg also served as financial adviser to the church. "Teaching them it's okay for these people to live outside the law?"

"I think it's about teaching them 'When I was in prison, you visited me. When I was thirsty, you gave me something to drink. When I was hungry, you fed me.' I think it's what we should be reminding ourselves." Shannon tried not to sound defiant, but she couldn't get the sight of the children crying for their parents out of her mind.

"I'll take my truck to load the groceries and follow the church van," offered Steve Nabors, a local pharmacist. Steve was always ready to lend a hand. He owned a small horse farm out from town and often used Hispanic labor.

That night at Walmart the youth filled ten grocery buggies with rice, beans, diapers, toilet paper, laundry detergent, and dish soap. As they were waiting in line, a young black coach from the local high school came up to Shannon.

"I know what y'all are doing," he said and handed her a one-hundred-dollar bill. "Thank you. Add this to your funds."

Shannon smiled and whispered her thanks. Most people get it, she thought. We need each other.

The pantry warehouse was chaos the first night. The intake workers were trying to get some basic facts on each family, especially the ages of the children to know what to buy for the next time. Did they need diapers? What size? Was anyone diabetic? What was the most needed item?

The clients had questions themselves. Could they get more supplies if there were several families at the same address? What if a neighbor was too scared to come? Could they sign up for the neighbor? What if they weren't caught in the raid but were afraid to return to work? Would there be more raids?

Then news came that one of the chicken plants closed its doors for good. Some workers at another plant went to work that morning and were fired. But even with all the anxiety and the unknowns, everyone was glad to have a place to gather. The doors opened at 6:00 p.m., and the last box was loaded into a car at 10:00 p.m. The volunteers were exhausted but exhilarated.

"Let's go next door, get some chips and salsa, and regroup," said Glenda. "I think Los Cazadores is open until 11:00."

"Pretty ironic, isn't it? Going to eat Mexican now?" said Shannon. "What would we do without all our good Mexican food?"

"Have y'all eaten the *pupusas* at Felicia's Salvadoran store?" said Steve. "They are delicious."

"Yes, they're my favorite," said Jill, a faithful volunteer. "But the most ironic thing today was getting a huge donation of frozen chicken nuggets from the plant that was raided."

"Guilty conscience or really wanting to help the community?" asked Glenda. "I guess we'll never know, but there are good people in this place. Let's order and then start a list of the most needed items to put out on Facebook and give to all our church connections."

"I think we served about 200 families tonight. Let's ask the blessing," Jill said. Then they all joined hands and prayed like a first-century church.

Chapter 34

2019
Mississippi
Itzel

Itzel had to do something. She couldn't work a real job with an ankle bracelet, and she couldn't pay bills without a job. Javi was still in detention in Louisiana somewhere, and her worst summer electric bill was past due. Javi called at 11:00 p.m.

"You've got to get me out. I can't help us from here." He was desperate. "Call my cousin Jesús in Ciudad Juarez. He has contacts. He'll know what to do."

"No, Javi, we already talked about that. It puts me and the girls in too much danger."

"It'll just be a one-time loan. You know we can pay it off quick."

"Javi, maybe I should go home and wait for your release. Mami and Papi will take me back in. They will be thrilled."

"Yeah, until they realize they can't feed more mouths and there is no remittance coming from the other side."

"That's not fair. They love us. They want to meet their grandchildren."

"I know, Itzel. I know. But you know there wouldn't be enough to eat. And the schools are so bad there, they probably wouldn't even have a spot for the girls until next year.

Let's try to hold on. Please call my brother. I've gotta go. *Te amo. Esfuérzate.*"

Itzel hung up and let her tears flow. The girls were asleep. *Esfuérzate.* Be strong. Give it all you've got. That was their encouraging word to each other since they met.

* * *

The next night, Itzel and Sandra waited in line at the pantry for food and supplies. Their girls adjusted to school, and there were no more raids, but Sandra had bad news.

"I can't believe they fired us," Sandra said. "Saul and I worked there for fifteen years!"

"Me either, Sandra. I'm so sorry. I thought you were both in the clear."

"At least our house is paid for. If it wasn't for Tito at the bank, we would still be paying rent and never getting ahead. I guess he really took a big risk on us."

"And neither one of you has an ankle bracelet! You can find another job, but what am I going to do about rent? Our trailer is paid for, *Gloria a Dios*, but the lot rent and electric bill come next week. And you know how bad my light bill is in August, running that air conditioning all the time in a mobile home."

"God will provide, Itzel. He has so far, hasn't He? And look!" Sandra pointed to a flier. "Sign-up for help with bills at the Methodist church. God's got this!"

"And a lawyer?"

"Well, did anyone ever call you back from that day you went to Forest?"

"No. I'm going to see what I can pawn or sell and go to that lawyer in Jackson. Javi said some of the guys have already been bailed out."

"Why don't we go to the Catholic church tomorrow night after you sign up for the rent help?"

"No, I'm not waiting on any more free help. I'm going to get my husband out. We can't make decisions with him in jail that far away," Itzel said as she stepped to the table for her turn.

"Print your *nombre* and *cuantos* are in your *casa, por favor*," said Jill, trying to use some Spanish. "Let us know how the food box is this week. Is there anything you would like to have next time or anything you don't really use?"

"No. Thank you for all you are doing," said Itzel. "We are so grateful. We would never complain about what is in the box. God bless each of you."

"Thank you," said the volunteer. "And here is a map and time for signing up for help with any bills for light, water, gas, or rent, but not cellphones. I know you need a cell to keep in touch with your detained family members, but we can't cover everything."

"God is so good to us. Thank you for hearing his call," said Sandra. "God bless you."

Chapter 35

2019
UTEP in Mississippi
Daniel

Aﬔer the long drive, the UTEP Students were all too happy to crash on the carpeted floor of a Sunday school room at the Morton United Methodist Church. Saturday morning the aroma of coffee and donuts pulled them from their air mattresses as they gathered for instructions. Then they were back on the van to Forest's Trinity Mission Center. Thirty minutes later they unloaded to meet Pastor Shannon at the distribution center.

"Good morning. Y'all sure have come a long way to help us, and we so appreciate it."

"Put us to work where you need us most," Mr. Acosta said.

"We are still working with several groups who are promising legal assistance. Volunteers from some of the agencies are signing up families at those tables. Do any of you speak Spanish? We could use more intake workers there."

Daniel raised his hand as Burly said, "I took two years of Spanish and can order a cold beer."

Mr. Acosta nudged Daniel forward. "Here's your man for the job. This is Daniel. He's from Juarez, Mexico."

Pastor Sergio smiled. "My wife is from the Chihuahua area too. *Bienvenido.*"

Mr. Acosta nudged the other student. "You go with Daniel, Burly, and see if you can learn something more useful." Burly grinned and followed.

The rest of the team divided themselves into groups of three, some distributing food, others doing crowd control. The news crews were worse at following the rules than the clients. They couldn't seem to stay within the yellow-taped areas, as if the rules didn't apply to them. Jennifer's personality came out as she bossed the media with a teacher's voice.

"Oh, no sir," she said. "You will have to stay behind the tape, and stop trying to get pics of the kids. You have been warned. Do you want to lose your press credentials here?"

The journalist backed away and did as he was told, but another young photographer approached her.

"How's your day going?" he asked. "Where are you from?"

Jennifer gave him a hard look. "You are not going to distract me with your Southern-boy charm. Get back."

"I'm interested in all the people who are helping here. What's your story?"

"I'm a pre-law major at UTEP. Now get behind the tape."

"I'm sorry, but a Southern boy like me doesn't get out much. What is UTEP?"

Jennifer rolled her eyes. "It's THE University of Texas."

"Okay, but what's the EP part?"

"El Paso, the farthest west city in Texas with over two million people. Just a small town as Texas goes. You do know, of course, that everything's bigger in Texas?"

"So, you came all the way from there to direct traffic in our little town?"

"I'm getting real-world experience here and community service hours to put on my law school application. You should get out more. Now get behind the tape."

"So, how are the lawyers going to help these people who have clearly broken the law?"

"Everyone deserves his day in court. It's the American way. Surely as a journalist you know that much. Or do they not teach that at the universities in Mississippi?"

"Oh, they teach that, but we also know that lots of lawyers are hoping to make bank on this raid. Politicians too. What is your take on the raid?"

"I'm not here to discuss the politics of the situation."

"Right! Crowd control and an entry on your resume. Got it!" This time the journalist rolled his eyes as he walked behind the tape.

Daniel and Burly got a hasty orientation on filling out the intake forms and a line soon formed in front of them. The first lady was from Guatemala, and a tiny baby peered out from her shawl.

Her sister translated for her as they whispered in their indigenous language. Daniel often heard the Tarahumara speak their language when they came into the flea market in Juarez, but he didn't understand any of either language.

"What's her full name, full name of her husband, and names of any children?"

Daniel listened closely as he filled in the information because the accent was different for him. The Guatemalan ladies were so small compared to the tall Tarahumara.

"Was her husband detained?"

"Yes. He worked at the main plant on the highway. He worked there for fifteen years."

"Has she spoken to him? Does she have his A number? His alien registration number?"

Daniel wrote down the information and asked about the children. "How old is the baby?"

"Only two weeks."

"Make sure she gets signed up for diapers and other baby needs in the last room. Use this link to locate detainees. Her husband could be anywhere. This detainee locator will track him if he is moved to a different location."

Daniel filed the paper, and Burly punched his arm.

"That was impressive, Dude. How do you do that?"

"Do what?"

"You know, switch so easily to Spanish."

"I grew up speaking it, you big dummy." Daniel laughed with his friend.

"I know, but I have to stop and think about each word before I say it."

"You need practice, that's all. I was that way when I first came across and was learning English. I would get headaches at night from focusing for so long."

Their next client was a young girl from El Salvador. She handed him a paper from Immigration and Customs Enforcement with a court date scheduled for February of next year.

"So, you already have a court date?" Daniel asked in surprise. "But in Laredo, Texas?"

"Yes. I have an ankle bracelet too. I was caught back in March at the border. My sister lives here and got me on at the chicken plant. I work nights so I didn't get caught in the raid, but now I hear they will be checking documents more carefully. I have to work. I can't sit at home until next February. I have to pay off the loan I made to get here. If I don't, they will do bad things. Surely, ICE knows I will be working somewhere. I'm afraid to go back to the night shift. So far, they haven't noticed my ankle bracelet, but now, who knows?"

Daniel raised his shoulders. *Who knows? Did these lawyers know, or were they only collecting fees to postpone the inevitable? And who was paying the "free" lawyers?*

He filled her form and sent her on to the line for food. Daniel listened to story after story, gathering A-numbers and contact information and sending the clients to the next line with the hope that their problems would be solved. But would they really?

The lawyers were supposedly free, but someone was paying for the assistance. Was it political parties, unions, philanthropists? Daniel wanted to know more. He knew how evil the cartels could be. He grew up during the worst drug war in Mexico, the worst of the violence occurring in Juarez. There were nebulous players on all sides of the immigration and drug problem. He didn't want to be a part of the wrong side.

"Daniel, let's go," Burly said. "We're loading up to go to Morton."

Daniel walked to the van and tried to reconcile all he saw and did that one day. Were they making a difference or just giving false hope? *Señor, ayúdame. I know you brought me this far for a reason. Open my eyes to what you are doing. I want to be a part of that, I want to be on your side.*

The UTEP team worked all afternoon at the pantry in Morton. Donations were arriving from everywhere. Amazon, youth groups, UPS, and individuals pulled into the parking lot with trunkloads and truckloads. Others came by with sweet tea, homemade sandwiches, and poundcake for all the volunteers.

That night, the team helped as they did in Forest. They loaded wagons with the appropriate food, diapers, cleaning products, and personal hygiene items and rolled them out to the waiting cars. Daniel helped at intake, hearing more stories from the frightened immigrants. A few clients already received donations the night before, but they said tonight they were registering for a neighbor or a relative. Daniel did his best to get all the pertinent information. He believed them. They were all truly scared. The rug had been pulled out from under them.

Chapter 36

2019
Mississippi
The Volunteers

Aᶠᵀᵉᴿ the pantry closed, the team went back to the church to sleep on the floor. Jill, Shannon, and Glenda went next door to eat Mexican food as was becoming their habit. Jill was a newlywed. She felt guilty about how much volunteer time she spent away from home. Glenda was raising her ten-year-old grandson and depended on her husband to pick up the slack at home. Shannon was a seasoned pastor who always spent too much time away from home on various outreach projects and resented time spent in meaningless committee meetings at the church. They discussed the details of the next food order, what they needed more of, and any changes to be made in the intake process.

"I think we need to do some home visits," said Jill. "Yolanda was translating at the intake table for me tonight. She thinks some people are not exactly being honest."

"I knew we would face this sooner or later," Shannon said. "The bill-paying will probably speed up the possibility of fraud."

"I think the majority are truly needy and are not providing false information. It's always a tiny few who make it difficult for the rest," said Glenda. "We have a few who always try to pull one over on us at the pantry during normal times."

Shannon pursed her lips into a grim line. "The immigrants' rights group still doesn't want us to ask questions, but I have a responsibility to our donors to be a good steward. The donations won't last forever. People will move on to the next tragedy."

All three nodded, each trying to come to grips with the magnitude of the undertaking. "Let's pray," Jill said, and they joined hands to pray for wisdom.

"I think tomorrow night we will begin to see what we need to ask for. Every case is so different, it is hard to have blanket rules," Shannon said. "Yolanda will be there tomorrow night too and a Spanish teacher from Pelahatchie. The team from UTEP will be here too. On Friday we have a meeting with all the leaders in the area again to compare notes. Hopefully, we will be on top of things by then."

As they moved to pay their checks, they noticed the servers crowding around the television mounted above the cashier's station. The channel was for a Spanish station, but they had no trouble understanding the captions as they scrolled by: *Memorial para las 23 Víctimas de la masacre en El Paso.*

"*Lo siento,*" Shannon said to the servers. "I'm sorry. We are glad you are here and are part of our community."

The head cashier smiled. "Thank you, Pastora. We appreciate what you are doing to help our people."

* * *

As Shannon and the others drove home, the Spanish teacher in Pelahatchie put her last graded test papers back in her briefcase. Brenda was tired from teaching all day and grading papers all night, but tomorrow would be different. She was excited about the mission opportunity in Morton. Teaching Spanish was okay, but using her Spanish to help was Brenda's passion. She hoped she was up to the task. Many of her students' parents worked for the now closed chicken plant in Pelahatchie. She worried about them. Would they move away? Would they continue their schooling elsewhere? Would they drop out to help their families? She had never had those struggles growing up. *These kids are so resilient. Lord, show me how to help them.*

Chapter 37

2019
Mississippi
Daniel and Itzel

Sunday night Shannon organized the fellowship hall at the Methodist church for intake with a copier from her tiny office ready to copy bills and lease agreements. File folders, pens, and forms were at each intake station, and an area was ready with books and toys to entertain children. The families began lining up at the door thirty minutes early. The desperation of the situation overcame the usual *hora hispana* custom of arriving late. The UTEP team divided up to help again, and as soon as all the volunteers were in place, Shannon opened the door.

The families who brought someone to help them translate went to Jill's table, and the others went to Brenda's or Daniel's. Burly stayed with Daniel, actually seeming interested in improving his Spanish. Jennifer asked to fix hair and nails on the little girls while they waited for their moms. Steve, the pharmacist, and a couple of youth did juggling and magic tricks for the kids. Tootie, a lifetime member of First Methodist, kept everyone plied with homemade cookies and coffee. Everyone found something to do.

Brenda's first family had four children, ages six, four, two, and two weeks.

"So, your husband was picked up on the day of the raid and you went into labor the next day?"

"Yes. He hasn't seen his baby. Thank God his sister lives beside us and helped me get to the hospital. Her husband kept the other kids."

The next client was a man with four children. "My wife was picked up in the raid. We hoped they would release the women, but she is still in detention. She was breastfeeding the baby, and he doesn't want to take a bottle. It's been so hard. He cries all the time. I used my last cash to put in Dish so the others could be distracted with cartoons while I try to take care of him. I borrowed $7,000 from my uncle to pay my wife's bail. She has to come home."

Story after story was gut-wrenching, each different, but with a common thread. One day they were working hard, paying bills, sending their kids to school, and the next day, an earthquake rocked their world. The volunteers did their best to get billing information and due dates, but many bills were in the name of someone who lived in the rental many tenants ago. Or a bill was subdivided each month between several tenants who were at the same address. Again, every case was different, and there were no easy rules.

Daniel's last client was a young mother with a child about four in her lap. She began pulling out her bills and looking for her husband's A-number. Her older daughter was nearby getting a new hairdo and fancy nails. When the young mother looked up, she stared and then exclaimed, "Daniel?"

"Itzel?"

They rushed around the table and embraced as Itzel burst into tears. Her sobs were heard all over the fellowship hall.

"I had no idea you were here," she said.

"I had no idea you were here. We are here for a week to help. Did your boyfriend get deported?" Daniel asked.

With that question, Itzel laughed. "He's not my boyfriend, Daniel. I guess we need to catch up. He's my husband, and we have two little girls now. Javi is in jail in Louisiana, but I'm trying to bail him out. OMG, you were still a little kid when I left. How old are you now?"

"I'm a senior at UTEP. And I wasn't *that* little," Daniel said, hoping to make her laugh again. "Do you have a lawyer yet? We helped sign people up in Forest yesterday."

"Yes, I signed up there too, but everything is moving too slow. I called a lawyer in Jackson today. They want $7,000 to open the case and try to get a bond hearing."

"Wow, Itzel, that's a lot of money even on this side. Don't you want to wait for a free lawyer?"

"Javi can't wait. He told me to get a loan from his cousin like we did before."

"Isn't that dangerous?"

"Yes, but last time we were able to pay it all back real fast."

"Yeah, but last time didn't you both have jobs?"

Itzel looked down. The tears were fighting to spill out again. "We want our family together again. We were doing everything right. Why did this happen now? Why?"

"I don't know, Itzel, but I do know that our being here together is not a coincidence. Let me look at your bills."

Daniel and Itzel exchanged phone numbers and promised to meet the next day. At the same time, they looked at each other and said, "*El mundo es un pañuelo,*" such a small world. No one could believe that Daniel found someone he knew from his neighborhood in Mexico in Morton, Mississippi. That encounter helped buoy the team. They were exhausted as usual, and not so exhilarated. The volume of need was overwhelming.

Shannon locked the front door. "Let's go into the sanctuary for a few minutes."

Jill, Brenda, Steve, Tootie, two youth, the UTEP team, and Shannon circled up for prayer. "Lord, we are exhausted. We are overwhelmed. We want to do your will. Humanly, we don't know how to do this, but we believe you do. We put all these needs into your hands. Give us wisdom, bring us donations, provide more workers, and most of all, Lord, be in the middle of this work. Or maybe we should say, we want to be in the middle of what you are doing. Thank you for bringing us all here together to serve you. Amen."

Chapter 38

2019
Mississippi
The Volunteers

T HE next day, Yolanda came to see Shannon.

"We don't need to be helping Felicia. She owns the Honduran store and has income."

"Is her store still open?" Shannon asked.

"Yes. She might not have as much income right now, but it is open. Plus, she has some rental property. Some of the bills you are being asked to pay will be paid to her."

"I haven't seen her name on any of the rent requests."

"They are under her husband's name. Didn't you get some requests for rent paid to Alejandro Ramirez?"

"Yes," Shannon sighed. "How can we check all this? After two nights of intake, we have over one hundred families requesting bill payments."

"We need to do some home visits. Even if we don't see them all, if word gets out that we are checking, then the few bad actors will disappear."

"And I'm going to have to separate what we as a church are doing from what the immigrant rights group is doing. Our funds are being donated to our church, not to a political action group. If our donors believe we are being irresponsible with the money, our donations will dry up."

"I could visit a few after work each day, but I don't know if someone from the community is the best person to do it."

"Let me think about it, pray about it. I do think we will have to have some guidelines. Some of the court dates are more than six months out. We can't support over one hundred families for six months. I'm going to pay every request we received this month. Then, before the next round of payments, hopefully we can do some home visits. Maybe the visits will trim the rolls a little bit."

Chapter 39

2019
Mississippi
Itzel

Sandra knocked on Itzel's door a few days after the raid. "I have some news, something I never thought about before."

"Come in. Want some coffee?" Itzel said.

"Sure, I've run out at home. Hope there will be some in the next box."

Itzel fixed their coffees, and they sat on the porch. Mississippi summer was still brutal, but she was trying to limit air-conditioning use.

"I was at the Catholic center yesterday. There was someone from a law firm talking to the other moms there about filing a power of attorney for your children. It's some kind of document that gives someone here the right to your children in case you get deported. That way they won't end up in government custody and sent to who knows where. Then that person would know your wishes and be able to send them to you or keep them here until you can get back."

"I never knew you could do that."

"Me either. I would hate for my kids to get split up in foster care. I was thinking, you could be my person, and I could be yours," Sandra said.

"Well, I would trust you with mine, but maybe we need to find someone with papers to be that person. What if we both got picked up again at the same time?"

"Yeah, but who?"

"Felicia at the store has papers."

"Yeah, but she would probably want to charge us to sign it."

Itzel laughed. "You're probably right. And Tito at the bank too. I think our Pastor and his wife would do it."

"Good idea. I've got extra forms in the car. Let's go see them. They may want to ask everyone at church to offer if they have papers and have one big signing day."

"You are full of good ideas today, Sandra. Thank you. Let's go by the church."

"Okay. And let's tell Lulu too.

Chapter 40

2019
Mississippi
Daniel and Itzel

THE next morning, Itzel dropped her girls at school and drove to the church. Daniel met her in the courtyard with coffee.

"I still can't believe you are here, Daniel. Tell me what you've been doing and how you ended up here."

"I've been at UTEP. I went there after graduating from La Lydia in El Paso."

"I remember you were going across to *prepa*. Ma told me about that, but I forgot. I just remember you always reading. What are you studying?"

"The group I came with, we are all pre-law students. I want to help with immigration problems, but I'm having doubts about becoming a lawyer." Daniel shrugged and looked at his cup.

"I went to see a lawyer yesterday. They want so much money. I have to find $7,000 just to get the bail process started."

"Yeah, that's the part that seems so unfair. I want to make money, but I don't want to take advantage of people in their worst days."

"Maybe it's not taking advantage. I don't know if some people get out and then disappear. Maybe they are covering those costs, like insurance in case Javi runs."

"So, besides the money, how can I help you?"

Itzel was quiet for a moment. There was so much need. She thought of the lady who took in all those children. She thought of the women who were not released. She thought of her neighbor, who was going to a coyote for a loan.

"I hate to ask for anything. I'm so much better off than most. I was thinking about going to Jackson to sell Javi's truck. It's like new and has low mileage. My car is in good shape for getting me and the girls where we need to go. I think if I could sell the truck, I could get him out on bail until a court date."

"Well, think about it. Maybe you should sell your car. He could do work with a truck when he gets out. Is your car paid for?"

"Yes, Daniel, that's a good idea. And yes, both are paid for. I hope Javi will call tonight, and I'll see what he thinks."

"How is Carmen handling this? My mom really wanted me to come home before I came on this trip," Daniel said.

"Mom really wants us to come back. I want to go home too, but how would we live there? I couldn't earn enough to feed my girls."

"Your pa seems to always find work, more than my pa."

"He does, but they always struggle. I hate to be a financial burden in addition to the pain I caused them by coming here to begin with."

"I'm just now beginning to realize how much Abuelo helped our family through the years. His help opened doors for me. I want to be like Abuelo for someone else."

"You will. God has a plan for us both. I didn't appreciate all we had growing up. I was probably a little arrogant, maybe entitled even. I want my girls to be grateful for the life we have. That's another reason I really want to take them back to Juarez. I want them to know our stories. We are so blessed."

"You know, I was in the Walmart parking lot when the shooting began."

"*Ay, Dios mío*, Daniel. How awful! Were you hurt?"

"No. I saw the people running out, some bloody, and I helped an older lady get away. That was close enough."

"I can't imagine. The raid here was horrifying enough, but at least no one was hurt or killed."

"These two events back-to-back have really made me think about what I want to do. Let me know what Javi thinks, and I'll see what I can do to help."

They talked a while longer, reminiscing about their neighborhood and old friends. Then the team began to load into the van, and Daniel said goodbye. Itzel tried to pray about the decisions to be made. She felt pulled in several directions, each from different sides of the border.

* * *

That night Javi called and agreed with Daniel that selling the car instead of the truck made the most sense.

"But please Itzel, do it fast. I know there's probably no one in Morton who would buy it, but what about Matías and his church in Jackson? They would probably help. Just get something to get the bail process going. I have to get out."

Itzel hated the desperation she heard in Javi's voice. She called the couple in Jackson, and they wanted to buy the car.

"We won't have the money until next week though. Can you wait?"

"No, I'm sorry. I'm afraid something will happen to Javi if I don't get the lawyer hired this week."

"Okay. Let us talk with our Pastor and we'll call you back."

Itzel knew it was pointless to try to sell the car in Morton. No one had any money or any certainty of a job. She had to get it to Jackson. She messaged Daniel.

"Could you go with me to Jackson tomorrow to try to sell my car? You could drive our truck to bring me back after I sell the car."

After checking with his teachers, he agreed to go. "My teacher will drop me off at about 8:00. Is that okay?"

"Yes. The girls will be at school. Thank you, Daniel. It's so nice to have someone from home to lean on."

* * *

Daniel followed Itzel down the interstate to the Pearl exit and parked behind her in front of a small house. A woman came out and greeted Itzel with a hug.

"Itzel, it's been too long. How've you been?"

"Ana, it's so good to see you! How's Matías? How are the kids?"

"We're all good. We stay glued to the TV though, watching for rumors of any future raids. You must be so scared."

"I'm okay. I got back to my girls that night, but Javi is desperate to get out."

"I'm sure. I can't imagine Matías being locked up and not able to provide for us."

"Ana, this is Daniel. He's from my neighborhood in Juarez. He's here with a group helping out at the mission center."

"*Mucho gusto*," Daniel said as they shook hands.

"Nice to meet you too. Thanks for helping Itzel out. And all of us."

"So, did Matías decide to buy my car, or does his friend want it?"

"Our neighbor wants it. He ran to the bank to get the cash. Come on in. He'll be right back."

The three visited and reminisced of good times in Mexico and the cultural challenges they each confronted arriving here.

"Ana, remember when we got off the bus in Jackson and wandered into your food truck area? What a blessing! Daniel, it was the middle of the night. They didn't know us at all but took us right in."

"You two were go-getters, though. We were pretty sure you would make it. Matías and I were the same way when we came. We had no idea what we were getting into. We believed all the myths about easy money. There's money to be made, but it's not easy."

Ana stood to answer the knock at the door and let her neighbor in. After introductions, Itzel gave him the keys for a test drive. Cash traded hands, and Itzel had enough to go to the lawyer's office. "When Javi is released, we'll both come back to visit again. Thanks so much, Ana. Thank Matías for his help."

With money from her savings and the cash from the sale, Itzel drove to the lawyer's office and signed the paperwork. If everything worked smoothly, Javi could be out in a week. Someone would have to pick him up or at least get him to a bus station. Itzel wasn't worried about those details. She only wanted forward motion.

"Itzel, where are the other women getting the money for lawyers? Not everyone has managed their money as well as you and Javier."

"I'm afraid they are borrowing from the same coyotes who took our money to get here in the first place. That's scary stuff. I don't want to be in debt to any of them ever again. I'm surprised the United States wants to have people here who are indebted to them." She shivered. "Daniel, those *narcos* have no conscience. The stories I've heard from the more recent arrivals are horrendous. If you can't keep up on the journey, they leave you to die."

"Yeah, I hear some stories in El Paso from Border Patrol reports. It's sick."

"Let's get back so I can cook you something before the girls get home."

"You don't need to waste your food on me. I have meals with the team."

"Not real meals. I'm cooking anyway, and I'm sure you would like some homemade tortillas better than a cold ham sandwich."

They pulled into Itzel's driveway as her neighbor came across the yard. Itzel introduced Lulu to Daniel, but the neighbor wanted to talk in private. The two women walked back to Lulu's yard.

"Itzel, I'm going to get the loan from my cousin's friend. What did you decide to do? Are you coming?"

"No, Lulu. I sold my car, and with our savings, I had enough. Isn't there anything you could sell to get together the money? Do you have any savings in the bank?"

"No, Itzel. We didn't plan for this. Who plans for something like this?"

"I'm sorry. I wish I could help. Do you have any relatives you could stay with to help with expenses? Think about it, Lulu. Do you really want to be under that kind of pressure, that constant threat of violence if you don't pay?"

"I don't have a choice. I've got an ankle bracelet and two mouths to feed."

The story was the same. The ones who managed to save some money were able to survive, but the others were at the mercy of the cartels.

"Just be careful, Lulu. You can't miss a single payment. You can't be late or not have the whole amount."

"I know, Itzel. I know. We should have saved more. We shouldn't have bought beer every weekend."

The two women hugged, and Lulu went inside. Itzel walked back to her house and let Daniel in, explaining Lulu's situation.

"It's the same back home," Daniel said. "So many people work all week just to spend it all on beer for the weekend. I thought things would be different on this side."

"Alcohol is the same everywhere, Daniel. Javi struggled with it when we first came. I had to be tough on him. The scare with the coyote taking our car should have been enough, but he still had a couple of times when the macho peer pressure got to him."

"I guess I thought that making it to the promised land would be enough."

"Nope. Even in the Bible, the people still messed up after making it to their promised land. We have to walk with Jesus every day. More money does not solve all problems. Sometimes it makes them worse."

Chapter 41

2019
Mississippi
The Volunteers and Daniel

Pastor Shannon sat at her desk at the church, staring at the pile of bills to be paid. "Lord, only you can solve this problem. It's too big for me, for us, for our church, or for our community. Show us what to do."

She sat in silence and waited. There weren't enough funds. She needed to make home visits. She needed to write a sermon. She needed to meet with the finance committee. She should spend more time with her husband. She had reports due for the bishop's office. Where should she begin?

Steve tapped at her office door. "I had an idea this morning that I wanted to run by you."

Shannon smiled. Steve always had big ideas, but unlike others, he was willing to help carry them out.

"I've been thinking and praying about the need to do home visits and how to help lift some of your load. We've got our bunkhouse vacant right now. I was thinking, what if we could get an intern to work with us maybe until Christmas? Somebody bilingual who could handle some of the day-to-day stuff that is putting too much on your plate. They could stay at our place and even use my old farm truck. Would the conference office have any funds to pay some kind of stipend for that?"

"That's a great idea, Steve! I thought about asking Brenda, the teacher, to do the visits, but she wouldn't have time. Too bad it's not summer or she would be all over it. Let me make some calls. Maybe one of the Christian student organizations would have someone interested. More kids are doing college online these days."

"What about the kid from UTEP who's here now? He's who got me thinking about this. He's so natural with the families."

"That's a long way from home for him. He might not want to stay here."

"He does know one family in town though."

"Yes, he does. Let me find some money first. We might need the intern to do some fundraising as well, maybe speaking to groups so people understand what we're doing here."

"Yes, there are still quite a few who don't get what happened, and how it affects us all."

They talked some more about the amount of the stipend, what expectations they would have for the intern, and how they could best use him or her. Steve would make some calls concerning insurance and liabilities. Shannon would look for funding from the conference. Together they prayed for guidance, and Shannon gave thanks for a speedy answer to her prayer.

* * *

Daniel sat in the church garden again with his coffee waiting on the team members to get a move on. Today was their last day in Mississippi. Tomorrow they would head back to El Paso and their regular life, but so many would never get their regular life back. *Lord, how can I help? What am I supposed to do with all this opportunity you have given me?*

For some reason, his thoughts turned to a memory of a bus ride with Cristal. She told him the same thing as Itzel. Money doesn't solve all problems. Cristal was going to be a teacher. A teacher in Mexico. She wanted to give back to kids like herself. What did he want to do? He used to want a big house and a nice car without worrying about a budget. But lately, those things seemed trivial. He remembered the warmth he felt in Itzel's little kitchen as she prepared tortillas. He remembered the warmth and joy he felt in the *señora's* house in El Paso as family gathered to thank him and enjoy being together.

Professor Coronado came into the garden with his coffee. "Buenos días. Mind if I join you?"

"Not at all. Is anybody moving yet?"

"I think a couple of the guys are. It's gonna be another long day. It's pretty amazing here, what so many Christians have done together. I hope they can hold out."

"Yeah, so many good people helping out. But also, I didn't realize that so many of our people were here. They've put down roots, become part of the community. I don't think they were planning to go back. Who knows now?" Daniel said.

"Yeah, I knew there were lots of Spanish-speakers in big cities across the United States, but I didn't realize there were so many in rural areas too."

"So, do you think being a lawyer will be the best way I could help? I'm kinda struggling with how much these lawyers are charging. I mean I wanna make money, but I wouldn't wanna charge my friend Itzel a fee like that during the worst time of her life."

The professor was quiet for a few minutes. Then he said, "I really enjoy teaching, seeing young people find their places in life. I was often told I could make more money in technology or in the medical field, especially being bilingual. But it wasn't for me. I can't tell you what to do except to tell you that money can't be your end goal. Money can have problems of its own."

"I keep hearing that," Daniel said smiling. "You're the third one. God must know I can be hardheaded if he sent the same message three times directly to me."

Jennifer came out to the garden with her ever-present Yeti cup. "Good morning, guys. Only one more day of roughing it. I can't wait to be home."

"Like I said," the professor said smiling at Daniel, "money can have problems of its own."

* * *

The team worked in Forest for the morning, had lunch, then returned to the Morton pantry and thrift store for their last day. They sorted and organized the food donations that arrived that morning and tried to streamline the pick-up process for that night. Clients began to arrive at 5:00, and things moved smoothly. By 8:30, they were finished.

"Let's go next door for one last-night celebration," Glenda said. "Y'all have done an incredible job this week. Thank you."

As the team headed for the door, Pastor Shannon called Daniel to the kitchen.

"Can I talk to you for a minute?"

Daniel followed her into the kitchen where Steve, Professor Coronado, and Mr. Acosta were waiting. Daniel's eyes got big.

"You're not in trouble, Daniel," Mr. Acosta said. "We have an opportunity you might be interested in."

Daniel relaxed and sat on a cooler.

"We are looking for an intern to help us manage the next few months," Shannon said. "We need someone bilingual to do some home visits. We also need someone to help with teams who are wanting to come help. We might even want you to help with fundraising. We thought you would be a great fit. Steve has a bunkhouse and an old truck you could use. The bishop has given us a small stipend for three months, possibly renewable for three more."

Daniel looked around and tried to think of questions to ask. He liked the sound of it all.

"You could do your classes online," said Professor Coronado.

"We would make sure you made time to study," Shannon said.

"We could look at your courses and see if you wanted to make any changes for this semester," Mr. Acosta said.

"So, do I stay and not go back with the team?"

"We thought about that," Professor Coronado said, "but we thought you would rather go home first. There are enough funds in our program to fly you back."

"You can think about it. You don't have to tell us on the spot, but I would love to have your help," Shannon said, giving him a side hug.

Daniel grinned. "But can I decide tonight?"

Everyone laughed. "Of course."

"I want to do it."

"Let's go celebrate then," Shannon said, and they all went next door to the Mexican restaurant.

They placed their orders and remembered the week. Daniel saw that Jennifer was finishing a margarita and signaling the waiter for another. He didn't care that she was drinking, but was she affected at all by the time spent here?

"Jennifer, what was your favorite part of the trip?" Professor Coronado asked.

Jennifer hesitated for only a beat and said, "Probably when the team from Ole Miss came to help."

Mr. Acosta tapped his glass with a spoon. "I have a big announcement to make. Daniel has been offered an internship here for the rest of this semester."

The boys clapped and began shouting, "Daniel! Daniel! Daniel!"

Jennifer looked at him with big blue eyes. "You aren't coming home?"

"I'm riding back with you in the van to get my stuff. Then I'll fly back out next week."

"I told you we shoulda flown. That's great, Daniel. You can help these poor people better than we can. And they are your people anyway."

Daniel smiled, but he really didn't know what she meant by that. He would never understand her. Her margarita came as their food did, and everyone dug in. Daniel thought of all the families he met this week and wondered how the others could just walk away and go back to their lives. He wanted to see the rest of the story. He wanted to be a part of their lives as they figured things out. He wanted to see what God had planned for them and for himself. He was excited to tell his family.

That night back at the church, Jennifer and two of the guys brought a bottle of tequila into the kitchen. They were playing an ABC drinking game of Spanish words. If they couldn't think of a word they knew with the next letter, they had to take a shot.

"Adios," Jake said.

"Burritos," Jennifer said.

"Cancun," Burly said.

"Diablo," Jake said.

"Enchiladas," Jennifer said.

"Fajitas," Burly said.

"Gorditas," Jake said.

"Daniel, come in. Come play with us. I'm winning. Tell me a Spanish word with an H."

"No. I'm going to call my family before it gets too late."

"Come on, Daniel. You won't ever have to take a swallow. You can always think of a word."

"No, Jennifer. I've got things to take care of."

"You're, like, so responsible. Loosen up a little. Life isn't so serious."

"Really, Jennifer?" Daniel didn't get it. How could anyone see families ripped apart and not be sympathetic? He went out to the garden to call home. He was about to hit Send when Burly came out.

"Hey, I'm sorry about that. I wasn't drinking. I guess I was trying to show off all the Spanish I've learned this week."

"You don't have to apologize, man. I get it. Y'all are here to get the credits and go back to your real life. It's okay."

"It's not okay. I learned a lot watching you this week. You switch so easily between the two languages, it's amazing. But it's more than that. You really care about these people. And they can tell. They gave you a lot more information than any of the other people doing intake. I wanna be serious in my Spanish class when I get back. Before, I just thought it was cool that I could communicate with my uncle's employees and learn some bad words. Now I see a reason. I'll never be as good at it as you, but I'm gonna put in the effort."

"That's good, Burly. Thanks."

"If you're still here during Thanksgiving, maybe I'll come out and lend a hand again."

"That'd be great. I might actually be glad to see you by then." Daniel grinned at his friend. They fist-bumped, and Burly went back inside. Then Daniel called his ma.

Chapter 42

2019
Ciudad Juarez
Daniel

DANIEL drove across the international bridge toward home. He glanced down at the trickle of water which formed the boundary and the looming fences that protected it. Immigration was a tough topic. There had to be some rules. Everyone locked doors and decided who to let in. There also seemed to be more than enough work in the United States for anyone who wanted it. So why couldn't more people cross legally? Why weren't there more visas available? Why couldn't someone make new lines to get in?

He made it to his neighborhood, named for a famous Mexican boxer, Jose Sulaiman. The streets, mostly paved now, were all named for other boxers. Trash and dirt blew as the ever-present desert wind came down from the mountains. He dodged a couple of dogs and watched for children playing soccer in the street. With his windows down, Daniel could smell the delicious aroma of tortillas on a comal, salsa in a blender, and carne asada on a grill. It was good to be home.

"Ma, ya llegué," Daniel called, and his ma and Memo came running.

"We missed you," his ma, Araceli, said as she hugged him tightly.

"*Carnal*," Memo said, with an air of toughness Daniel could see through.

Memo tried to fist-bump, but Daniel grabbed him into a back-pounding hug while they both laughed.

Araceli smiled at this unusual display of affection.

"Where's Pa?"

"He's on his way. He had a big job this week, plastering the ceilings at the new store opening beside Coppell."

"That's good, but doing ceiling work all week will kill his neck. He needs to slow down some."

"That's what I tell him, but you know your pa."

They heard the loud muffler of Pa's truck and turned to welcome him home too. Daniel was glad they would all eat together. He remembered too many nights when his pa would not come in until late, trying to finish a job.

During a supper of chicken legs in *mole*, with his ma's perfect rice, Daniel told them about his trip and the plans for his internship. As usual, his ma asked all the questions and his pa only listened. Memo wanted to know about any cute girls on the trip.

"Carmen is so worried about Itzel and her granddaughters. She was so relieved when she found out you were there."

"That was a real surprise," Daniel said. "I think she and her family will be fine. Most of the families I interviewed had it together. They had savings and a plan. There are others though who are borrowing from coyotes. I don't know how they will ever pay that much back."

"That's so hard to understand," Araceli said. "How do they not have any money?"

"They took the same problems with them that they had here. Alcohol, no money management, vices. It's sad they didn't value what they had."

After supper, the guys went out to kick the soccer ball around while Araceli washed dishes and cleaned the kitchen. When she finished, she called to Memo to take out the trash.

"Aw, Ma. Daniel's home. Let him do it."

"Are you really still whining about taking out the trash?" Daniel took the bag and walked to the big container.

"Thanks, Man. I didn't want you to get the big head, going off in an airplane and all."

"Yeah, that's gonna be the scary part," Daniel said.

"All my life I've watched planes flying over Ciudad Juarez and wondered who was on them. This time I'll know," Pa said.

Daniel looked at his pa in surprise. "One day I'm gonna buy you a ticket to the United States, maybe you can go watch Mexico play their soccer team."

"Thanks, *mijo,* but I'm fine here. Just finish your studies."

"I will Pa, I will." Daniel couldn't believe his pa shared that much with them. He was going to get that degree and keep his promise. His pa worked way too hard. He needed a vacation.

"I'm walking over to Fina's for dessert. Wanna come?" Memo said.

"Sure," Daniel said. "Let's go."

* * *

Fina served them a new *chocoflan* dessert she was perfecting. It was a cake with a chocolate flan layer in the middle and whipped cream on top.

"This is better than gringo brownies for sure," Daniel said.

"She's going to enter it in a contest," Cristal said. "The winners get a partial scholarship to culinary school."

"She should win," Memo and Daniel said together.

The young people sat outside, and Pati and Miguel gave them their privacy. When they finished the dessert, Daniel turned to Cristal.

"Wanna go for a walk?"

"Sure. I want to tell you about my student teaching."

They started their usual stroll around the park, passing Carmen's store. "I need to stop by there tomorrow to talk to her about Itzel."

"You'd better! Everyone's been talking about the crazy coincidence of you being in her town."

"Tell me about teaching first."

Daniel listened as she described all she was learning. She bubbled over as she described each student. Then she described Quetzali and her face showed the pain she kept guarded inside. Pain for Quetzali, and pain for her own lost childhood.

"I'm sorry, Cristal. I don't think I really understood your life before, and why you were always on me about money not being the main thing. I can see how you are giving back. I felt the tug to do that too when I was in Mississippi. I could give back as a lawyer, but I'm not sure my heart is in that anymore. I'm hoping this time as an intern will help me see other options."

"Daniel, there aren't many families like yours, or many couples like Pati and Miguel. I want to help as many children as I can to have some unconditional love. They need to know there is at least one person who truly cares for them. I haven't made a dent in Quetzali yet. She is so empty, it's gonna take a lot to fill her up."

They sat on a bench and watched some of the neighbor-hood children play on the broken slide. A dog slept under-neath, and music blared from a car that zoomed by.

"You know, I haven't really talked much except to Ma about the shooting. It was horrific, and I didn't even really see the bodies. I can't imagine how the people who were inside felt. How do they ever get those images out of their minds?"

"I can't even imagine, Daniel."

"But also, that day, I heard God speak to me. That's never happened to me before."

Cristal grabbed Daniel's hand and squeezed it. "I under-stand," she said. "You know, one time when we still lived in the pallet shack, it snowed. It was so cold, but I peeked out the little window. Everything was so white and clean. I felt like I heard God's voice that day. I thought he was telling me everything would be okay, everything would be white as snow again, to trust him. So, I do, every single day since. Tell me what he said. I won't think you're weird."

Daniel told her about his experience after the shooting.

"I felt him telling me to grab his hand, to trust him. So I did," Daniel said. Then he squeezed her hand with both of his. "You know, I always wanted to hold your hand when we would hang out with Memo and Fina, but I was afraid I would ruin our friendship."

Cristal smiled at him, placing her other hand on top. "I wouldn't have minded."

Daniel smiled at her. "And when I saw Memo sneak a kiss from Fina on the Ferris wheel, I wanted to do the same, to you."

"I wouldn't have minded."

Daniel kissed her then and thought his heart would ex-plode. Why had he waited?

"When do you leave?" she asked.

"I fly Monday morning. I'll probably go across Sunday night to get the rest of my things from the dorm."

"I'll miss you."

"Can I call you?"

"Yes, but not during school hours. And I'm working most days after school at S-Mart, so late night is probably better."

"Okay. I'll be an hour ahead, so that'll work. I want to know what happens with Quetzali. I know if she can be reached, you will be the one to reach her."

"Be careful over there, Daniel. We're living in crazy times."

"I will, and you, too." He kissed her again, and they walked hand-in-hand back to her house.

Chapter 43

Fall 2019
Back in Mississippi
Daniel

DANIEL hit the ground running. He picked up the files from Pastor Shannon and using his GPS he began the home visits. The farm truck was a little ornery at times, but Daniel enjoyed driving it around. He soon became a familiar site in the small town of Morton. Gringos and Hispanics waved as he passed by.

One of his first visits was out from town. He finally found the house back off the road, turned in, and started to get out. A large black dog growled and came to his side of the truck. Quickly he pulled his foot back in and slammed the door. Heart pounding, he called out to the lady of the house.

"*¡Señora! ¡Señora!*" When no one came, he honked his horn several times. He called the number in the file, but it went straight to voicemail. When no one came, he drove on to his next home visit.

The next few files were several families in an apartment complex. He found the first apartment and knocked. A young mom with a baby on her hip peeped out, then opened the door.

"I know who you are. Everyone knows your truck. I'm Sonia. Come on in. Can I get you something to drink?"

"Water is fine, thanks. Who else is living here?"

"My husband, his brother and sister-in-law and their five kids, my sister and brother-in-law and their three, plus our two, and another guy who is a friend of my husband's."

Daniel tried to count.

"It's sixteen of us. We're supposed to be getting a four-bedroom next month. We're trying to hold expenses down while we all find new jobs."

"Who's working and who was detained?"

"My husband, his brother, and their friend were all detained. They got bail money together from family in Mexico. At least that's what they are telling us. I pray every day that it didn't come from a cartel."

"So those three have ankle bracelets?"

"Well, they were supposed to, but my husband didn't get one. We don't know why. And none of them have a court date yet. Their lawyer told them all the dates were filled through next year, but they would be getting a letter as soon as they start making appointments for the next year."

"So, are they working at all?"

"Yes, my husband got on at another plant last week. The others started with a construction crew from Jackson yesterday. The crew chief said he would pay them cash."

"Are you or your sister-in-law working?"

"I'm not. I'm home with the baby and get all the other kids off to school, and I'm here when they get off the bus. My sister-in-law is still working at the plant. She was out sick the day of the raid. No one has checked her paperwork or said anything to her."

"What are your main needs?"

"We so appreciate the food boxes from the pantry. Everyone has been so wonderful. I can always use more diapers and wipes. The rent will be higher next month. Hopefully the guys will keep getting work, and together we can make the rent. I'm sure our electric bill will be sky-high this month. Do you think we could get some help with that?"

Daniel explained that they would need to bring a copy of any bills to the church on the next Tuesday night. They would try to help them pay utilities, but not cellphone or cable.

"*Gracias,* Daniel. Please let them know how much this helps us all."

Daniel left there and went back to the house on the edge of town. A truck was parked in the driveway, so he once again called, "*¡Señora!*"

A lady came out, and the dog joined her at his truck. "*Hola,* Daniel. Come on in. I just got home."

Daniel hesitated, but the lady said, "He won't bite. Come on in."

Daniel opened the door and eased out.

"I've been trying to get my propane tank filled to finish cooking, but I can't get the hose off. My husband always did that."

"Maybe I can. I always did that for my ma and carried it to get filled."

"Here's the wrench he usually uses, but see? It won't turn at all."

"Oh, you're turning it backwards. Gas is opposite from water." Daniel quickly disconnected the tank and carried it to his truck. "I'll go fill it for you. They have a gas exchange by McDonald's. I'll be right back."

Daniel drove and thought of his ma. She was such a good cook with her tiny stove and tinier countertop. He was glad he could help this lady. He exchanged the tank, drove back, and hopped out without remembering the dog. As he lifted the tank, he felt the teeth sink into his elbow. He screamed, dropped the tank, and jumped back into the cab.

The lady came running out, picking up a big stick to chase the dog away.

"Daniel, I'm so sorry. He's never bitten before. Are you okay?"

"Yeah, I'm fine, just embarrassed for screaming."

"I won't tell anyone, but seriously, did it break the skin?"

Daniel saw the rake of teeth marks already turning blue, but no blood. "I think he was giving me a warning."

"I'm sorry. He's my husband's dog, but he's been so protective of me since my husband got detained."

"Is he still detained?"

"Yes. We haven't gotten enough money together yet to get a lawyer, and I'm not going to a cartel."

"I hate he's still there, but I think you are making the best decision. That cartel stuff is scary."

"Our house and land are paid for. Our son lives in Alabama and sends me money for the light and water bills. I clean three houses a week and with the groceries you are handing out, I make do. Our daughter lives in Texas and just had our first granddaughter. We were planning to go visit that weekend after the raid. But I'm okay. His brothers are working to get him out. Let those funds help a family who doesn't have any help. I'll make it fine. Thanks for stopping by and teaching me about the gas. If you reconnect it for me, I'll keep the dog away."

Daniel drove back to the church to update Shannon on the families he visited and to show off his battle scars.

"Oh, Daniel!" she cried when he showed her his now purple elbow. "When's the last time you had a tetanus shot?"

"I had one when I started college along with meningitis. I'm up to date." Daniel grinned.

"Okay, but you be careful going into this apartment complex. It can be a rough place too, and I don't mean from dogs."

"I will. I'm always on the alert, especially since the Walmart shooting."

"You were there?"

Daniel told her his story.

"I'm so sorry Daniel. I can't imagine."

They were both quiet for a few minutes. Then Pastor Shannon said, "Just be careful. I know young men think they are invincible. Even old men do. Just be careful."

* * *

Daniel finished home visits without incident and ate supper with Tootie. She was a great cook, but Daniel had never eaten fried okra before.

"This is great. What is it?"

Tootie got some uncut pieces from her refrigerator to show him. "Fried's the best. If you boil it like other vegetables, it's a slimy mess. It's good in gumbo though."

"What's gumbo?"

Tootie enjoyed teaching Daniel about Southern foods. She really could not believe he'd never tasted banana pudding.

When he got ready to leave, Tootie just had to ask, "Daniel, do you have a girlfriend waiting on you back home?"

Daniel grinned.

"I knew it. I knew it. Who wouldn't want a hardworking, compassionate young man with a million-dollar smile? What's her name?"

"Cristal, but I'm not sure we're official yet."

"Have you kissed her?"

"Yes, the night before I left," he said as his cheeks reddened.

"Oh, I love it. Have you called her?"

"I'm going to when I get to my apartment."

"I'm gonna be praying for you two. What does she do?"

"She's a student teacher right now and will graduate in May."

"Oh, that's perfect. I used to be a teacher too. Did I tell you? Taught kindergarten for thirty years."

"She's teaching kindergarten too. She loves it. But if you're going to be praying, pray for her student named Quetzali. Cristal says she needs to be filled up with love."

"Well, I'll never remember that name, but God knows who she is. Now get on home and call that girl. She sounds like a keeper."

Daniel smiled all the way out to the ranch. He took the stairs two at a time to call Cristal.

Chapter 44

Fall 2019
Mississippi
Itzel

JAVI was released in Louisiana and managed to get a ride to Jackson where Itzel and the girls picked him up. The first thing they did after their joyous reunion was drive to the church that first took them in seven years ago. Pastor Matías met them at the door.

"I'm so glad to see you all together. Come in, come in. Let's praise God for guiding you through this ordeal."

They kneeled at the altar, and Pastor Matías prayed over them. "Dear Lord God, we give you thanks and praise for holding this family together. Thank you for all the hands across this nation who have donated to these shattered families. Thank you for the tireless volunteers manning the pantries and making decisions about how to best manage the funds they're entrusted with. We ask for wisdom and guidance for next steps for this family and all the others affected by this raid. We pray for those still in detention as well as those who have sold their souls to the devil to be released. Protection, Lord. They have entered into a dangerous contract and can see no other way out. Give them, give us, more faith. We also remember the families affected by the shootings in recent days. Forgive us, Father. Amen."

"Thank you, Pastor. I can't believe I am free. I will do my best to serve God by helping others. I see now how Americans work together in a crisis. I saw it during hurricanes and floods. We may have our differences, but together we can make a difference. I want to build others up instead of pulling them down when they seem to get ahead of me. Thank you."

"That's good news, Javi. God may surprise you in his next moves, but he is always in control."

"Amen," Javi and Itzel said together.

Javi lost no time finding work with his truck just as they planned. The men in the crowded apartment joined Javi's crew, and together they started a successful roofing company. They began each day with prayer together and began roofing their first house as the sun was rising. They were honest perfectionists, leaving a spotless worksite when the job was complete. Word of mouth was their best marketing tool.

As more people found work, Itzel cooked her mother's best recipes, borrowed Sandra's car during her shift, and sold plates of food from the trunk. The men brought their containers back each day, and she piled them with rice, beans, and a different meat cooked in a different sauce each day. Hot, homemade tortillas were the crowning glory. Lulu often helped her, especially on Fridays when she made dozens and dozens of tamales. Even the gringos came around then.

Itzel now talked to her parents almost every day. They FaceTimed at night so the girls could get to know their grandparents better, and Javi checked on his ma at least once a week. As the trauma of the raid faded and income stabilized, Javi and Itzel were able to help some of the families who were still struggling.

Lulu came by one day while Itzel was cooking.

"Itzel, I don't know what to do. We have a payment due on Friday, and Chino hasn't worked at all this week."

"How much do you need?" Itzel dreaded the answer.

"A thousand."

"What's Chino gonna do?"

"He just buys more beer. I've got $800 put back, but do you think you could lend me $200? I'll pay you back next week. I've got a big house to clean this weekend."

Itzel hesitated. She had the money, but was it wise? Was she feeding the irresponsible behavior of Chino? *Lord, tell me what to do.*

"Okay, let me finish this sale today and I'll have it for you tonight. But please don't tell anyone, okay?"

Lulu hugged her tightly. "Thank you, Itzel."

Late that afternoon, Itzel parked Sandra's car at her house and knocked at her door.

"Hey, Itzel. How were sales this week?"

"Great. Here's some extra for letting me use your car. You're a good friend, Sandra."

"I'm so glad it's working. I sometimes feel guilty that we didn't get caught in the raid. I'm glad to help out."

"Yeah, I sometimes feel guilty we are doing so well again. Poor Lulu and Chino, not so much."

"Did she hit you up for money again?" Sandra asked.

"Yes, and I told her I would lend her some tonight, but it gets harder every time I see Chino with another bottle of beer."

"Sometimes we are so hardheaded in our vices, we can't see the grace God is offering."

"Yeah, and the ones who suffer from that are not always that person. Consequences may not make a direct hit," Itzel said. "What's that phrase they use on the news? Collateral damage?"

"Yes, that's it. So sad. But hey, who's the little girl I've seen at your house? Are you babysitting?"

"I'm letting her come home on the bus with my girls. She stays until her uncle gets off work. Sometimes 'til 9:00 or 10:00 at night."

"Where's her mom?" Sandra asked.

"Apparently, she's at the border waiting for asylum."

"Where are they from? Why did she cross and not her mom?"

"Well, they're from Guatemala. They were part of that big caravan. When the uncle heard they were not accepting single men, he carried the little girl so he could come in as a single dad with a child," Itzel explained. "The mom and older kids got picked up in the river and sent to the Immigrant House in Mexico to wait."

"Oh, that's awful. Has she talked to her mom?"

"Yes. I let her FaceTime when I get home. It's so sad. The uncle really doesn't have a use for her now."

"What's her name?"

"Yamilet."

Itzel walked to Lulu's, left her the money, and with a hug, went on to her house to meet her girls as they got off the bus. She was so blessed. Her family was back together. Then she thought again of Lulu. How could she help her more?

As it turned out, Itzel never got the chance.

Chapter 45

2019
Mississippi
Daniel

Daniel organized his day using early morning hours to do his online courses. Then he helped at the pantry. He'd found that the best time to catch people at home was afternoon. He also visited the schools and talked to the counselors to make sure no one was falling through the cracks. The soccer fields were also a great place to see the mixing of local families. Soon Daniel was coaching the ten and under boys' team. Having only a part-time job, Daniel stayed steadily busy.

One morning during his call-in with his professor, Mr. Acosta, Daniel asked him about teaching.

"I love it, Daniel," he said. "Yeah, sometimes the paperwork gets ridiculous, but it's a flexible job that allows me to also coach my kids at soccer and serve as a pastor. I can see where I really help make a difference."

"I'm wavering on law school, and I don't know what to do."

"You're not locked into that path. Getting a teacher's license would probably only mean a few more classes next semester and taking the professional exam."

"I'm really liking coaching these kids."

"I'll look at your transcript and email you a list of what courses you are lacking. You'd be a great teacher, and a bilingual male teacher is really needed in our schools."

"What's the pay like?"

"It won't be like a lawyer for sure, but there are lots of perks. And compared to teachers in Mexico, I think you'll be surprised."

Daniel hung up. He had three home visits today and promised Glenda he'd go to Sam's Club in Pearl to pick up an order. He also wanted to talk to Shannon about her life as a Pastor. God was putting lots of new ideas in his head.

Late that afternoon, Daniel reported to Shannon on the progress the three families were making. Slowly they were trimming their list of families needing rental assistance. Some simply moved away in the middle of the night. Others had family elsewhere who sent money. Many found cash jobs in construction, cleaning houses, and selling food. They were all so resourceful.

"I guess that's why many of these families made it here to begin with. They have that special umph inside to keep going. I wish I could bottle that," Pastor Shannon said.

"Yes. And others are dragging bottom or doing the same thing expecting a different outcome. I'm so glad there's not been any cartel activity. I guess those who borrowed from them are keeping up to date on their debts."

"Scary thought, isn't it? What else did you wanna talk about, Daniel?" Shannon said.

"Well, I've been having doubts about law school. I talked to my professor this morning about education, but I also wanted to talk to you about being a pastor."

"Wow, Daniel. That doesn't surprise me at all. You'd be a great one, and we need more bilingual pastors."

"I don't know. I can see myself doing the pastoring part, but I don't know about the preaching part."

"When I first started investigating being a pastor, someone gave me a questionnaire to help me discern my gifts. It was very helpful. Of course, it was paper and pencil back then in the dark ages, and I had to wait forever for the results. But I bet it's online and instant these days. Let me look."

Daniel waited patiently. He liked Pastor Shannon. She worked so hard for everyone and didn't seem to play favorites or politics. And she was the one who offered him the opportunity of this internship.

"Yes, here's the link. I'll send it to your email, and you can do it at home. It takes about thirty minutes. After you do that, let's talk again about the results."

"Thanks, Pastor Shannon. I really appreciate it."

"You know, another area you might want to research is being a chaplain, a bilingual chaplain. Anyway, God has a place for you, Daniel. The harvest is plentiful, and the workers are few. Don't grow weary in doing good."

Daniel nodded and smiled.

"I'll stop preaching, but ask God for discernment. He'll open the doors for you. Thanks for all you are doing."

* * *

That night, Daniel had lots to think about. He read over the course list from Mr. Acosta and took the survey from Pastor Shannon. Then he read the qualifications for being a chaplain while waiting for the results of his quiz. He was surprised there were so many places to be a chaplain. He only knew about hospitals, but there were chaplains in many branches of the medical field plus the jails and prisons, the armed forces, and even on ships. He also hadn't thought about the Pastors who lead the student groups from different denominations on campuses of universities. Suddenly his world seemed bigger with lots more options.

When his report came in, Daniel couldn't believe what he saw. The results showed his greatest strengths were in teaching, organizing, and compassionate care. Now Daniel wanted to talk to Cristal. He really missed her. Her number was on speed-dial.

"Cristal, how was your day?"

"Busy, busy. I just got home from S-Mart. I forgot I told Maestra Beatriz I would grade papers for her tonight. I can't wait not to have to work another job. I want to teach full-time, maybe even two shifts. What do you think?"

"I think you're a natural teacher. But what do you think about me becoming a teacher?"

"You? I thought you wanted the big bucks. Teaching sure isn't the path to riches."

"Well, I'm looking at lots of things. That's why I called. But if you need to grade papers we can talk tomorrow."

"No, Daniel. I wanna hear."

They spent almost an hour talking of Daniel's options. Daniel was happy Cristal was interested in his ideas.

"Okay, enough about me. Tell me how Quetzali is doing."

When they finished catching up, Daniel let Cristal go grade papers. He appreciated her input, but he also loved hearing her voice. Then he called his ma. It was an hour earlier there, so they were still awake.

"Hey, Ma. How are you doing?"

"I'm good Daniel. I'm so glad you called. Carmen told me she talked to Itzel today and Face Timed with her granddaughters. I was hoping to hear from you too."

"Ma, would you be very disappointed if I didn't become a lawyer?"

"Not finish school?"

"No, Ma. Just change direction. I'm thinking about teaching and maybe being a chaplain too and maybe coaching soccer."

"That sounds very busy, but I think you would be good at all those things."

"I'm still getting advice from my teachers and from Pastor Shannon. And I talked to Cristal."

"I'm glad you and Cristal are still friends."

"Well, it might be a little more than friends, but don't go telling Memo I said that, or Carmen. It'll be all over the neighborhood."

"I already heard it," Memo cut in. "You know you can't keep gossip from spreading here. I already knew when you came home last time with those moon eyes. Then Fina told me. Then Carmen heard it from Itzel."

"How did Itzel know?"

"She heard it from some lady at the clothes shop next to the pantry in Morton."

"Tootie! The international gossip line is faster than the local one," Daniel said.

They talked and joked together like old times. Daniel missed them. He couldn't wait for Christmas.

"But guess what. Remember my friend from El Paso, Burly? I went to church with him some? He's gonna come here for Thanksgiving to help out."

"That's nice, Daniel. I bet you've made an impression on his life. God's using you."

"Thanks, Ma. See you soon. Love you."

"*Buenas noches, mijo. Te amo mucho.*"

Chapter 46

Thanksgiving 2019
Mississippi
Daniel

DANIEL picked up Burly at the airport in Jackson on the Saturday before Thanksgiving. They ate lunch at a diner Tootie recommended that had lots of Southern vegetables and fried chicken. Burly cleaned his plate and ate two cornbread muffins before the waitress brought the banana pudding.

"Oh, I'm gonna die. I thought my granny could cook. I'd be big as a barn if I lived here."

Daniel laughed. He'd learned to like the Mississippi food too. He had plans to take Burly to an all-you-can-eat catfish restaurant next week. Tomorrow Tootie was having them for Sunday dinner after church.

"Did you wanna do any sightseeing before we go to Morton?" Daniel asked.

"Ride me downtown by the capitol building. Then maybe drive some of the Natchez Trace?"

As they drove, they caught up on people they both knew.

"So, are you still planning to take the LSAT in January?" Burly asked.

"No, I've changed my plans. I'm looking at being a teacher /soccer coach/chaplain."

"Well, I've never heard of that combo, but I'm sure you'll be great. Your old roommate Kevin is going into the ministry. He might even become a priest, but I think he really wants to direct a Newman House at some university."

"He'll be good at that. What about Jennifer? Still the same?"

"Oh, yeah. Going to law school on her daddy's money. She did do a fundraiser and sent a bulk food order to your pantry when she got back though."

"That's nice. Maybe something rubbed off on her from the trip. What about you, Burly? Still going to coach?"

"That's the plan."

"Got a local girl on your arm?"

"Nah, football always keeps me too busy. If we'd made the playoffs, I wouldn't be here."

"I'm glad you came. We'll go by the pantry first. Then I'll take you to my mansion."

* * *

Sunday, they attended Pastor Shannon's church and ate lunch with Tootie. After a nap from calorie overload, they went to Itzel's church. Everywhere they went, Burly was amazed at how many people greeted Daniel and wanted to check on him. He was walking easily between both cultures, and everyone obviously loved him.

"I don't know how you do it, Daniel. How do you keep it all straight?"

"I think when you love what you're doing, you don't think about it. That's when I started doubting my law school path. I think I could have completed it, but I don't think I would have liked it very much."

That night Daniel made another happy call to Cristal. "I don't think the gossip line made it into El Paso. Burly hasn't asked me about you yet."

"Yeah, I didn't know it could travel so fast and so far. Only three weeks until you come home?"

"Yes, Baby. I can't wait to see you."

He ended the call, and Burly stuck his head into his bedroom. "These walls are pretty thin, Daniel. I'm sure that wasn't your mama telling her baby goodnight. Who is she?"

Daniel covered his head with a sheet. "Goodnight, Burly."

* * *

Monday morning Itzel put her girls on the school bus. There were only two days of school this week, and they were looking forward to Thanksgiving Day at Doña Elia's house again. Daniel and his friend would be joining them, and she hoped to FaceTime her parents again. She saw Lulu's boys get on the bus for the high school. Then she saw Lulu get in their car and drive away. She didn't know where Lulu would be going so early.

Itzel turned to go back to her kitchen. She needed to sell extra food these two days so she could buy ingredients for her contribution to Thanksgiving dinner. Then she heard what sounded like a shot, and then a crash. She ran back to the street and saw others coming out from their homes as well.

"What was that?" everyone seemed to be asking at the same time. Soon they heard sirens. An ambulance and a Jaws-of-Life firetruck raced down the highway. A neighbor, who just dropped her kids at school, drove up. She got out, white and shaking.

"Someone got assassinated driving down the road. I never saw anything like that in Mexico. I passed the car right when blood plastered the inside of the windshield. Then the car went off the road. It could have hit me, either the car or the bullet. Who would do something like that in broad daylight?"

Then Itzel knew. "Oh God Almighty, help us all. Is it Lulu, Lord? Oh, God, is it Lulu?"

Itzel called Javi, then Daniel. Both came to the house. After confirming their worst fears, Javi, Daniel, and Burly went next door to find Chino and deliver the news. Once again, the small town of Morton was making national news. Chino didn't make that week's payment. Lulu was leaving him. But the assassin's bullet changed her destination.

Chapter 47

2019
Ciudad Juarez
Cristal

CRISTAL was running the classroom more and more each day. Maestra Beatriz trusted her with every aspect of her schedule and recommended her for a position that was opening in the spring semester. Cristal worked a miracle in Quetzali's life. Even after her mom brushed them off, Cristal persisted. Quetzali's classwork and participation were evidence.

But Quetzali was not in school today. After checking with her older brother's teacher, Beatriz found that he was absent also. The children rarely missed school. As the day came to a close, Beatriz said, "I suppose you'll be going to check on Quetzali?"

"Yes, I'm kinda worried. I'll take her work and some snacks."

"You're gonna spend all your salary on that little girl," Beatriz said.

"She's worth it." Cristal smiled and headed out the door.

As she got closer to Quetzali's home, Cristal picked up on a vibe. Finally, she stopped and asked a neighbor. "What's going on?"

"Didn't you hear? The little boy in that house got electrocuted this morning. The mom was out working the streets, and DIF came and took the little girl into care. It was so awful. That baby was crying so hard for her ma, and her ma never gave her the time of day."

"Did her brother die? Did it kill him?"

"I don't know. The ambulance came and took him away, but he wasn't moving. We kept telling that mama to raise the power line off that chain link around her outhouse. She wouldn't listen. I guess the fence wore a place in the line. Somebody said he tripped and fell against it. Somebody else said he was carrying a bucket of water when he tripped. I don't know."

"Where's the mama?"

"The police took her."

Cristal didn't know what to do first. She remembered when Pastora Pati came to the DIF home and rescued her and Fina. Could she do that for Quetzali? She had to talk to her own mom. She quickly dialed Pastora Pati and explained what happened.

"Let me make a few calls. In the meantime, catch the next bus to Zaragoza and I'll meet you there."

Cristal ran. She thought of all the love she poured into Quetzali. Would it all be for nothing? Would the little girl ever trust anyone again? And where was the brother? She didn't want to think about it.

She met Pati as planned.

"I'm sorry, Cristal. The brother didn't make it."

Tears rolled down Cristal's cheeks. "Haven't those kids suffered enough?"

Pati wrapped her in her arms and let her cry. Then they took another bus to the closest DIF office.

At the office they learned that Quetzali was at the same home where Cristal and Fina stayed the last time they were picked up. Her mom was in jail pending an investigation but would probably be released by morning. Pati did not confer with Cristal, and Cristal didn't have to ask Pati. Together they said, "Can we take Quetzali home until her mother is released?"

Some papers were signed, and some documents were copied. Then the two ladies with the big hearts took the next bus to the DIF home to find another lost little girl.

Late that night after Quetzali was sound asleep as close to Cristal as she could get, Cristal called Daniel. It would be midnight there, but she needed to talk to him. She saw many missed calls from him as well.

"I'm sorry, Daniel. It's been a really awful day here," she said when he answered on the first ring.

"Here too. That's why I was calling. But tell me your news first."

Cristal told him everything, trying to talk without crying. Then Daniel told her everything, trying to hold his voice steady.

"Daniel, our world is so crazy. What is happening?"

"I know, Cristal. And that's when our faith has to be even bigger. God is still in control."

"Ugh, but that sweet little boy. Why?"

"Yes, and this mother. She left two boys behind with an alcoholic father to care for them. Why?"

"And Quetzali's mother leaving them all alone at night, like Rubi did to us. Why?"

"I don't know Cristal. I don't know. I just know I have to hang on. God is calling us to be the comfort in these situations even if we don't understand them."

"I hope you'll be home soon. I miss you."

"I miss you too."

They disconnected and lay awake most of the night trying to understand the evil of this world. Morning would bring new strength and God's mercies.

Chapter 48

Thanksgiving 2019
Mississippi
Daniel and Itzel

THANKSGIVING at Doña Elia's was subdued this year in light of all that happened. This year there was no Tom in the backyard, but the pantry donated whole turkeys to every family on its list. Burly and Daniel were new additions as well as Lulu's two sons. Their father Chino disappeared. Itzel and her family and all of Elia's children and their families arrived. Tables were set outside, and the children ran around glad to be free from school for a few days. The men watched as Burly deep-fried the turkey. The women gathered in the kitchen, chopping, stirring, and gossiping. Delicious aromas floated around the room.

When everything was ready, they formed a huge circle around the table, joined hands, and prayed. Everyone prayed aloud together for different things at the same time. The praises and the cries floated up to heaven. When Doña Elia said a loud "Amen," everyone else did too, and plates were served.

As the ladies washed dishes in the kitchen, the men supervised the kids and cleaned the tables and the fryer. Itzel called her girls to a quiet spot to FaceTime their grandparents.

"Hey, Ma, Pa. How is everything?"

"Another regular workday for us," her pa said.

"Pa, that's why I was calling. You work too hard. I've been able to save some money to get you two tourist visas. Would you come for a visit?"

Her pa pretended to have something in his eye. He took out his handkerchief and wiped his face. He took a drink of water. "What do we need to do?"

"First step is for you and Ma to get passports. I'll send you the money for that first. It might take a while to finish the process, but I think you should be able to come. You own your house, you have a business with regular income, and you're getting close to being senior citizens." Itzel grinned at them. "I'm kidding, Pa. But will you do it?"

"Yes, *mija*. We'll start on it tomorrow. Thank you. *Te amamos, mija.*" He wiped his face again and passed the phone to his wife.

"*Gracias, mija.* We will be praying for God's will to open doors for us to come. *Te amamos. Cuídate.*"

Chapter 49

Christmas 2019
Ciudad Juarez
Daniel

Dᴀɴɪᴇʟ made it home for Christmas. He flew into the El Paso airport. Burly picked him up and gave him a back-pounding bearhug.

"Merry Christmas, bro," Burly said. "Glad you're back. How did you leave everything?"

"I think Morton is in good shape. There are still a couple of families getting assistance, but most have found a way to get by. And, by the way, no one has been charged with Lulu's murder. If there were any clues, no one would dare speak up. Everyone is sure it was a cartel hit."

"Man, I couldn't get that out of my mind. So, I wanted to tell you in person. I'm buckling down. I'm gonna keep working on my Spanish, and I'm planning to go to law school, maybe for immigration law."

"Wow, man. What a change!"

"Yeah, it might take me a while to get in, but I'm deter-mined to put in the work."

"That's great, man. You'll be a good one." They back-pounded again.

"Thanks, Daniel. You're mainly responsible. These trips to Mississippi really opened my eyes."

"Ma invited you to come over for *pozole* Christmas Eve. She makes the best."

"That'll be great. Thanks. So, are you going home to reconnect with your girl?"

"That's the plan. I saved a little for a ring. You'll have to meet her. What about you, man? Any luck on that front?"

"I don't know how to explain it, Daniel, but ever since I got back, the girls here seem shallow."

"I think that's called reverse culture shock. You'll get over it."

"That's just it, Daniel. I don't think I want to get over it. I want to help."

Daniel smiled at his friend. He knew exactly how he felt.

* * *

Christmas Eve morning, Daniel waited at the bridge for Burly to cross. When Burly got the green light, he came through the barrier, recognized Daniel's beat-up car, and followed him to the neighborhood where Daniel grew up.

"This is it, the famous Colonia Jose Sulaiman, home of Daniel Hernandez. *Bienvenido.*"

"This is so cool but embarrassing at the same time. I've lived about five miles from you my whole life. I never knew any of this existed. Show me everything."

Daniel introduced Burly to his parents and Memo.

"*Mucho gusto,*" Burly responded in Spanish.

"I'm going to the hardware store for supplies. When I get back, I could use some help repairing the roof."

"Sure," Burly responded quickly.

Pa grinned. "I was talking to my sons. You are a guest."

"I'm happy to help."

Daniel and Burly walked around the neighborhood, stopping to visit with Carmen.

"We have an appointment next month to get our passports. We're going to visit Itzel."

"That's wonderful! She will be so excited. I'm praying for everything to fall into place for that to happen," Daniel said.

They walked on to Cristal's house. She was outside with Quetzali.

"*Es un placer*, Burly. This is Quetzali. She's staying with us for a few days while her mom gets some things done."

Later Cristal told them more of Quetzali's story. "Quetzali's mom agreed to go to a Christian counseling retreat Pastora Pati recently discovered. Our church is covering the cost. Quetzali never asks about her, but she does ask about her brother. I hope we are giving her the love she needs to find her way."

"Will she get any counseling?" Burly asked. "She witnessed him getting electrocuted?"

"Yes, but there just aren't any children's counselors around here. I can't imagine what she's feeling. We are doing our best to help her through it."

* * *

Daniel, Burly, Memo, and Pa spent the afternoon reroofing their house with hot melted tar. They worked hard, but Daniel was glad to see his pa relax and joke around with Burly. When the work was done, they took cold showers and sat outside. Ma served them a typical Christmas *ponche* to drink while the *pozole* finished cooking.

"I have an announcement to make," Ma said. Everyone turned to her in surprise.

Memo, always the jokester, said, "Please don't say you're having another baby."

Everyone laughed, but Ma wore her serious face. "I finished *prepa*!"

Then everyone cheered as she pulled out her certificate of high school completion. Daniel picked her up and swung her around. "Way to go, Ma. But when did you find time? I thought taking care of baby Memo was a full-time job."

Burly came to Memo's defense. "Don't pick on the baby. It could be worse. I have three older sisters."

The pozole was delicious as always, lots of pork, hominy, and broth, with radishes and cabbage on top. Burly ate three bowlfuls, not realizing Fina provided a *chocoflan* dessert.

"She did win the contest," Memo said. "She starts culinary school in June, right after graduation."

"And you, Memo?" Burly asked. "What are your plans?"

"I'm going to work full-time at the mechanic shop. I'm saving to open my own."

"And he's going to take an advanced diesel course this summer too," Ma said.

The air got cooler as the wind from the mountains blew down into Juarez. Burly got up to leave. "Thanks so much for inviting me into your home. I hope you don't mind if I come back more often. I see why your *Abuelo* was so attracted here. I can feel the love. *Feliz Navidad.*"

"Gracias, Burly," Araceli said, laughing as she pronounced his name as a Spanish word. *"Y Dios nos bendiga a todos en el año nuevo, 2020."*

"God bless us all in 2020."

Chapter 50

Early 2020
Juarez and Beyond

IN January, under the guidance of Mr. Acosta, Daniel enrolled in four education courses at UTEP and an online chaplaincy course he could complete by March. For the first time, Daniel enjoyed studying. He always was a good reader, but now he read with a purpose. He continued his part-time job at the athletic department, but also made hospital visits with the chaplain at the University Medical Center when he had free time. He learned that most of the shooting victims from that awful day in August were taken to this hospital.

Cristal began her first teaching job in January. She still had two more courses and a professional exam to take to be certified, but thanks to Beatriz, she was given the teaching job at the same school as she finished her coursework at night. Quetzali often stayed at her house and rode the bus with her to school. Her mom was stable for the moment, and Quetzali stayed in her own home on the weekends.

Memo and Fina got engaged. No one was surprised, but Pastora Pati kept asking them to wait until Fina finished culinary school. Memo would finish his diesel course in August, but Fina wouldn't finish for another year. They compromised on a September wedding, and the planning began.

In Mississippi, Itzel continued her food truck business from the back of Sandra's car, and Javi's roofing company could barely keep up with all the work that poured in. Their girls were excelling in school and were excited about the visit from their grandparents, scheduled for April during Holy Week. Pastor Shannon cleared the final families from the assistance roll, and most families were getting by as they waited for their immigration court date.

Carmen and Humberto took photos, copied documents, paid the fees, and made an appointment for their passports. They had to go all the way downtown, and each had an appointment on a different day.

"I guess it was too much to hope we could both go at the same time," Carmen said. "What if one of us is approved and the other isn't?"

"I guess I'll go without you," Humberto teased her. "Don't worry, *mi amor*. The passports are the easy part. The visa will be the hard part."

Humberto was right. They did finally get their passports, requiring one more trip to the busy city center to pick them up in person. Then they had to make appointments at the United States Embassy for their tourist visas. To make the appointment, they had to have a credit card and pay online. They had to pay for the appointment whether or not they were approved. They called Itzel who quickly made the arrangements from her home in Mississippi, and Carmen was amazed.

"*Gracias, mija*. All this technology and all this money just to come visit my baby and my grandbabies."

Their visa interviews were for the first and second of March, on different days of course. Itzel wrote them letters of invitation, promising to cover all their expenses during their visit. Visas were usually extended for three, six, or twelve months. Sometimes at renewal they could be extended for five years. They all hoped for a long-term visa, even though they could only stay a maximum of six months at a time. Itzel knew they probably would only stay two weeks, but she hoped her mom would stay longer.

Carmen went to Araceli's house the day before her appointment.

"How's your job hunting going?" Carmen said.

"I've applied for a few office jobs, but I don't really have any experience. I could always go to a maquila, but I'm still holding out for something better."

"Well, it's not exactly an office job, but I was wondering if you would want to run my store while we're gone?"

"Oh, yes, Carmen. But only if you think I can handle it as well as you do."

"You've been hanging out there since you were a kid. I think you know what to do. I can show you how to keep the books and deal with the deliveries. Maybe that would count as office experience."

"Do you know when you're going yet?"

"No. Humberto is at his visa appointment now. Mine is in the morning. I'll let you know. We plan to go as soon as we get the visas, primero Dios."

* * *

Daniel called home almost every day and visited every Saturday or Sunday, depending on his volunteer chaplain hours. During the week, he and Burly often met over wings or occasionally to drive up to his grandparents for a good meal. And Burly came across with Daniel on Saturdays for a different home-cooked meal. Daniel was impressed at how quickly Burly's Spanish was improving.

One night Burly and Daniel were studying in the student center when Jennifer came through. She was with a group of girlfriends and didn't stop to talk.

"Is she really gonna go to law school?" Daniel asked.

"Yeah. She took the LSAT last fall and passed, but she's going to take it again in June when I do to raise her score. She must be really smart because I don't know when she would have time to study," Burly said. "She's always partying or shopping or planning a party."

"And you would know this how?" Daniel teased his friend.

"I just know. I guess I'm jealous because it doesn't come that easy to me."

"You'll pass it though. I know you will, but have you thought about asking her for help?"

"*Claro que no*," Burly burst out in Spanish indignation, trying to turn so that Daniel couldn't see his reddening cheeks.

"Okay, just asking. I know Cristal is a good tutor for me. She always thinks of different ways to teach me and shows me how to practice something 'til it sticks. I guess that's what makes her a good teacher."

"Yeah, and it doesn't hurt that you're in love with your tutor."

"That's what I was thinking too."

"Back to the books, *güey*."

* * *

Itzel phoned home almost every day now too. Finally, she heard the news she was waiting to hear.

"We both got our visas!" Carmen said. "We had to leave our passports for them to insert the visas, and we can pick them up next week. Our bags are packed."

"Oh, Ma, that's wonderful. We're all so excited. But listen, Ma. They keep talking on the news about this new virus. Have you been hearing about it?"

"Yes, people are talking about it here too, but it's probably just another flu. Your pa and I, we never get sick. Nothing will keep us away now."

* * *

Daniel passed his Chaplaincy Licensing test and was issued an official identification card at the hospital. To celebrate, he took his meager savings and made the last payment on a ring. Then he drove to Juarez to visit Pastor Miguel. His heart was pounding as he got closer.

"Daniel, come in. Cristal is still at school."

"I know, Pastor. I came to see you."

Pastor Miguel raised his eyebrows but took a seat in the small living room. "What's up, Daniel?"

Daniel cleared his throat, and Pastor Miguel smiled. He remembered how he felt when he talked to Pati's father.

"Go ahead, Daniel. You'll be glad when it's over."

"You know?" Daniel said.

"Yes, but I still want you to finish. Go ahead."

"Okay. I love your daughter and I want to marry her. I don't have a house yet, but I have a job lined up on the other side and I can go across each morning so she can keep her teaching job here. And I promise to take care of her."

"Breathe, Daniel. You want some water?" Pastor Miguel brought a glass of water and said, "Of course, Daniel. I can't think of a better son-in-law. Welcome to the family." He gave Daniel a bearhug as Pati came in. "We're gonna have two sons-in-law, *mi amor*." And all three hugged again.

Daniel drove to Cristal's school to surprise her with a ride home. He told her about his new chaplain card and job possibilities.

"Do you feel like strolling around the park for a little bit?" Daniel said.

He parked at his house, and they walked the circuit around the neighborhood park.

"You know, this park is the same one where my ma and pa met and decided to marry. But they never really married. Did you realize that?"

"What? No! How?"

"Pa just said, 'You wanna get married?' and Ma said she thought about it and said yes. The next day he picked her up with her little bag of clothes and moved her to his rough pallet shack."

"*Ay Dios mío*," Cristal said. "I could never do that."

"And I don't want you to," Daniel said. "I'll finish my courses in May and take my teacher's exams. Mr. Acosta wants me to go on and apply for some openings at local El Paso schools. He said I might even be able to get on at La Lydia. And the hospital wants me part-time to cover for the full-time chaplain I've been working with. What I'm thinking is that with a teacher's salary and a part-time chaplain job, I could live on this side and drive over each morning. You could keep teaching here. What I'm trying to get to, Cristal, is will..."

"Yes, Daniel! Yes!" She wrapped her arms around his neck, and he squeezed her tight. How did everyone know the rest of his sentences?

"I love you, Cristal. I want to spend the rest of my life with you."

"I love you, too, Daniel, and I want to spend the rest of my life with you. I know you'll be a good teacher too. You were always a good English teacher on the bus."

"Do you want to crash Fina and Memo's plans and have a double wedding? Or do you want your own day?"

"Fina and I have always done everything together. If she's okay with it, I want to have the double wedding."

"In the meantime, I've been saving up for this." Daniel slipped a silver ring with a tiny diamond on Cristal's finger. "I love you, Cristal."

"I love you too, Daniel. God put us together from the beginning. Let's keep him in the center."

"Always."

They kissed, a long kiss, under the few trees of the park. The stars were beginning to come out, and a cool breeze blew down from the mountains. The time change was next weekend, but a much bigger change would soon rock Daniel, Cristal, and the inhabitants of Sulaiman. They walked to Cristal's house to share their big news with Pastora Pati and Pastor Miguel.

Chapter 51

March 2020
Covid 19
Juarez and Beyond

CARMEN and Humberto had never crossed the river, never flown in a plane, and never been farther than ten miles from where they were born. Itzel made the airline reservations for March 23, 2020. Daniel would drive them across to the El Paso airport, and they would fly to Jackson, Mississippi. Carmen had gifts for everyone, including a care package from Javi's mom.

But on Friday night, everyone gathered around their televisions as the news anchor informed them of the serious novel coronavirus, also called Covid-19, rapidly infecting the world. A strict travel initiative between the United States and Mexico would be imposed starting at midnight, restricting border crossings to essential travelers only. The news anchor reported, "Non-essential travel includes tourism. This collaborative and reciprocal initiative is an extension of our nations' prudent approach that values the health and safety of our citizens. Out of an abundance of caution, we are encouraging people to avoid unnecessary contact with others."

Everyone was stunned, but Pastor Miguel called his flock. "Let's gather at the park in one hour. Invite your neighbors."

At 9:00 p.m., the faithful and the fearful gathered to pray for God's protection and for wisdom in the days to come. "May our fears not overtake us. May our faith be found enough to guide us through these coming hard times. May we be good neighbors and shining lights to those still in the darkness. We thank you and praise your name, Lord. Amen."

* * *

Daniel and Burly were eating wings at their favorite restaurant when the news of the border closing interrupted the ballgame. They looked at each other in surprise.

"What does that do for you, Daniel? Can you go home?"

"I can probably go home, but I don't know if I can get back. I need to talk to Mr. Acosta. Let's get out of here."

Daniel's recent certification as a chaplain turned out to be gold. With a letter from the hospital, he was able to travel back and forth as an essential worker. But as an essential worker, he would encounter a whirlwind of tragedy that no amount of training could have prepared him for.

* * *

As schools shut down, Cristal scrambled to learn new ways to stay connected with her students. Very few of her students had Wi-Fi at home, and most only had access to one or two cell phones in a family with many kids. She sent homework assignments in a WhatsApp group and asked the moms to take a picture of the work and send it back. A few did, but it was discouraging.

She began making videos of herself reading books to her students. Quetzali was often at her house and would be her student to interact with. Using a small dry erase board from their church, she made videos of counting and adding any items she could find. Every day she made a video of calendar time to keep the kids ready for when they returned. She even did silly exercise videos and had Daniel film her doing a homemade obstacle course in their tiny yard. She was sure they would return to class soon, but the number of cases and, even more alarming, the number of deaths continued to rise.

The *colonia* of Sulaiman seemed to be immune in the first few weeks. The kids played outside together, and stores were still open. But the moms began to worry. The stores had less food on the shelves, and hand sanitizer and masks were nowhere to be found. Daniel brought some items from the other side when he could. One day, he called his ma to tell her about making hand sanitizer from scratch.

"I saw a YouTube video about it, Ma," he said. "Take your big *sábila* leaves and scrape out the aloe gel from inside the biggest leaves. Then mix the gel with alcohol in a blender. That's all there is to it. You could even make a bunch and sell it."

"Daniel, I want to help, not make money. The problem is there isn't any alcohol to be found on this side."

"I think I can get some at the hospital. I'll bring it on Sunday."

By the weekend, the rising statistics were alarming. Videos of the temporary morgues outside the main hospitals of downtown Juarez were horrifying. City officials rigged their maintenance vehicles with spray equipment to disperse an antibacterial chlorine mixture down the streets. Hucksters sold a variety of suspect vitamins and immune-boosting pills to ward off the disease. Fumigation tents outside the emergency rooms sanitized hospital personnel so they could return home to their families for the night.

Daniel arrived Saturday night with a case of rubbing alcohol. Araceli cut the aloe vera leaves and scraped the insides clean. They didn't have bottles to pour the gel into, so Pastora Pati brought her salsa bags she sold with her tamales. Cristal came over to help, taking some to distribute to her students. Fina and Memo took a boxful to distribute to the neighbors.

"Ma," Fina called from the door. "I think you'd better come. Carmen's husband is barely breathing."

Everyone ran to the corner store. Carmen was frantic. "He had a little fever last night, but he said he had a headache. Then in the night, he started coughing. I gave him honey for the cough and of course vapor rub, but his fever seems higher, even when I bathe him down."

Daniel stepped inside. "Don Humberto, can you stand?"

Humberto tried but sat back gasping. "I think he needs to get oxygen right away. That's what they are doing on the other side. I can take him in my car."

Carmen nodded, seemingly unable to make a decision on her own.

Pastora Pati stepped in. "Memo, will you go get Pastor? Carmen, we need to get him to the hospital. I don't think the clinics are gonna have any oxygen. When Miguel gets here, the men can get him in Daniel's car. Let's get your purse and a sweater. Where's your cellphone?"

Daniel drove. Humberto leaned back in the front passenger seat. Pastor Miguel and Carmen sat in the back. Thirty minutes later, they arrived at the emergency room. A technician came to the car, did a Covid quick-test, checked oxygen levels, and raced back with an oxygen tank.

"It's positive and with these low oxygen readings, he needs to be admitted. I'm sorry, but no one can come in with him."

"What? No. I have to be with him," Carmen began to wail.

"It's okay, Doña Carmen. I can go in." Daniel showed the tech his chaplain identification. Then they loaded Humberto into a wheelchair. Daniel handed his keys to Pastor Miguel and wheeled Humberto inside.

"I can't leave him here. I can't," Carmen sobbed.

"Let me call Pati."

Memo brought Pati and Araceli to the hospital in Humberto's truck. There was still no word from Daniel. When the ladies arrived, Carmen said, "I need to call Itzel, but I hate to tell her this news. She is crazy about her daddy."

"She needs to know, and you need her," Pati said. "Here, use my phone in case Daniel calls you."

Itzel answered immediately. "Ma? Is everything okay?"

"No, *mija*. Your pa has the virus. They just admitted him, and they won't let me stay with him." She couldn't hold her tears back, and Pati took the phone.

"We are all in the hospital parking lot with your mom, Itzel. Daniel was able to go inside with his chaplain card. We'll let you know as soon as we hear from him."

About an hour later, Daniel sent a text, "He's admitted, but there are no rooms. He is on a bed in the hall with full oxygen. He's resting now. I'll stay the night. Hope to have a room tomorrow."

* * *

Itzel was in a panic. This virus was making everyone crazy. The girls didn't go back to school after spring break, and now with her dad in the hospital, Itzel was once again thinking of going home.

"Javi," she said, "what if the girls and I went back first? You could keep working and try to sell the house. Then you could come home in the truck and use it to work in Juarez. I know it won't be the same money or as many opportunities for the girls, but we would be together. When the girls are older, they can come back. My parents really need me right now."

"We're doing so well here. Do you really want to throw it all away?"

"I don't think it's throwing it away. I think it's choosing to believe that God will honor our decision."

"Let me think about it," Javi said.

But the numbers in Mississippi continued to rise, and the situation in Juarez worsened.

* * *

Daniel called his ma to give an update. Araceli answered on the first ring.

"Ma, it's not good. They moved him straight to ICU. They are going to put him on a ventilator. He can't finish a sentence without gasping for air. I'm going in there now if Doña Carmen wants to talk to him before they put him on the vent."

Araceli quickly explained the situation and passed the phone to Carmen. They listened as she told Humberto she loved him and was waiting for him right outside. Carmen hung up and cried silent tears. Pati prayed for them.

An hour later, Daniel came out to the car. "He's sedated until he can relax with the ventilator. His oxygen is much better. This would be a good time to go home and regroup."

Daniel slept a few hours, then left for his shift in El Paso. Carmen drove Humberto's truck back to the hospital now equipped with pillow and blanket, snacks in a small cooler, and a phone charger. She wanted to be as close to him as she could.

Daniel returned every two days. He would place his phone beside Humberto's ear so Carmen could encourage him and pray for him. Itzel called when Daniel was there as well. Daniel used FaceTime also, and he could tell Humberto was pleased. His vitals always improved. Then Carmen would go home for a shower, restock the truck, and go back to the parking lot. Araceli manned her store since she planned to be working there anyway, although they hoped she would work there for happier reasons.

* * *

After the last FaceTime with her mom, Itzel could wait no longer. "I have to go, Javi."

"I know, *mi amor*. I understand, but I don't want to be alone here. You three are my whole world."

"I love you, Javi. We've been through many adventures together. God has always been with us. We can do this. God will provide."

* * *

Daniel alternated between the two hospitals, but he soon heard that his dorm would be closing. He would have to move home. Without his small income from the athletic department, he really couldn't afford the gas to cross back and forth either. During his last week at the University Medical Center, he was surprised to see Jennifer in the parking lot. He could tell she'd been crying and wasn't wearing all the make-up she usually did.

"Jennifer, what's the matter?" Daniel asked as he approached her.

"My daddy is in ICU, and I can't go see him. He's on a vent and can't talk to me."

"I'm so sorry, Jennifer. But look, I'm a chaplain now. I can go up and call you. He can at least hear your voice. What's his name?"

Jennifer hugged Daniel so tight he could barely breathe. He'd never seen her this way before, so desperate, so out of control. "Jennifer, do you believe in God? He's got this, you know."

"I do know, Daniel, but I haven't really made him a part of my life. Why would he care about me now?"

"He's always loved you, Jennifer. Just let him know you need him. He's always there."

Daniel hurried to the entrance and up to ICU to find her father. He hoped he said the right things. He didn't know how anyone made it in this crazy world without knowing God was right beside him.

Daniel found Jennifer's father, tried to wake him, and called Jennifer. "I'm right beside him, putting the phone to his ear. Tell him everything you want to say."

Daniel was amazed again at how the vital signs improved at the sound of a loved one's voice. He didn't think keeping everyone out of the hospitals was the best protocol, but he had to follow the rules. When he saw her father doze off, he removed the phone.

"Jennifer, you really helped him. He relaxed and drifted off to sleep with a smile."

"Thank you, Daniel. I didn't know what to do."

"Where's your mom, Jennifer?"

"I don't know. She ran off when I was little. It's always only been me and my dad."

"Are you going home?"

"No, I'm staying in my car."

"I understand. I have another family doing the same thing on the other side, but they have a good support system. I'm going to call up a team for you."

Daniel called Burly, who enlisted his mom and a group from church. Soon they would all be taking turns with Jennifer in her vigil. Burly's dad even offered to cover Daniel's gas expense each week if he would stay on at the hospital. As Daniel drove home, he thought of Abuelo and gave him a call.

"I was worried about you. Are you taking care of yourself?"

Abuelo answered right away. "I'm in hibernation. I'm a prime candidate for this monster bug. I'm old, fat, and diabetic. I'm not even going out to the mailbox 'til this thing is gone."

Daniel laughed and filled him in on his chaplaincy work.

"I'm proud of you, son. You aren't mean enough to be a lawyer. Sounds like you've found your path."

* * *

In Mississippi, Itzel packed the most basic things for each of them. She hated leaving so much behind, especially from her kitchen.

Javi watched as she made her choices. "*Amor*, why don't you take the truck and drive home. That way we could really fill it with everything we need, and even things your mom needs. Stuff you've always wanted to take her."

"What about your work?"

"Well, you're not going to believe this, but the chicken plants are hiring back people with ankle bracelets. Apparently, chicken is an essential, and I'm an essential worker. Isn't that crazy? Think of how much money was wasted wrecking our homes, keeping us in jail, instead of paying taxes. Anyway, I can walk to the plant. I'll work as many hours as I can and try to sell the house. When it sells, I'll come home. Or if we need me to stay longer, I'll go back to Doña Elia's. Full circle, huh?"

They laughed and hugged. Maybe one day they would even finish at UACJ.

* * *

Cristal sat in a circle on the ground in front of her house. Quetzali and five students who lived nearby listened carefully as she read the story of Doña Chana and her *rana*, a cute rhyming story about a frog that soon had them all reading along. When they got too silly and wiggly, she taught them to play leapfrog, then "Mother, May I," using different frog steps and jumps. Then they sat back in their circle and practiced their addition facts.

Daniel watched from the street, amazed at how Cristal kept their attention and had so much patience. He hoped he would be as good a teacher and coach. How did he get so blessed to have such a beautiful woman as his future wife? Not wanting to interrupt her, Daniel walked back to his house and found his pa under the hood of his truck.

"Anything wrong?" Daniel asked. His pa was always tinkering on his truck. It was unbelievable the thing kept running.

"No, just checking the oil and fluids. Did you check on Humberto?"

"Yes, Pa. He's about the same. That's good though. So many go in and go down. Carmen has some good news too. Itzel and her girls are coming home."

"That's good. I know they appreciate the remittances she always sends them, but having her home will probably make Humberto well."

"Yeah, I think daughters do that. I've got a similar situation on the other side. The daughter went on the trip to Mississippi with us. She only has her dad. I'm so glad I became a chaplain. God must have known all along."

"I'm proud of you, *mijo*. I don't say it enough. It shouldn't take a worldwide pandemic for me to tell you, but I love you."

The two men hugged and pounded each other's backs. "Thank you, Pa. I love you too."

Araceli watched from the front window as her oldest son and her husband seemed to connect for the very first time. Love was always the answer, and there was no need to be stingy with it. God poured out an abundance. We should all share it more often.

THE END

Chapter 52

Frequent Terms in Spanish

ABUELO–GRANDFATHER
Ay Dios mío–OMG
Ayúdame–help me
Bienvenido–welcome
Cariño–dear, sweetheart
Chido-cool
Colonia–a neighborhood
Comedor-–a place for a free meal usually for children and sponsored by a church
Conchas–Mexican pastry
Coyote–someone who charges a high price to lead a person into the USA illegally
Cuídate–be careful, take care of yourself
DIF–Desarrollo Integral de la Familia, child protective service
Dios te bendiga–God bless you
Disculpe–excuse me, pardon me, forgive me
Doña–a title for an older woman used with her first name
Elote–corn on the cob with mayonnaise, chili peppers, cheese, etc.
Es un placer–it's a pleasure
Esfuérzate–do your best, strive
Felicidades–congratulations

Gloria a Dios–glory to God
Grito–Independence Day celebration in Mexico
Güey-dude, guy, man
Hasta luego–see you later
Maquila–an international factory located along the Mexican border with the United States
Maestra–teacher
Mija–my daughter, term of endearment
Mijo–my son, term of endearment
Mojado–undocumented or illegal alien
Mucho gusto–glad to meet you
No te preocupes–don't worry
Novela–a soap opera
Paquetero-delivery driver
Pozole–a hearty soup made with hominy
Prepa–high school
Primaria–elementary school, usually first through sixth grades
Primero Dios–God willing
Pupusas–Salvadoran meat pie
Raspones-snowcones
Quinceañera–celebration of a fifteenth birthday
Rueda de la fortuna–Ferris wheel
Segundas–a flea market of second-hand and discount goods
Te amo–I love you
Tío–uncle
Uni-university
Válgame, Dios–goodness gracious
Vato–dude

Teacher, missionary, immigrant helper, Marion Surles wears many hats. Teaching English as a Second Language, high school equivalency, citizenship, and swimming, Marion helps immigrants reach their full potential in a new land. Her mission, Love and Literacy, bring books and activities to the impoverished neighborhood of Sulaiman in Juarez, Mexico. The mission is supported by the sales of her books. Follow her Facebook Page Love and Literacy.